Forgotten Bloodline

A Guardian Series: Book Two

Danielle M Pepe

3

Prologue

He stood in front of the council, all eyes on him as he gave his final testimony. He knew there was nothing he could do to change their minds, but it was his job to try. He would do anything for her. Month after month, he had been going back and forth from England to America, without her knowing. He wouldn't put her through the worry if it turned out to be nothing.

He watched as her family, too, gave their testimonies, but they did it without putting her best interest first. They spoke as if they didn't care about her feelings, and about how valuable she was as a fighter, not as a person. He was speechless by their actions. He knew that if it had been Peter and Alexandra standing up there, all hell would've broken loose to defend their daughter, but these people couldn't care less, at least not anymore.

"You allowed this to happen. You even encouraged it from what I hear," the woman's voice rang through the large circular court room, made of all white marble from floor to ceiling.

In the front of the room, opposite the glass French doors, a large dais, carved from black marble into the form of a large horseshoe, gleamed in the lowlight of the chamber; atop it sat nine identical leather thrones. The walls were lined with framed photographs of every council member that ever existed, most merely paintings.

The man looked over to see Peter's portrait hanging on the far wall, a man who had entrusted his daughter to him to protect, a man who had never judged how different they were from one another, and still was a good friend—the best. He was a man who had died too young, the same as his love, and he would be dammed if this life took the only person he had left.

"Is there a question in there?" he replied, sarcastically.

"Boy, it is not the time for jokes," she snapped. "Now, why would you allow this to happen?"

"Why? Because I would do anything for her, I would never tell her how to live her life, and honestly, I'm glad she found a life that truly makes her happy. I will back her actions one hundred percent," he roared through the room, feeling as if he was the only one there to defend her.

He watched as the council members stared at him in shock. They didn't expect him to say that. They expected the same reaction as her family, but he wasn't like them.

After what felt like hours, they dismissed him from the stand. Feeling alone in a room full of people, he slumped down in his chair, waiting for the verdict, a verdict he never expected.

They came back into the room after mere minutes. The entire room silenced, as they watched wide-eyed. The man didn't wait to hear what they had to say. He read it in their minds, and before anyone could stop him, he was gone.

Chapter 1

One week earlier.

I looked out at the two story, white wooden, Victorian house. Blue shutters framed each window, and a porch wrapped around the front. The lawn was well kept, with large Quaking Aspen trees blanketing the ground. The driveway gave way to a cobblestone walk, which led to the porch by a variety of flowers and shrubs on either side, stretching up to the bright summer sun. A moving truck pulled into the driveway, and I watched as a new family took ownership of the North Carolina home; my family, my new home.

It had been a year since the incident that took place in Hidden Falls, the night I put my friends in danger. It was that day Andy found out the truth of what I was. On accident, because of me, my friends and I were forced to stay the night in a town being run by a pagan god. It was a fight to the death and with the help of Shasta, Derek and Lucas we were able to save the innocent humans and free the town.

I never regretted the choices that I made since then. I spent the last year finishing up my senior year with Kady, my best human friend. I graduated with honors and, because I brought the soccer team to another winning season, I was rewarded with a full scholarship to the University of North Carolina; which just so happened to be the same college that Greg, Kady and Andy attended. Now the four of us were moving in together with just one other addition to our little group.

"Hey princess, are you going to just sit on your ass while the rest of us do all the unpacking?" Andy yelled from the truck. He was struggling with the large copper sectional, as Greg held the other side of it. His messy brown hair stuck to his forehead, sweat dripping down his shirtless body. Andy's body was always well toned, but after spending a year in college, he was more ripped than ever; with his muscular biceps, wash board abs, and the V at his hip bones that drove me crazy when his jeans would hang down, exposing his happy trail.

"Um, last I checked, I offered to pay someone to do the moving, but you guys said no. So I'm saying no now. It's too damn hot, and I just got my nails done," Amanda yelled back from the front porch, as she laid on the swing, sipping her tea. A ceiling fan was keeping her cool. "Plus, Alikye could do all of that in like two-seconds, just ask her."

So, as it turned out, our fifth addition just happened to be Amanda. No one would have ever thought that Amanda and I would be living together, let alone become friends, but it surprised me as much as it did her how close we grew over the year.

"Hey, what do I look like?" I grunted. I made my way towards Andy, wrapping my arms around his stomach, and showering kisses all over his smooth back. I glided my hands up his torso to his silky, hairless chest. Standing on my tiptoes, I planted another kiss on his cheek.

"Okay, you keep doing that, and I'm going to drop this couch, baby."

He turned his face towards me, bringing his lips to mine. The heat from our bodies radiated around us like throwing gasoline onto an already lit fire. My body shivered with pleasure as the electricity ran from my fingers to my toes, my heartbeat speeding up to match his. He pulled away smiling, pausing to catch his unsteady breath.

"You want some help?" I asked breathless, pulling away from his body.

****

The sun started to set over the hills as I brought the last of the boxes inside the house. From the entryway, there was a large living room. To the left, a staircase led to the second floor, and to the right there was a huge bay window where you could see the front yard. The floors were made of mahogany wood, and the walls were painted a light natural brown. Towards the back of the living room was the kitchen, with white tile floors and off white marble countertops. The cabinets were the same mahogany as the floors, and the appliances were made of stainless steel. In the middle of the kitchen, a large island sat, and a skylight illuminated the room in brilliant colors of red and orange. To the right of the kitchen, there was a dining room. The upstairs had three bathrooms and four bedrooms, one of which we used for a game room, complete with a pool table, flat screen TV, and numerous game consoles; there was also a mini bar, plush seating, a poker table, and a state of the art stereo system.

Since it was Amanda's parents who bought us the house, it was only fair to give her the master bedroom. Andy and I took the room down the hall on the opposite side. The room was beautiful, and had a conjoining bathroom that we shared with Kady and Greg. One wall was taken up almost entirely by a window with the view of the backyard, while the opposite wall held a much smaller window. Next to the bathroom, there was a walk in closet big enough to fit a twin sized bed in, with room to spare. Andy and I had decided on picking out a bedroom set together, and after about two hours in the store arguing over vintage or modern, I had won with the simple style of dark wood. A king-sized, four poster bed with a simple green blanket and pillow casings, two end tables, a dresser, and an armoire, which was Andy's choice since I hadn't had a clue what it was, were now arranged in our new room.

I ran downstairs in a flash when I heard Greg call out that the pizza had arrived. It had not dawned on me just how hungry I was until then. Within a second, I was at Greg's side. I was about to take a few slices when he jumped, dropping the three boxes. I caught them before they had time to spill on the floor, and set them back on the counter as the room grew quiet.

"Damn it, Kye, you scared me!" Greg yelled, shaking his head while he laughed. "I still can't get used to it. I always forget how fast you are."

They all still treated me the same as before, making it comfortable to be myself around them, but sometimes I forgot that my powers were still new to them. Outside, in the human world, I posed as human, but as soon as I walked into my own home, I was free to be me. They all knew my secrets, and accepted me without judgment. My own family did not. The night I told them my choice, all they could do was walk away without a word, never speaking to me again.

"Sorry," I said, as I grabbed a Mountain Dew from the refrigerator. Amanda was seated at one of the bar stools, laughing. She put her head in her hands, as tears ran down her cheeks. I turned to her, furrowing my eyebrows, but not saying a word

"What? I'm sorry, but it's funny. Who would have thought I'd be the only one not affected by your supernatural ways?" Amanda giggled.

"Maybe it's because you had practice the last year, and because my girlfriend is normal, so it's not every day I get to see crazy things happening," Greg grumbled.

"Don't worry, dude. I still have trouble with this whole thing," Andy added as he walked into the room, putting his arms around my waist, and kissing my neck from behind.

10

As I lay back into his chest, the electric shock from his body engulfed me, sending tendrils of heat up and down my body. My marks started to glow brighter, lighting the dim room in a brilliant blue. It was nice never having to hide around him, which included not hiding my Enochian marks that covered my body in blue scriptures. Andy preferred it that way; he wanted me to be real with him, and when I was around him, touching and kissing him, it was hard to keep my emotions in check, bringing out the marks in bright Persian light.

"Um— gross. Get a room," Amanda groaned.

"Fine, I just may do that."

I grabbed a few slices of pizza and Andy's hand, pulling him towards the staircase. It had been so long since we had a chance to be alone, and right now, feeling the way I was feeling, all I wanted was to be curled up with him; his body against mine, feeling his heart beat for only me. I wanted to look into his sapphire eyes and feel how much he loved me. At times, he would ask if I made the right choice in choosing him over my family Every time, without hesitation, I would tell him that I never wanted to be anywhere that he wasn't. I loved him with every breath I took, and every time I told him how he made me feel, it was God's honest truth.

We walked into our room, and just as I set our food and drinks down on the table, he grabbed me, throwing me onto the bed. His body moved on top of mine, pushing me into the mattress. His lips were soft on mine as he parted my mouth, finding my tongue with his. As his hands moved up my thighs to my ribcage, our kiss deepened, causing me to moan, and him to make a growling sound in the back of his throat. His body trembled, his hands making tantalizing movements against my skin. I moved my fingers to his hair, gripping harder while he pushed me deeper into the mattress, his muscles moving against me. He smelt like his cologne; sweet, but spicy and boyish. He tasted like mint and the beach. I rolled on top of him, sitting astride him as my auburn curls fell around us like a curtain.

It took me a minute to catch my breath before I could speak, "I'm starving. I really need to eat. You know how I get when I'm hungry."

He lay smiling underneath me. He grabbed the plate from the table, and placed it on his stomach.

"Okay, baby. You eat, but I'm not moving," he said, choosing a slice and taking a bite. All I could do was laugh as I sat on top of him, leaning against his knees while we both finished the plate in silence.

Chapter 2

"What are you thinking?" I asked, while Andy lay next to me in our bed, tracing my Enochian marks on my stomach with his index finger. The blue markings curved around my ribs and hip in all different patterns and letters.

"The same thing I'm always thinking, pretty girl, when I'm laying next to you in our bed."

He smiled his boyish smile. I rolled my eyes at him, rising from bed to get ready for the day. Before I had the chance to get up, I was pulled back down, falling on top of Andy and causing him to grunt.

"Where do you think you're going?" he said jokingly.

He pulled me in to him, bringing his mouth to mine for a moment. I sunk into his kiss, savoring his sweet taste. Then, in less than a blink of an eye, I was gone, listening to his laughter from outside the bathroom. I took a quick shower, using Andy's shampoo and body wash. I loved the way he smelled, and even more, loved the way he smelled on me.

Bang, bang.

"What do you want?" I asked when I heard his footsteps enter the bathroom. I was in the middle of washing the soap out of my hair when Andy turned the sink on, causing the water to shoot out ice cold. I jumped backwards, knocking over all of our toiletries. "What the hell?" I screamed.

"Sorry baby," he laughed, continuing to brush his teeth.

When we got downstairs, the smell of grease and sweetness filled my nose, causing my mouth to water.

Kady was in the kitchen dancing to her music, as she twirled around readying breakfast. Amanda sat at the table flipping through some fashion magazine, while sipping on her vanilla latte. She looked up at us as we pushed through the kitchen door. Without a word, she pointed to the counter where two coffee cups sat, steam rising from the tops.

"Thanks," I mumbled as I took my first sip, savoring the sweetness of the caramel.

"Um-uh," Amanda mumbled back. Then, placing her magazine on the table, she looked up again with a playful smile on her beautiful face. Her hazel eyes brightened in the sun light filtering in from the window. "Hey, have you heard from Shasta lately? He's not picking up his phone."

"No, not in the last week. Why, are you having boyfriend troubles?" I smirked.

Amanda and Shasta started dating the summer after she graduated. At first, it was weird, and the age difference was a little gross. Soon after, I realized that it was as normal as an eighteen year old and twenty-six year old dating, and she made him happy, which was a surprise to me. After my choice to stay, I needed a Guardian, by human law, to look after me until I turned eighteen.

Apparently, before my parents died, they had already discussed matters of Guardianship with Shasta. He had agreed that he would care for me if they ever passed. Unfortunately, the council wouldn't allow a Legacy to be in the hands of a Demon, so Jack agreed to take me. Knowing he couldn't win, Shasta handed me over. Since my decision was to stay, Shasta moved in with me for my senior year, and pretended to be my brother. The arrangement worked out for Amanda, because for the first time in centuries Shasta was staying in one place, and with his abilities to teleport their relationship grew into something stronger. It worked out for me, because any time I wanted to see Andy he was only a jump away.

"No!" she exclaimed. "He has just been really secretive lately, and in the past week he's been distant. I figured it was one of your things."

"I don't know. I haven't heard anything yet."

"Hey!" Greg yelled from the front door. "Can someone give me a hand here?" I walked around the corner to see Greg standing by the door, struggling to keep his balance while carrying an armful of beer. I walked up to him and, without any kind of effort, took the multiple cases from him into the living room. "Wow, Kye, way to make me feel like a man."

School wasn't scheduled to start for another two months, but soccer practice started the last week of June, which gave us a few weeks to move in and meet new people. Since Greg, Andy, and Amanda had already spent a year there, we had planned to throw a huge party at the end of the week so that Kady and I had the chance to meet our future classmates, and I could meet my future teammates. So for the rest of the week, Amanda was in charge of throwing orders around from food to drinks to decorations. She went to extremes to prove that her house was going to become the place to be seen. I just went along because, to be honest, I kind of wanted the same thing.

"Aw, baby, you're my man," Kady cooed, coming in from the kitchen with a dish rag in her hands, smiling. She walked up to Greg and planted a quick kiss on his lips. "Breakfast is ready whenever you guys are."

"The rest of the things are in my truck. Make yourself useful, I'm starving," Greg smirked, making his way to Kady.

Within five minutes, our living room turned into a brewery, and our kitchen was stocked with all types of food and desserts.

"Damn, Amanda, how many people are coming, the entire school?"

"Oh, please. If I invited the entire school, where would the challenge be? Besides, half of the school is still home for the summer. It's only going to be like sixty people, mostly the sports team since they're the only ones on campus, plus a few locals," she grinned, tossing her long blond hair over her shoulder.

****

Andy and I decided to spend the day getting to know the small college town. I was in awe as we walked down Franklin Street, checking out the numerous shops and restaurants. One shop impractically caught my eye; it was a small boutique that sat in between a coffee shop and book store. Eyeing me, Andy noticed my awareness of the store and pulled me with him to the door.

"You want to go in, pretty girl?" Andy asked, holding the door open for me.

Almost two years ago, my interest in clothing consisted of black shirts and dark jeans. Anything that I could fight in and wouldn't worry about blood and dirt smeared all over. Since being around two fashion fanatics, day in and day out, I learned to appreciate colors. I found a dress that I thought would go perfect for our party Saturday night, so I grabbed it and headed for the changing room. The dress fit beautifully; the light blue chiffon clung to my small body. The straps were thin, crisscrossing down my back and showing off more skin than I would prefer. The length was a couple inches above my knees, showing off my tan, toned legs. I twirled around in front of the mirror, and it was love at first sight. I changed quickly, leaving the room and meeting Andy at the register.

"Are you hungry, babe?" Andy asked, as I stopped by a display full of vintage rustic jewelry.

An owl pendent strung on a copper necklace hung low, catching my eye. I grabbed it, placing it with the rest of my order. I raised my eyebrows, pulling half my lip up in a slight smile before turning around and shaking my head as to say, "Really, you have to ask?" I handed my money to the boy behind the counter.

"Yeah, I got it, dumb question."

"You think?" I questioned as I took my bag from the boy's hand. Taking Andy's arm in mine, we walked out of the shop.

"Well, before you just had to be all rude, I was going to tell you that Jake called while you were trying on clothes. He asked if we would want to meet up with him for a quick lunch."

Jake was a junior, and also played soccer with Andy and Greg. I met him plenty of times while visiting Andy last year. Jake was always a great guy, just a bit inappropriate at times. Andy never seemed to mind his behavior towards me, as long as Jake never made me feel uncomfortable. But the boy was harmless, and nothing I couldn't handle on my own; he was also really sweet, and we got along great.

"Um, of course! I haven't seen him since school ended in May."

Large murals painted each building, as Andy and I passed by numerous shops and restaurants; from the history of the town, dating back to the civil war, to pictures of turtles and a pencil. We walked to the neighborhood restaurant that specialized in sandwiches and burgers. People walked in the streets enjoying the bright sunny day. A light summer breeze blew through the town, bringing along with it the smells of freshly baked bread and cut grass. Jake was already waiting for us at the counter when Andy and I entered. Bypassing Andy, Jake came to me first, greeting me with opened arms.

"Damn girl, I've missed you," he said, pulling me hard to his chest, and lifting my little frame off the ground. I started laughing, pushing at him to ease up before he crushed my sternum.

Jake was like a large, lovable teddy bear who handed out hugs to whoever would take them. He had blond hair, cut short, and dark chocolate eyes. Sizing him up to Andy, they were both the same height and build; six feet tall with a lean swimmer's body.

"It's good to see you, too. How's your summer going so far? Breaking all the girls' hearts yet," I joked.

To say Jake was a player would be putting it mildly. The boy certainly got around, and made quite the name for himself freshman year. Still, somehow, the girls still flocked to him like he was God's gift to the women of Earth. The girls were even dumb enough to believe that they would be the one who could change his ways. Andy also attracted many women; I had seen my fair share go after him, knowing he had a girlfriend. They believed that they could persuade him to break up with me by offering absurd requests.

Unlike Jake, Andy did not give these girls much of his time, other than being friendly, because that was the type of person he was. I like to think it's because our love is something different, something magical like fate, and that we are meant to be together for eternity; I like to believe that nothing could ever rip us apart. I know, in a way, this is the reason; but I also know Andy would never be stupid enough to cheat on a girl whose best friend is a magic-wielding Demon that can read minds and jump dimensions in the blink of an eye.

"You know me so well," Jake said, placing me back down on my feet.

"And yet she still talks to you, and lets you touch her," Andy retorted, scrunching up his nose as if he smelled something foul.

"That's because she thinks she's safe with me," Jake said slowly, allowing each word to roll off his tongue seductively.

"Yeah, that's not creepy or anything," I huffed, scrunching my brows together.

The guys burst out laughing as I side stepped them to speak with the girl behind the counter. As I told her my order, I also gave her Andy and Jake's orders, seeing as they couldn't stop laughing for a second to speak one coherent sentence. Her eyes wandered back and forth between the guys, as they bent over supporting their weight with their arms on their knees. I watched her as she slowly punched the order into the computer, taking seconds in between each question she asked.

Jake came up from behind me, throwing an arm around my shoulder, pulling me tightly to his side, and asked, "Did you order for me woman?"

"Hands off my girl," Andy said, shoving Jake's arm away from me and playfully punching his shoulder.

"First of all, call me woman again," I said, pointing my finger in Jake's face, "and I will hurt you. Second, can you two knock it off? We are in public."

I was never the type to draw attention to myself for various reasons; I liked going about my day with as little excitement as possible. I spent too much of my life in the spotlight, never knowing what was around the corner. I liked having a stable, predictable life now. As much as I had changed over the year, Andy had too. He was still the most loving, amazing boyfriend ever, but he could now get loud at times, especially when he was with his teammates. I accepted his changes just as he accepted mine, knowing humans change with their environment.

"Sorry," they said in unison, glancing down at the floor as if they had just been scolded by their mothers.

As I handed the girl the money for the food, I pointed over to the corner booth and told the boys to go sit down while I waited for our lunch. Without so much as a glance up, Andy and Jake moved to the table, knowing not to back talk me. I wasn't a bossy person, and most of the time they would ignore my plea to behave, but in a place where people come to enjoy a meal, they needed to be respectful.

"Wow, that was pretty good. Would you mind showing me the secret to controlling the opposite sex?" the girl behind the counter asked, as she handed me the food.

"You just have to show them who's boss; train them like puppies," I joked.

The three of us kept a steady conversation as we ate, talking mostly of our plans for the rest of the summer. Since soccer training would take up most of our weekdays, as well as some weekends, we planned to make the most out of the time we had off by traveling to the beach or the mountains. Once school started, I would be busy with classes. I had decided to take six this semester, and piled them on top of each other in order to have Fridays off. To be honest, I was nervous. Hell, at times I didn't think I would be able to do it. Having a normal life felt so surreal, and with college it was a bit overwhelming; but I promised myself I could do it. I gave up everything so that I could have the life I truly wanted, and I would be damned if I failed because it was more than I expected. With that pep talk in mind, I finished the rest of my Thai veggie wrap and smiled.

Chapter 3

"So, what are the plans for tonight?" Kady asked. "I heard there is a great band playing at some local bar in town."

We all sat around the living room, enjoying some down time. Amanda was sitting in the love seat, re-painting her nails for the twentieth time, while Andy sat on the floor, my head in his lap, playing with my hair.

"Sounds good to me, but can we please eat first? I'm starving," I complained, while my stomach rumbled despite it being only a few hours after lunch.

"You're always starving, O.M.G. If I get fat because we are living together, I am kicking your ass out," Amanda laughed, putting the finishing touch on her pink toes. "Fine, I guess I can go for something light."

****

We headed to a hot spot on the corner of Franklin and Columbia Street, a local restaurant and brewery. The inside was large with windows covering the side wall. Brown tables and chairs filled up the spacious room with a bar off to the side. The food was delicious, and the freshly brewed beers were crisp and ice cold. I looked around the place smiling, still not believing that this was my life. For the first time since I was a child, I felt like I had finally found my happily ever after.

I still wanted to be a Guardian and protect the earth, but for now I just wanted to go to college and be a normal girl. I still didn't know if I would ever be welcomed back by my race, and after a year of not hearing from them or my family, I figured I would give them time before speaking to Anastasis about living both lives. If I couldn't, I would always have Andy, my friends, and a degree in something where I could still try to save the world. Maybe I would become a cop or something. I mean, I definitely had the skills to do so, and I could still make a difference by bringing justice to both human criminals and Demons.

We left the restaurant just as the streets started to fill with anxious party goers trying to find a crowded bar. We walked a few blocks up, and finally found the right place for us after hearing loud music billowing up from an underground bar. The place was large, filled with booths flushed up against the walls. The dance floor took up most of the center area, with a small stage to the side. On the opposite side of the stage was the bar. I took a booth closet to the stage, while Andy and Greg went to the bar to get drinks for the girls and me.

"This place is awesome!" Kady yelled to us over the music.

The band was made up of a group of local guys that had made it big a few years back. Every now and then, they would show their appreciation by playing for free a few nights out of the year. Their music was a little heavy, but it was really good and upbeat. Their sound was a mix between 30 Seconds to Mars and Imagine Dragons.

"I know, right? And the band is so hot," Amanda replied.

"Amanda, this morning you were talking about how much you missed your boyfriend who, by the way, is my best friend," I said as Kady shot me a dirty look. She always challenged Shasta when it came to the title of being my best friend. I rolled my eyes, continuing, "and now you're drooling over a bunch of punk looking kids."

"Are you kidding me? Alikye, my young grasshopper, boys are like shoes," she said as she pointed to the boys on stage. "Yes, they are great to look at, but that doesn't mean I'm gonna try them on when I have the perfect pair already at home," she grinned. We all laughed just as the boys arrived.

"What are you girls giggling about?" Greg asked, wrapping his arm around Kady. He handed her some fruity drink, and gave Amanda an Apple Martini. Andy handed me a Mountain Dew, while he and Greg set their beers on the table.

"Just about how amazing Shasta is," Amanda blurted. I shot her a look as Andy tightened his grip around my shoulder.

"Oh, really?" he asked.

I held my hands up, palms out. "She said it, not me," I smiled, forging innocence.

Within the hour, the bar filled to capacity. Sweaty bodies clung to each other on the dance floor, while the band played another upbeat hit. Kady stood up, yanking Amanda and me up from our seats to join her in front of the stage. Amanda looked up at the lead singer as he wailed his lyrics in the microphone. He must have felt Amanda's penetrating stare, because he looked down at us and winked.

The girls around us swooned, screaming out the band's name, hoping to steal their attention. Kady grabbed my hand, twirling me around the dance floor. I took a second to feel the beat of the music inside my chest, moving my hips to the song. Sweat dripped from my brows as more bodies were pushed up against me.

Lost in the music, I didn't feel him behind me. He wrapped his arms around my waist, pushing his body into mine. Heat spread up my body as a bolt of electricity shot through me.

He moved his lips to my ear, whispering softly, "Have I told you today that I love you, pretty girl?" He ran his hot tongue along my neck, driving me crazy. I rested my head on Andy's chest, as we moved together to the beat of the song.

After the song ended, I grabbed his hand and led him off the dance floor. I turned, grazing my lips against his. I ran my hands through his hair, pulling him closer to me. I could feel my markings slowly seeping up from my skin, and it took everything in me to command them to stay hidden.

I never had a problem hiding my tattoos from the world, but they seemed to be making more of an appearance lately. Every time Andy touched me it was hard not to glow. Around the house, when I was just amongst friends, I let the markings come to life. In public, I tried to keep them under control. I pulled away, breathing more heavily.

"We need to stop," I whimpered. I looked down to see a faint blue line running from my wrist to my shoulder, lightly faded symbols coming off of the line.

"Sorry, baby. But damn, I couldn't resist. Every guy in this room was staring at you dance, and I needed to show them that you're mine," Andy said, kissing my forehead.

I rolled my eyes. "Baby, I highly doubt that."

Andy threw his head back and laughed. He headed back over to our table, pulling me along with him. Kady was already there sitting on Greg's lap. She kept laughing at nothing in particular, sucking down her drink through double straws.

Kady didn't really drink much. In all the time I've known her, I have only seen her drink a handful of times, and usually it was merely a glass of wine or two. Watching as she drank down her third Vodka Bay Breeze, I knew my girl was wasted. I had to laugh, though, because she was entertaining. At home, where I know I'm safe, I don't mind having a few beers; but out in public where danger could be lurking around each corner, it was best I stuck to soda.

"I'm going to the bar, does anyone want anything?" I asked, noticing everyone's drinks getting low, including mine.

"Me!" Kady screeched, jumping off Greg's lap and barreling into me.

"Whoa there, babe, maybe you should slow down with the drinking," Greg said, grabbing ahold of her waist and pulling her back.

Kady turned around, glaring at him. I had to laugh, because she did not look too happy. Andy nudged my arm, giving me that look as to say, "Stop it." I laughed harder.

"Do not tell me I should slow down. I am fine, and as you can see, I am still sober, unlike you and Andy over here who have sucked down half the bar in beers," Kady said pointing to the table which housed at least ten empty bottles. "I know damn well when enough is enough. Do you understand, Gregory?"

"Oh my god I love this girl," I thought to myself.

I threw my hand over my mouth, trying so hard to contain my laugher; but it was near impossible, and I burst out laughing. Both Andy and Greg sat there, dumbstruck, nodding their heads. Kady let out a small squeal before jumping back on Greg's lap.

"Good! That's what I thought." She kissed Greg on the lips and turned back to me. "So, about that drink."

"Well, hell, how can I say no to that? Anyone else?" I raised my eyebrow at Greg. He raised his beer bottle to me, bringing it back to his lips as he downed the rest. I took that as a yes.

"Hey, just put it on my card," Greg yelled out as I made my way over to the bar.

I found an empty seat by the end and took it, waiting for the bartender to notice me. After a few minutes, he looked my way, holding up his finger to signal that he'd be right over. I nodded once, smiling.

"Is this seat taken?" I looked over to see some guy in a white polo and khakis, gesturing to the empty seat next to me. I opened up my senses, flipping through my mind for any indication of knowing him. I came up empty.

"It's all yours," I smiled. Just then the bartender walked up to me and leaned over the bar.

"What can I get for you, babe?"

He was kind of hot in that bad boy sort of way, but he still had nothing on Andy, and had way too much metal in his face.

"Water, beer, and a bay breeze, please. You can put it on Greg Sardinia's card."

"You got it, babe," he said, walking away to make the drinks.

"So, is Greg your boyfriend?" the guy next to me asked, moving closer to me.

Was this guy serious? I wondered.

Pausing, I said, "Um, no, he's just a friend, but I'm actually..." I replied, before being cut off by his interjection.

"I'm Billy," he said, offering out his hand.

"And I'm taken, sorry," I smirked.

The nerve of this guy. He wasn't even my type. I mean, if I had a type. His blond hair was slicked back by gel with not a single strand out of place. He was maybe a few inches taller than me at 5'10, with soft brown eyes. The best part was that he had a popped collar.

"Well, too bad. Do you go to school around here?"

Apparently, it didn't matter that I just told him I was taken, because he didn't move from his seat.

"Yup, UNC. I play soccer."

He raised his eyebrows. "Well, damn, a jock. I'm not too much into the whole contact sports thing, I much prefer football. You know, Quarterback—starter," he joked, wiggling his brows up and down. I had to laugh because the look on his face was priceless.

The bartender set my drinks in front of me, walking over to the next waiting customer. I noticed Billy had a full drink in his hand the whole time. Well played. "You have a beautiful laugh," he said.

"Do you use that line on all the girls?" I rolled my eyes. "I should get back to my friends."

"Do I at least get a name?" Billy asked.

"Yeah, it's 'not interested,' Billy," Andy growled. I looked over my shoulder to see him behind me. He wasn't very happy. I didn't know what his problem was; I was barely taking to this kid.

"Don't tell me this is the guy you're dating," Billy grunted, now void of any playfulness he had shown earlier.

Whoa, what the hell was that all about? Andy pulled me behind him; I grabbed ahold of his arms, keeping him out of reach of Billy's face. These two had history; it wasn't hard to sense it. It was how rapid their heartbeats were, just by looking at each other, that made me believe they hated each other. It was times like this that I wished Shasta was around, so I wouldn't have to play the guessing game.

"What the hell is that supposed to mean?" Andy snapped.

"Only that I know the type of guy you are," Billy turned to me. "Let me guess, sweetheart, this is your first year, and you guys have been together for a while, right?"

"You might want to watch your mouth, Billy," Andy hissed.

"And you might want to tell your girl here how you tried to sleep with my girlfriend last year," Billy yelled.

Andy lunged for Billy, but I was able to get in front of him. I took his face in my hands, trying to calm him down. This Billy guy could say whatever he wanted, but I knew what he was saying was a lie. Then, in that moment, it all clicked. I did know this guy; not personally, but if it was the same Billy I was thinking of, then I knew of him. It was Jake who slept with his girlfriend last year. Andy knew about it, but didn't feel it was his business to get involved. The only reason I knew this was because Shasta felt the need to dip inside Andy's head all the time, making sure he didn't have any intention of cheating on me. I guess, in a way, it was sweet. But really, my life would never be normal.

"Baby, you need to chill!" I pushed him hard, causing him to take a few steps back. I turned to Billy. "And you need to go now!"

"Just thought you should know, sweetheart," Billy said, giving me one last wink before he walked away.

Andy lunged for Billy again, but he wasn't quick enough. I caught him, pressing my body hard against his.

"Andy!" I yelled. We had already started to gather a crowd around us, but once they realized there would be no fight, everyone went back to their own things.

"What the hell, Alikye?" Andy yelled back. "You say you're going to get a drink, and I find you laughing with Billy Johnson."

I took a step back from him, feeling like I had just been slapped in the face. Could he be serious right now? All of the sudden, I'm the one to blame because I said two words to a guy I've never met, trying to be polite. Oh, hell no. Anger bubbled to the surface, and before I knew it, I was seeing red.

"Excuse me! Don't you dare blame this on me," I shoved my finger into his chest. "Honestly, if anyone is to blame it's you. You knew his girlfriend was screwing your friend the whole time, and didn't say anything. I would be pissed, too, if I were him," I yelled.

Oh crap. I threw my hands over my mouth. Andy's eyes widened, realizing I knew something he never told me. "Andy," I whispered.

"You have got to be kidding me. This whole time you never really trusted me, did you? So what, you asked your little Demon to spy on me? Is that it?" Andy ran his hands through his hair, yanking at the ends.

He turned, and walked down a hallway. I followed after him. I knew I messed up, but I never asked Shasta to do that. He did it on his own, and told me things now and again.

"I cannot believe you, Alikye! Dammit!" he yelled as he threw his fist into the wall, startling two girls exiting the bathroom. I walked over to him, taking his injured hand, but he pulled it away.

"Don't!" he snapped.

"Will you stop acting like a five year old throwing a tantrum, and let me explain?"

Okay, not the best thing to say in this situation, but I was never blessed with a mind to mouth filter.

"Seriously! I just find out my girlfriend has been using her Demon to read my mind, and I'm supposed to be okay about it?"

"First of all, stop calling him my Demon friend. Second, I never asked. I can't control what he does. You know that as well as I do. Third, yeah, what's the big deal? He reads my mind all the time. You don't see me acting all crazy!"

Again, not the best choice of words. Andy definitely didn't think so either.

"I'm done with this conversation. You just don't get it, do you?"

"Babe, I do get it, but all you're really trying to do is pick a fight with me because I laughed at something stupid a guy said to me," I said as I touched his arms, placing my face in his chest. Andy relaxed, taking a deep breath. I thought it was done, but I was wrong. He moved me from him, storming off in the direction of the bar.

Wait, what the hell just happened? I rubbed my hands over my face, chasing after him for the second time tonight.

This shit was getting old. I made it to him, just as he reached for the drink he must have just ordered.

"Stop walking away from me!" I snapped. How did this night go from fun to crap in a matter of minutes? "Why don't we just go home and talk about this?"

Andy tipped his beer back to his lips, drinking half the bottle down. He looked at me for a long moment, taking in a deep breath. He drank down the rest of his beer, signaled to the bartender for another one, and asked me, "Why is it so hard to love me and want to be with just me?"

"I'm sorry," I pleaded. "The next time I see Shasta, I'll threaten to stab him if he gets into your mind again, but you need to believe that I never asked him to spy; he just likes to be annoying." I ran my hand down Andy's cheek, forcing him to look me in the eyes so he would see I wasn't lying to him. "I trust you would never do anything to hurt me. I need you to do the same thing."

Andy closed his eyes, shaking his head back and forth. I didn't know how else to apologize, but it seemed like nothing I said was getting through to him. Just then, a small smile played on his lips.

"I'll take care of Shasta," he said, wrapping me in his arms. "And yes, baby, I do trust you." His lips met mine.

✳✳✳✳

By the time we arrived home, it was past two, and I had to deal with four drunken idiots, including my boyfriend who didn't know how to keep his hands off me. I got him upstairs in a flash, regretting that idea when his eyes rolled to the back of his head. I put him in bed, pulling off his pants and shirt. He started squirming around, mumbling incoherent thoughts.

"Mmmm baby, are you trying to seduce me? If so, all you have to do is ask," he mumbled, with the most devious smile on his face.

"Yes, honey, that's exactly what I'm trying to do. Now go to bed," I demanded.

"Or we could play a little," he said, running his hands up my legs.

"Andy, you're about to pass out, and I would prefer not to mess around with you when you won't remember anything in the morning," I argued.

At this point, it didn't matter; by the time I looked down, he was lightly snoring. I laughed, rolling him over and pulling the covers on top of him. He looked so sweet sleeping, and I couldn't help but wonder how I got so lucky to have the most amazing guy in the world love me.

Chapter 4

Over the next few days, we were able to get the house completely unpacked. We ordered a large canopy for out back, and set it up under the plentiful American Elms. Our outdoor costume bar and grill was fully stocked, and the red brick fire pit that sat off to the side had a variety of seating. I was pulling the last of the wooden pallets from the truck, stacking them near the fire pit, when Andy came up from behind me and took me in his warm arms.

"Hey baby, you almost done here?" he asked.

I turned in his arms, placing my lips on his. Andy's hand moved up my back, stopping at my neck, pulling me closer. Just as his kisses became more intense, I pulled away, breathless, watching his eyes burn with passion. "Is that a yes?"

"I'm done, what do you have in mind?" I asked, wiping my dirt stained hands on my jeans.

His lips barely touched mine as he whispered, "Well."

I smacked his arm, moving away from him. "Whatever, perv," I said, leading him over to the back porch. I sat down on his lap, grabbing my soda. "So, what do you really have in mind?"

"I was thinking we could take a trip to the mountains, do a little hiking, and have a picnic," he said.

"Sounds good. Go get everything ready, but we are taking my baby," I said, pulling up from him and walking inside.

Yes, my car, a 1968 fire engine red Mustang GT convertible, would be perfect for a day like this, riding with the top down. It belonged to my dad; he left it to me when he died. Jack had it in storage, until the day I moved to Florida, when he handed me the keys.

We were out the door within twenty minutes, heading west to Asheville, about three hours away. It was almost noon when we arrived, taking the back roads to where the forest surrounded us. I looked over to Andy, who all of a sudden was completely silent; he was looking around anxiously.

"What's wrong, baby?" I asked, worriedly.

"Nothing. Just, last time I was in the woods isn't the greatest memory."

It wasn't long after the incident at Hidden Falls that Andy started to have nightmares, and it didn't help much when I told him about everything that I did. He would tell me everything was fine, but occasionally he would get flashbacks. It was the same for the rest; they all handled it, but every so often, something would trigger that night, and the nightmares would start.

"Aw, baby, we don't have to do this," I said, soothing him.

"No, it was my idea. Let's go."

We walked through the forest, coming to an opening just before reaching the mountainside. The day was bright and sunny. The cool breeze felt good as we made our way up the mountain path, passing an assortment of wildlife. We were given stern warning to stay on the path, and not to veer off into unfamiliar territory, worried we would run into a bear or mountain lion. Little did they know, I could take care of a situation like that, but I kept to the rules for Andy's sake.

After about an hour on the trail, Andy's demeanor started to lighten up as he took in the beauty. We stopped for lunch, indulging in fresh fruits and the most amazing sandwiches we had gotten from a deli down the street. Still trying to get me to give up Mountain Dew, Andy brought along water and tea, saying soda was not a good idea when hiking. I told him it didn't really matter in my case, but he wouldn't allow it. All I could do was laugh it off and agree to drink water, which I hated.

Standing on top of one of the smaller mountains, I was mesmerized by the view. All I could think about was the feeling of freedom, being so far away from civilization and the stress of everyday life. Here, there was nothing but peace. It was the same feeling I got sitting on the beach of my Florida home, or laying out in the fields, looking up at the clear night sky in Colorado, where my parents used to live. This kind of tranquility was what I wanted one day, after Andy and I got married; to build a house in the middle of nowhere, where we could run and hide away from everyday life, just the two of us. Maybe we would live in a cabin by the lake, where we could teach our kids how to swim, and watch them play hide and seek in the woods. Our beautiful kids, who would most certainly have my eyes, but I hoped at least our daughter would have his.

"Hey, what are you thinking, babe?" Andy asked, bringing me back to the present.

"Our kids, and watching them grow up. I was thinking that, one day, I would like to have a place away from everyone where we could escape," I said truthfully. Andy got this dazed look in his eyes, and I could only imagine he was thinking the same thing.

"So, kids, huh?" he asked, with a playful smile on his face. "That will take some practice."

"Way to ruin a moment," I hissed.

"I'm just saying, you talk about wanting kids with me, yet we have never had sex."

"Andy, we've talked about this. It's not that I don't want to, because trust me, I do. You know what would happen if we do," I reminded him.

Andy and I had this conversation about a year ago; he knew what I would be giving up if I gave him my virginity. Back then, he understood why I couldn't, but now even I didn't know why I kept waiting. I wanted to spend the rest of my life with him, and I knew he wanted the same. Our love was different from anyone else's. Reason being, I was different; but it was still a lot to give him all of me.

When two Guardians commit to each other, sex is a way of sealing their bond; they become one, and their hearts are given to the other forever. After that, they are mated for life in a primal kind of way. Humans are different. They can fall in and out of love in the blink of an eye. If that happened with Andy, then I'd be left alone for the rest of my life, never being able to love another. Right now, there was no point in trying to explain it to him again; I couldn't, because either way, I wanted him forever.

"I guess I'm just scared that you'll change your mind one day. After all, you are only human," I laughed at my own stupid joke, which Andy didn't find funny. *Yeah, I wasn't really a funny person.*

He rubbed his hands over his face, not wanting to explain to me, once again, that he wouldn't ever not want me. This only got me more frustrated, because I never second guessed anything in my life until him. For the first time ever, I had a weakness; I had something in my life that made me vulnerable.

We sat in silence for a few more minutes, looking over at the darkened blue sky.

"Trust me, Kye, there is no one out there that could hold a candle to you. You stole my heart a long time ago."

After that, we just sat talking about everything on our minds; from school to the upcoming parties, and what life would be like after college. We continued to talk as the sun started to disappear over the mountains, streaking the sky with millions of stars. Once the night started to get cooler, we decided it was time to go. Curling up in Andy's arms, we drove home in the darkness, watching the mountains take on a whole new level of beauty.

****

Our plans for the night were ruined by a storm that came in from the East. The rain fell down in sheets, flooding the streets in minutes. Thunder roared in the sky, shaking the windows in the house. I came downstairs wearing a pair of grey sweats and a white tank, bypassing the boys sitting on the couch as they watched the rest of the game. I walked into the kitchen where Kady stood by the stove, cooking her famous fried chicken. Amanda sat at the bar mashing the potatoes. I was never much of a cook; I lived mostly on fast food growing up. Kady offered to teach me, starting with the basics, but it always led to putting out a fire and calling for takeout. Kady was patient with me, and I was finally able to put together a decent meal with the help of one of my housemates.

"What can I help with?" I asked, grabbing a Mountain Dew from the refrigerator.

"I'll go get the fire extinguisher," Amanda snorted, moving from her bar stool to the nearby closet, where we did indeed keep the extra extinguisher. It was a necessity after the last incident, when I almost burnt down Kady's house in Florida, not even a month ago.

"Ha ha, very funny. I will have you know that back when you two were learning how to cook, I was learning how to fight and kill Demons. All so that you humans wouldn't become slaves, and spend an eternity being tortured, living in a real life hell where, by the way, you wouldn't be cooking anyway. Most likely, you would be eating scraps off the ground or starving to death."

I tried to keep a straight face so that I sounded somewhat threatening, but one look from Kady's frightened face, and

I couldn't hold it in any longer. Amanda rolled her eyes, taking her seat and finishing up with the mashed potatoes.

"Kye, that's not funny. Why don't you come and stir the green beans? The seasoning is already mixed in the pot, so just stir slowly that way it will all cook evenly," Kady requested.

Always the mother in the group, Kady was the one to get in between Amanda's and my catty fights. As much as I loved Amanda, we fought like an old, married, human couple, and disagreed on everything. Kady handed me a wooden spoon, again explaining what had to be done, as if I was a child. You would think this crap would be easy, but take away the basics, and I would be in trouble.

"Yes, Kye, very slowly. You wouldn't want to burn the beans," Amanda's words came out sarcastic.

"Amanda!" Kady shrieked.

"Keep it up, if you want a face full of potatoes," I said as I turned, still stirring the green beans.

"Kye, you're not helping," Kady threw down her spatula, splattering grease everywhere.

"Oh, I would like to see you try—," Amanda trailed off.

Just as I was about to hyper-speed my butt over there, and show her just how serious I was, a loud, thunderous boom ricocheted off the house. The lights flickered on and off, before settling back on again. We all stopped for a minute, waiting to see if the lights would hold. When they seemed to be steady, I drew my attention back to Amanda, daring her to finish her sentence.

"Crap!" Kady cried. "Babe, will you go and find some candles and flashlights?" she yelled out into the living room.

"Babe, it's the ninth inning, and the Phillies are killing us," Greg whined, hollering something absurd at the television, as if the players could really hear him.

"Fine, but if the lights go out you're gonna be the one scrambling through the dark to find them!"

"Whatever, we can send Kye. She's the one who can see in the dark!" Andy hollered back.

"Thanks, jerk, just take advantage of my awesomeness. Is that the only reason you guys keep me around?" I joked.

"Pretty much! Now hush!" Greg shouted.

"Wow, I feel loved." I turned, Amanda had a shit-eating grin on her face, and I knew she was about to say something smart. "Don't even think about it," I grunted.

"Oh my god, will the two of you just stop?" Kady screamed.

"What the hell is going on in here? Can you guys stop yelling?" Andy asked, walking into the kitchen.

With one look at us, he saw me glowering at Amanda, who was halfway from rising out of her seat with a hostile look in her eyes, and Kady still standing by the stove, one hand on her hip while the other hand held a spatula in the air. He turned and walked back out, mumbling something to Greg about not going into the kitchen. I looked over to where Andy had just stood, and burst out laughing. Both Kady and Amanda followed suit, and within seconds, laughter bellowed out of the kitchen. I held tight to my side, leaning over to catch my breath. Like a line of dominos, I couldn't stop; making the girls laugh even harder, and when one would stop, they would just start back up again.

"Maybe we should think about getting our own place," Greg said to Andy, as he switched off the TV.

After we all finally settled down, we set the table together. Whatever Amanda and I were fighting about was in the past. Just as I placed the last of the silverware down, lightning illuminated the sky, followed by another fit of thunderous booms, and then the lights turned out.

"Tomorrow, I am sending the boys to the store to buy a generator. The last thing we need is to be stuck in the dark during hurricane season," Amanda said, setting down a dish of piping hot chicken. A loud crash sounded in the kitchen, followed by a few choice words.

Kady's screams broke out, saying something about, "I told you so."

"Kye, can you please help out the two morons who refused to find a light when they could still see? I think they're making a mess in here."

"No. Let them figure it out," I snapped.

"Please, babe, I can't see a damn thing," Andy muttered.

"Nope," I said, popping the P.

"Kye!" they all yelled at once.

I rolled my eyes, making my way to the kitchen. The contents of the closet were scattered on the floor around Greg's feet. A broken mason jar, filled with some smelly liquid, pooled around Andy, who was on the floor trying desperately to clean up what he could. I thought that if I had a camera right now, it would have been the funniest picture; but I didn't think it was an appropriate time to locate my phone.

When a human walks into a dark room, it takes their eyes minutes to adjust. Even then, all they can see are the shadows of their surroundings. To me, it's like every object hidden in those shadows lights up; a shiny outline is drawn in front of me. Colors and textures are non-existing. It's not like walking into a bright room, seeing every detail displayed in from of me, but I can still see like it's second nature. I stepped between the two morons, as Kady had called them, grabbing ahold of the basket full of emergency candles and batteries. On the top shelf, I located the bag of flashlights, handing one to Greg and one to Andy. I grabbed Kady by the arm, steering her safely to the dining room.

Chapter 5

Every candle was lit around the house, illuminating each downstairs room with a soft glow. We all settled in to eat, stuffing our faces with delicious food. Outside, Mother Nature pounded down on the world, trying to rip it apart, piece by piece. Inside, as the candlelight flickered and danced in the darkness, it was calm and comforting. After the leftovers were put away and the kitchen was somewhat clean, we moved over to the living room. With not much else to do, Kady pulled out a deck of cards.

"Okay guys, the game is called Scat. Each player gets four chips. The object of the game is to get as close to 31 as you can. I'll deal out three cards each. Face cards are 10 points, A's are 11 points, and number cards are that many points. Got it?" We all nodded, as Kady dealt us three cards each.

I looked at my hand. I had a king, a five, and a seven; all different suits.

"Now, the cards have to be the same suit," Kady continued.

Just my luck.

"We go around in a circle. You pick up a new card, if you want it, and discard an old one. If you feel you have a good hand, knock on the table. That means everyone else only has one more try to beat you. Whoever has the lowest hand, throws in a chip. If someone has 31, yell the word Scat, and everyone throws in a chip. If you run out of chips, you get what is called a 'your honor,' meaning you can play until you lose. Whoever is left holding a chip at the end, wins the pot."

My turn came. I picked up a Queen of Hearts, the same suit as my king. I moved the new card to join my other cards, and plucked out the five. Just as I threw it on the pile, my phone blasted "Little Talks" by Of Monsters and Men. That song was my new obsession lately. I played it around the house every chance I got, even hooking it to our surround system.

I let it ring for a full minute, listening to the chorus, when Amanda slammed her hand on the table.

"Oh, for shit's sake, please answer your phone before I claw out my eardrums."

"When you say things like that, it makes me want to replay the song over and over again," I replied, sarcastically.

"ARGH! Stop it now, Kye! Answer your phone!" Kady roared.

I jumped at her sudden outburst, grabbing my phone from the table, and looking down at the caller ID. I smiled to myself when I saw whose name flashed across my screen. Holding the phone up, I shoved it in Andy's face so he could see.

"Put it on speaker," Andy said with a smile.

"Hello, you're on speaker," I said into the phone.

"Is it a good time to talk about—" Riker trailed off, waiting for me to give him permission to speak freely about Demon stuff.

It didn't take long after the incident for Riker to put in his resignation. He loved teaching, but he wanted to do more with it. Only a year away from his Master's degree, he took extra courses in Demonology at the University of Florida, where he soon started to teach that very same subject.

He never really talked about what had spiked his interest in delving further into the world of the supernatural, but the night after I had sat in the room with my friends answering all their questions, Riker stayed out in the living room with Sarah and Shasta, talking privately.

"You're all good," I answered.

"My class discussion for this week is a Demon you call Abaddon. I just wanted to get the inside story on the guy to make the class a bit more exciting."

Abaddon was once an angel who chose to follow Lucifer. As the angel of destruction, the destroyer of everything, Abaddon was the first to turn his back on Michael, becoming Lucifer's right hand man; he also just so happened to be Shasta's father.

"Did you try Shasta? He would probably know more about the guy than me, given the circumstances."

Shasta hated his father; it was the main reason why he never turned. He swore he would never be as cold and heartless as the man who hurt his mother. He also thought him to be a coward, for turning his back on his own kind for greed and power. Shasta met his father a few times over his life span, but never once gave into his pleas to join him in his army.

"Yeah, already tried calling a few times, but he seems to be busy," Riker replied.

"Yeah, same here. None of us have heard from him in awhile," I added.

It was a bit strange for Shasta to just disappear, without so much as a word to where he was going or what mission he was taking.

Back before I moved to Florida, I would go months without speaking to him, but that was my own fault. I was too self-absorbed in my own personal demons to allow Shasta to get close. Even though he was always my best friend, I never appreciated him as much as I did now. So, going a few weeks without hearing from him was starting to worry me.

"Is everything okay? You guys aren't in danger or anything?" Riker asked.

Not that I knew of, but like I said before, it had been over a year since the council, or any of my kind, had contacted me. I took it as their way of getting used to me being away, and with time, I hoped I would be welcomed back. But, I just didn't know. It wasn't long after I left that there was a Demon attack too close to home. Shasta and I had gone out on our own to take care of it. I had missed homecoming my senior year because of it; but it was my duty, and I understood that. I hadn't been on a mission since then. Either the Demons didn't see me as a threat anymore, or I was too much of a threat, causing them to stay away from my friends and me.

"Everything's great, actually. He's probably busy with a mission," I said, trying to sound convincing.

"Well, that's good. So, Abaddon—" Riker trailed off, waiting for me to fill in the blanks for him.

Everyone sat quietly around the table, listening closely. They loved to hear my war stories of the past; Andy especially, because it gave him a better understanding of me.

"Like I said, Shasta would be better help than I am. I've never met him, thank God. He would kill me before I had the chance to say hi. Abaddon is as powerful as Lucifer and Michael, but because he isn't an archangel, he isn't bound to hell," I started.

Abaddon was able to walk the earth, but only every two hundred and fifty years. I didn't know why, but Shasta said it had something to do with the planets and stars aligning. Or maybe it was something with portals opening when the world is at its weakest. I had zoned out the day he tried to tell me. Back then, I wasn't too interested in knowledge that wasn't relevant to me at the current time.

Now, I kind of wished I had paid more attention.

"I can tell you, for certain, that he's a mean son of a bitch that destroys everything he touches. The angels used him to fix their mistakes back in the beginning. Lucifer found his skills worthy of his own mission, and recruited him, promising him his own empire to rule as long as it didn't interfere with his own. Abaddon, in return, created his own army of minions bound by blood to one day overpower Michael himself. Lucifer thought he could tame Abaddon, but what Lucifer failed to realize is that Abaddon's a ticking time bomb," I continued.

"So when it comes time for him to walk the earth, then what?" Riker prodded.

"Well, have you ever heard of the War of 1812? Let's just say Abaddon got bored, and was able to manipulate both Americans and the British into fighting for no reason," I said, with an eye roll.

Abaddon was an egotistical child who took pleasure in watching the pain and suffering of others. To be honest, he was kind of annoying, as Shasta would put it. To say the guy was unstable would be putting it mildly.

"He actually took part in that war, playing spy for both sides, jumping from one team to another, as twisted as that sounds."

"Umm—" Riker went silent on his end, his breathing was the only indication that the line didn't go dead.

Finally, after a few minutes, he spoke.

"They were that involved in our history? I mean, actually starting wars," he said quietly, allowing us to hear the typing of keys on his end.

"Well, yeah. Most of the violence that humans endured is because of the supernatural. We try to stop them as soon as we can, but it's harder the more powerful they are. Plus, once something starts, humans take over. At that point, there is nothing we can do but try to persuade them into stopping. They use humans because they know we can't intervene if it's human on human violence, even if Demons started it," I explained.

As twisted as it sounded, there was only so much we could do.

"But if the Guardians were never created, the world would be in ruins. The humans they decided to let live would be nothing more than slaves, and in more ways than just serving the Demons' every needs. Trust me, when they say there is a fate worse than death, they aren't joking," I continued.

"Thanks, Kye. I think I've got more than enough."

Riker stayed on the line for a few more minutes, catching up on all of our lives, as we talked about college and sports. Like a proud father, Riker's voice lit up every time soccer came up. Amanda bragged about our upcoming party, saying it would be the party of the year. Riker laughed, telling Amanda only she could throw a celebrity-worthy party that people will talk about all year. Way to boost her already huge ego. It's what made Amanda and Shasta the perfect couple. They loved themselves more than each other, so they never had any drama.

After I hung up, I excused myself for a minute, stepping outside onto the porch. Bringing up my supernatural past made my heart hurt a little. I missed my boys, and I missed fighting; not as much as I thought I would, but sometimes I felt a part of me was empty.

Shasta was also running through my head. He didn't even call to make sure I was moved in or anything. It's not like he was obligated to play my family anymore, but I still missed hearing his stupid condescending voice. I trailed down my phone to his number, pressing call. It went straight to voicemail. I stared at my phone for a minute, before scrolling up to a number I hadn't used in over a year. I took a deep breath, closed my eyes, and hit call. It rang and rang, until it went to voicemail.

"Hey, you've reached Derek. You know what to do."

I didn't think he would answer, but I hoped he would. I hoped he would forgive me for picking Andy over my destiny, but it wasn't just Andy I chose. It was everything that came with being with Andy. It was the darkness that had finally lifted from me the day I met him. It was the anger and rage I carried, blaming everything and everyone, which vanished the day I moved to Florida. It was the peace that came after I made my decision to stay.

If I left, if I had never experienced the things I did, it would be only a matter of time before I was dead. If I chose to stay with Lucas, it would only have resulted in me resenting him one day. They didn't understand that my reasons weren't just to have fun and live a normal life; it was the change in me that I grew to love. But the biggest thing they didn't want to realize was how hard it was for me to say goodbye to that life—to them. It was a sacrifice that, after weighing my options, I had to make. I just wished they would tell me it was all okay.

"Hey, it's me," I paused as tears filled my eyes. "Just wanted to hear your voice. I miss you. Tell everyone I love them, and that I'm doing really well. I just wish you would all talk to me."

I wanted to say more, but the lump that formed in my throat stopped me from baring my soul. I hung up, dropping my phone onto the nearby chair. I looked out into the storm, feeling the same way it looked; cold, miserable, and sad. I also knew that when the storm passed, in the morning, the world would be bright and happy, refreshed after a long night. I looked forward to that. That feeling kept me going.

Andy came up from behind me, slipping his arms around my waist. I heard him coming when he got up from his seat inside, but I didn't bother to move. I lay my head against his chest, hearing the thumping of his heart beating faster. Blue symbols appeared, running down my arms like liquid running down a pipe. The symbols grew larger,

47

connecting to one another as my emotions swirled through my head.

"Hey, what's wrong?" he asked, knowing my emotions were what triggered my markings coming to life.

"Nothing," I lied, watching the rain fall from the sky.

He pulled his arms away, grabbing my shoulders. He turned me around so that I was facing him. His blues eyes grew dark, seeing my wet face.

"Kye, talk to me, please."

I didn't know what to say. I hated bringing up that I was sad that my family wouldn't talk to me, because Andy would think it was his fault. I didn't have to say anything; he knew.

"It's your family isn't it?" He looked down at my phone lying on the chair, still opened to Derek's name. "What did he say?"

"Nothing. He didn't answer. I don't know why I even called. I knew he wouldn't. They all hate me because—" I stopped short, wiping at my face.

"Because of me," Andy finished.

He pulled me to him, wrapping me securely in his arm. I rested my cheek on his heart while he placed his head on mine. I breathed in his scent, finding peace in his smell. My body started to calm, dimming my internal light.

"I could have used your glowing body earlier," he joked, referring to the mess still in the kitchen that was caused by him and Greg knocking down two shelves. His chest rumbled as I started to laugh. "You ready to go back inside before they think we got taken by the storm?"

I wiped at my face, nodding. Andy moved his mouth to mine, kissing me with so much love and passion that it wasn't long before I started to glow again, but for different reasons.

"Unless you want our neighbors to think aliens are invading our house, I wouldn't do that!" Greg yelled from inside, as my light grew brighter. I laughed into Andy's mouth, pulling away before I slobbered on him.

"Let's go," I said, pulling us both inside the house. I saw our curtains were pulled back, exposing the living room. I yanked them together, walking back over to the table to start playing.

Chapter 6

Saturday morning I was awoken early by Amanda running up and down the hallway, screeching like a banshee on Christmas morning trying to wake the parents. She banged once on my door, not waiting for me to open it before she came billowing in.

"Let's go! We have lots to do, kiddies!" she yelled, throwing back my comforter.

Thank god I slept in clothes. I laid there, watching her stand over me, with her hands on her hips and an annoying smile on her face. I rolled over, curling into Andy's chest; he was still sleeping and barely wearing any clothes, other than a pair of basketball shorts that didn't do much to cover him up.

"Ah, go away," I groaned, reaching for my covers. "What time is it anyway?"

"It's time for the two of you to get up. Come on, I got everyone coffee."

After ten minutes of early morning torture, I rolled out of bed, stumbling downstairs to find Greg and Kady looking just as miserable, chugging their coffees.

"Seriously, guys, you're acting like I woke you up at the crack of dawn," Amanda said, grabbing her coffee and taking a seat at the bar.

"You know, you guys really suck. If I'd know we were getting up this early, I wouldn't have gone out so late last night," Andy said, walking into the kitchen as he rubbed the sleep from his eyes. His beautiful dark hair fell in a mess around his face. He came up behind me, and planted a kiss on my head, while scowling at Amanda.

"Oh, please. It's almost noon, cry babies," she whined.

****

The hours ticked by as we prepared for our first party. By the end, the place looked immaculate. The living room furniture was moved around to put together a makeshift dance floor. The food was set up in the kitchen, and the outside bar was fully stocked. We set up the sound system to play around the entire house, and a seating area was placed around the fire pit.

Finally, around four, I walked upstairs to get ready. After a very long shower, I stepped out and wiped the steam from the mirror, small droplets of water glistening from my tanned skin. Wrapping a towel around me, I ran my fingers through my hair. My natural curls fell down my back. I applied shimmery blue eye shadow and black eye liner, bringing out my bright silver eyes.

"Damn, you're beautiful," Andy growled.

"Did you just growl at me, love?" I asked, watching him through the mirror.

"Err, when you look like that, wearing nothing but a towel, how can I not?"

I laughed, watching his hungry eyes sweep up and down my body. Before he knew what hit him, my towel slid down me. Falling into a pile on the floor, I was left standing in nothing but a bra and matching panties. His eyes widened in surprise as I pushed him through the door, locking it behind him.

"That wasn't very nice, Alikye," he said, emphasizing my name.

"Well, Andy," I said back in the same tone, "it's not very nice to growl at people."

Another growl erupted from deep in his throat. I couldn't really blame him. We've been together for nearly two years, and still haven't done much besides kiss. Every night we shared the same bed, always touching, but never once doing much more. It couldn't be easy on Andy. He was, after all, a guy.

I opened the door, smiling at his tortured face, fully wrapped back in my towel. Wrapping my arms around his waist, I kissed him gently.

"I love you, baby. Soon."

He smiled back, knowing what I meant. It was more than just sex to him, though. He knew that by me giving myself to him, I would be his forever. It was rough for me to give up my independence, but giving my heart to him fully only meant that I would love him forever. And that I could live with. Knowing I wasn't his possession, but his soul mate, his equal, and together we would get our happily ever after.

*****

The party was in full swing by eight o'clock, and the sixty guests that were invited turned out to be more like ninety. Barreling my way through the crowds of testosterone filled frat boys and girls whose daddies would have heart attacks just by looking at their tiny outifts, I finally made it to the back yard to find my housemates together around the fire. Andy's eyes caught sight of me the minute I stepped onto the porch. Tilting his head a little to the side, his eyebrows shot up. I twirled around once to show him my dress, before walking over to him. He was talking with a few guys that I recognized from his soccer team.

"Well, hot damn, girl. Why not dump this loser, and me and you can have a little fun?" Jake said, throwing his arm around my shoulder and pulling me away from Andy. Jake was a good looking guy, but compared to my boyfriend—well, there really wasn't any comparison, because my man was gorgeous.

"Sorry, honey," I said, shifting my eyes from him to Andy, "but I'm good. Have you seen my boyfriend?"

Andy laughed, punching Jake in the arm before pulling me from his grip and slamming his lips to mine. "You are beautiful."

He ran his figure tips down my exposed back.

"Speaking of your boyfriend," Jake began, "I think I owe you an apology for that whole Billy incident."

"Don't worry about it. It's not like I didn't know about it the whole time," I said, looking at Andy. "Plus, it's whatever. It's just who you are," I shrugged. The guys started to laugh.

"Wow, you make me sound so dirty," Jake grumbled.

"Sweetheart, you make yourself sound dirty. All I say is the truth. So if you don't like it, start making me a liar, and get yourself a real girlfriend," I chimed.

"I have plenty," Jake managed to say, before I stopped him with my hand over his mouth.

"Oh, no, I mean monogamy," I replied.

Jake threw his hands up to his ears, shaking his head back and forth like a child. "Nope, don't say it. I can't."

We all laughed.

"OK, I need to steal you away for a minute," Kady interrupted, grabbing ahold of me. She pulled me from Andy. He gave me a smile, before returning his attention to his teammates. Kady and I walked into the house. "So, I wanted you to meet the team."

A group of girls stood by the inside bar, passing drinks around. They stopped when they noticed me entering the kitchen. Before Kady had the chance to introduce me to any of them, a petite redheaded girl threw her arms around me, taking me by surprise.

"Holy shit, I can't believe we will be playing on the same team. I have heard so much about you. You were like a legend at my old school," she squealed.

For a moment, I was taken back to the first time I met Kady. Although they didn't have any kind of resemblance, save their size, their bubbly personalities and contagious smiles were identical. Thinking back to that time, I remembered that all I wanted was to be left alone, and to get through my time in Picture City as fast as possible, with no kinds of attachments. I was glad Kady had other ideas, and had forced me into a friendship that changed my life. It made me smile, because I knew right away that these girls and I would soon be friends.

"Alright, Kathy, you don't want to scare the girl away before our first practice," said a girl with bleached blond hair and a killer tan.

After a minute of silence, Kathy's face reddened, only making me like her even more.

"It's very nice to meet you, Kathy," I said, matching her smile.

For the next hour, after I was introduced to the rest of the girls, they gushed over my skills, replaying each of my games back to me in vivid detail. Andy finally made his way over to us, bringing his teammates with him. We all laughed and joked, and I found myself loving each minute of it. This was my life now. People liked me for me, and not because I was the best fighter, or because I was bonded to the hottest Guardian. Yes, there were certain similarities, but really they just wanted to be friends with me, without having a reason for it. We were already planning trips to the beach. Monica, my teammate with the blond hair, even offered to teach me how to surf, scolding me for not learning the two years I lived in Florida. Andy then scolded me for taking up her offer, when I had denied his a million times. Until now, I didn't see the need for it, but I finally realized that it would just be fun to learn something, without having a need for it.

"So, I was also thinking that maybe next weekend we could all go camping up in the mountains. It is supposed to be nice weather," Monica suggested. She moved here a year ago from Cali, and you could just tell by her appearance that she spent most of her time outdoors.

Kye, we need to talk, a voice entered my head.

Before I could answer Monica, I froze from hearing his voice.

Where are you? I asked, telepathically.

"I mean, yeah, sounds good to me. What do you think?" someone asked.

About to walk inside, the voice replied.

"Hey, Kye, what do you think?" Kady asked, breaking me from my conversation with Shasta.

"Umm, yeah sounds good," I said, only catching bits and pieces of the conversation around me.

Kye, now! Shasta's voice boomed in my mind.

Okay, meet me in my room, I sent quickly.

"Hey baby, everything okay?" Andy asked in a hush whisper.

I hadn't heard from Shasta in weeks, and now all of a sudden he shows up without so much as making an appearance. He just walks in, talking privately in my head, and sounding a bit urgent. Something was wrong, and all I could think was something bad had happened to my family. If something did, the council wouldn't have contacted me. No, they would send Shasta to give me the news. I looked over at Andy, seeing the concern in his dark eyes.

"You look a little spooked," he said.

NOW! Shasta's voice reverberated in my head.

I jumped.

"I'm fine. Just give me a minute, and I'll be right back," I assured him.

I walked out of the kitchen, a little too quickly, making it up the staircase as fast as humanly possible. Something bad must have happened, and all I could think was the worst possible scenario— my family. If I lost them, I would never forgive myself. I never even got the chance to say goodbye.

I took a deep breath to calm my nerves, chanting over and over that everything was fine. I burst into my room to find Shasta sitting on my bed. A look of horror shadowed his handsome face. His long black hair was down, curling around his neck, and day old scruff dusted his face. His icy blue eyes looked haunted but determined.

Even with something dark looming over him, he still felt like home to me, and I couldn't help but throw my arms around him. He wrapped me up tightly in his arms, cradling my face in his neck. If it had been two years ago, I would have said something sarcastic to him, and perhaps even hit him in the shoulder. That was the extent of me showing any kind of affection towards another.

"Please tell me they're all okay," I questioned, against his skin. He took a deep breath, nodding up and down.

They're fine, he sent.

What then, Shasta? You're scaring me.

"It's you, Kye. You're the one who is not okay," Shasta groaned.

Chapter 7

Me? Why would I not be okay? I was fine, at least I thought I was. Was something after me? Was my being here putting my friends in danger? Did the Demons find me? Why would they be after me now? I've been out of the game for almost two years, and the incident in Hidden Falls was just a fluke.

Shasta stayed silent while my mind was going back and forth to different scenarios.

"Love, just stop. It's not the Demons you should be worried about. Look, the past year I have been going back and forth from here to England. I was summoned by Anastasis," Shasta said aloud.

"Wait. What? Why would she have anything to do with my well-being?" I said in a panic.

"They don't like the choices you have been making. Other Guardians are talking, Kye. Anastasis said she needs to make an example of you," Shasta answered.

I was definitely confused. I knew Guardians would talk. Hell, I did the one thing no Guardian has ever done; I quit so I could live with humans. What I didn't understand was why Ana would summon Shasta, of all people. This couldn't be good.

Shasta was scatter-brained, stressed, and his hair looked like he'd been running his hands through it for the last few hours. I knew he was hiding something big.

"Kye, I just don't know if you should know everything right now," he said, warily.

"So what does she want to do then, lock me up? Force me to work under her until I turn 18, and then make me take over as the head of the council? Electric shock therapy because I'm the worst Guardian ever?"

Please don't make me go back there. The idea of living at the council and working under Ana was disturbing.

"Kye, this isn't a joke; she means business. She's pissed about what you did, and she's been holding a trial the past year," Shasta barked.

"A trial," I repeated.

"To figure out what to do with you," he answered.

"And they didn't think to invite me to my own trial? That's shit and you know it."

That was so like them, to think that they could do whatever they wanted, without so much as consideration for the other party involved. It angered me to think that for the past year they held a trial about me, to determine my future, without even asking how I felt about it. I was terrified of what they were going to do to me, but I was also angry with them. They could do what they wanted, but I wasn't going down without a fight.

"Give it to me straight, Shasta. What did they say?" I snarled.

"They said you were compromised. They said that what you were taught is now gone. You're not worth the trouble, and although they would like nothing more than to shun you, your actions will one day create waves to the younger generation. There is only one thing they can do that will ensure the safety of your race, and make sure that no other Guardian will ever think this is okay to do," he answered.

"Okay, so what? Spit it out. I can't take the suspense," I pleaded.

"Kye, they sentenced you to death."

My breath caught in my throat, silencing my next words. My chest felt like I had a hundred pounds weighing against it. Could they really do that? Justify killing their own kind over something so trivial? I put my head in my hand, trying to steady my nerves before I passed out. There was only one thing for me to do.

"How long?" I asked in a shaky voice.

Not long, maybe an hour. I got out as quickly as I could. They have a bounty out on me now, and on anyone else who helps you. They're sending their best hunters to bring you in; dead or alive. Anastasis doesn't care, she just wants you dead. I have a plan, but we have to leave now, Shasta explained, returning to our private thoughts.

"You risked your life to warn me. Shasta, are you kidding me?" I asked aloud, too panicked to steady my thoughts.

"You really think I wouldn't? Even they knew I would. Ana was betting on it, actually. She wants us both gone, and now she has a reason to execute me."

I had to run, it was the only way. First, I needed to say goodbye to Andy. I couldn't just leave without telling him my reason. The party was still going on downstairs, and it was still too early before anyone would leave. Amanda needed to say goodbye to Shasta, also. Even if he wouldn't admit it, I knew it would be hard for him to see another person he cared about leave.

Andy's worried about you. Some girl told him you went upstairs with a hot guy. Regardless, he is on his way up with every one of your housemates. You need to say your goodbyes, Shasta told me.

I grabbed my bags from the closet. In case of an emergency, I always had a packed bag that was small enough to travel and held everything I needed. Just as I was looking through my things, Andy came rushing in, eyeing my stuff.

"What's going on?" Andy asked.

Shasta took Amanda by the hand, leading her outside, probably to her room to talk.

"I need to go. I don't know for how long, but I promise I'll be back for you," I said through unwanted tears.

How long could I really run? My race had unparalleled resources throughout the entire world. Unless I could somehow make my new home on a different planet, I was shit out of luck. Shasta was smart. He was able to stay off the grid for over a hundred years, but that was also back in the fifteen hundreds, and he wasn't a wanted fugitive. So, there was nowhere to hide.

"I don't understand. Why? What happened?" Andy questioned.

The only way I could explain was to tell Andy the whole truth, and not to sugar coat it as Shasta liked to do. So, I did. I told him everything, and it crushed my heart to watch him so broken.

Death seemed to be an inevitable obstacle in our relationship, and I couldn't help but feel like it would never change. I really thought it would be acceptable for me to just get out of the game for a while, and to live a normal life, but I guess it was never okay. It was a delayed act from my race, and eventually, they would take everything from me.

"If you're running, Kye, I'm running with you," Andy added.

"Umm, no way. This is too dangerous," I retorted.

"Not for me. I'm human, they can't touch me."

"Andy, I'm sorry, but I'm not letting you get mixed up in this. Shasta will be with me the whole time, and we can figure something out so I can come home to you," I added.

As if I were talking to the wall, Andy ignored me, pulling clothes from our closet and folding them into a duffle bag. I glared at him, but he just glared back at me, shaking his head.

"Andy, I'm serious," I scolded, "you're not coming."

"No, I'm serious," he said, his features softening, "and yes, I'm going. Look, when you chose me, I told you I would never leave you, no matter what. I meant it. I love you, and there is no way I'm allowing them to take you from me. So just deal with it, please."

Before I had time to argue, Amanda and Shasta walked in, holding a pink carry-on bag. I looked over to Shasta with a look that said, "Are you kidding me?"

I'm sorry. I told her no, but as you can see, that didn't matter. She said that if I left without her, she would somehow find me. So, there was no point in arguing, Shasta explained.

I turned to Andy, who was watching Amanda.

"No, not happening!" I yelled.

Don't bother. His mind is already made up, Kye, and we don't have time for this.

I can't put them in danger, and you're permitting this? I was angry.

You know as well as I do that they will be safe. The Guardians can't hurt them.

"Then you better promise me now that nothing will happen to Andy. Shasta, promise me," I begged aloud.

"I promise."

****

Andy and Amanda left right away on a red eye to Venice, Italy, where Shasta owned a flat overlooking the Grand Canal. As for Shasta and I, time was not on our side. The council made sure of that, knowing Shasta would be the one to warn me. As if reading their minds, which Shasta did, they had hunters already posted outside of Chapel Hill, awaiting orders. The party saved my life, because in no way were they going to come in with that many witnesses.

Hunters were Guardians that belonged to the council, usually Legacies that weren't in line to take over their family name. They were ruthless and emotionless; they hunted their own kind, and played by the book. They were the council's secret service, and they were after me.

The one thing I hated about jumping was the sick feeling you get after you appeared at the place you imagined. It's like eating a dozen cookies, and then being thrown around in one of those fair rides that leave you heaving in the garbage. Luckily, unlike those rides, the feeling only lasted for a minute.

We arrived in Italy just as the sun started to rise. Shasta's flat was truly breathtaking. There were three bedrooms on the third and fourth floor, with high ceilings and wooden floors. On the far wall in the central living room, overlooking the canal, were floor to ceiling windows, draped with turn of the century linings. The walls were entirely authentic frescoes and stuccos.

Along with the three bedrooms, the flat also had two separate living areas, a grand dining room, four bathrooms, and a white stone balcony wrapping around the front of both floors. Shasta owned a few different places around the world; Paris, Sydney, Tokyo. The council didn't know about most of his properties, so not even the hunters would be able to figure out where he lived. He liked it better that way. I was one of the only people to know how much he owned, and where the locations were.

"What now?" I asked, as I threw my belongings on the floor.

I opened my duffle bag, taking out my bow and arrows and a few other weapons. Shasta had a large cabinet built in to one of the walls, full of weapons from all over the world and all over time. It was every Guardian's dream. Without a word, he walked out, coming back a few minutes later with a stack of folders. With a loud thump, he dropped them on the floor in front of me.

"Now, we figure out how to get you out of this mess, but first, you want me to make us breakfast?" he asked, coyly.

"It's still twelve thirty in the morning to me. So, no, I would rather get started," I growled.

"Well, I'm on England time still, so its breakfast time for me. Oh, and watch the attitude. I just saved your butt," Shasta countered.

He left me alone in the smaller living area, while he went into the kitchen. I had at least twenty different folders to go through, each with about fifty papers in them. The first one I opened was the private file of an old Guardian, Natalia Van Der Will. She was my father's best friend, and ex-lover, before the council bonded him with my mother.

Natalia was also the Legacy who went dark when she was twenty-three; the same year I was born. Some say she was so broken from watching my father be happy without her, while others say she was destined to turn. I put that file down, not wanting to read more. I already knew the ending to that story; she was killed by my father, because she tried to kill my mother while still pregnant with me.

The next couple of files were on the council members; each family tree, each Legacy. Everything I already knew, and yet for some reason, Shasta thought this information would be my lifeline. I couldn't see how any of this was helping.

"Because, like I said, I have a plan. It involves Natalia and the rest of the council, but it won't be easy," Shasta said, coming into the room with a plate of Eggs Benedict, complete with a creamy hollandaise drizzle and a hot cup of black coffee.

I grabbed the coffee, taking a large sip and silently thanking him.

"Natalia is dead, and even if she was still alive, how in the hell would she be able to help? She went dark for shit's sake." I took a bite of my food, moaning as the tastes melted together in my mouth.

Holy crap this food is amazing.

Without saying another word, I finished my plate, not realizing how hungry I had actually been. Shasta stayed silent the entire time, watching me carefully.

"That's not exactly true, Kye," he said slowly, wearing a very guilty look on his face.

"What are you not telling me? Enough with this sugar coated cryptic bullshit."

It was getting late for me, and I wasn't in the mood for this. I was tired, and pissed off that my own people would do something like this to me, just because I fell in love with a human. I mean, what did they think would happen? It was Anastasis's idea to send me away to live like a human for eight months. Did she really think I wouldn't grow some sort of bond with the people I was with every day? Did she think that I would be able to just leave them all to go back to a life that I truly never wanted? It was her fault this all happened, and instead of taking responsibility for her actions, she was throwing all the blame on me. It was all leading up to my death, and yet another Legacy name that would be wiped off the map, bringing Lucifer one step closer to breaking down the gates of hell, bringing Hell on Earth.

"So, all that rambling in there," he said, pointing to my head, "and you still haven't figured it out? Okay, so you want the whole truth, everything I was able to get out of her. For starters, she did all this betting you would become attached to this life. Therefore, she would have a reason to finally get rid of you, since you were never able to get yourself killed on your own. With you gone, she will bear all the power in the council. She will have no one to stand in her way. Like I said earlier, you have been compromised, and if you take your place as head chair, you will hold all the power to change the rules. But, now that you have been sentenced. There is nothing you can do, even if you can make it to your eighteenth birthday."

"So, this whole time she wanted me dead so I'd be out of her way, and she could take my spot. But, why?" I stood up, walking out through the French doors onto the balcony.

The morning breeze blew through my hair. The day was sunny and bright. Along the canal, people rode on their gondolas. They were starting their days off, whether it was going to work or just enjoying the beautiful morning. The view was something else, like something out of a storybook. Multicolored buildings lined the canal; old eighteen century architectural structures with high arches and hand carved bricks, created by some of the greatest artists in history.

Italy was one of my favorite places on Earth, but I couldn't enjoy myself. The beauty that surrounded me felt more like a calm before the storm. The peacefulness felt right before the world gets ripped apart was exactly what my life had become. After a few minutes, Shasta came out, handing me another cup of coffee. I took it gratefully, finally ready for him to finish explaining things to me.

"It's because of who you are, mainly who your father was. Peter was a pistol, fully loaded at all times. He was so different from his parents, so opinionated. You're the same way. Your father believed that while the world evolved, the council stayed set in their ways, scared that change would destroy them. He tried to explain that change was good, that if your race was able to have a little more freedom, then perhaps you would thrive. But, your grandparents were stuck in their ways, and believed that being a warrior was a full time job. After your parents died, Anastasis thought that if you were to be raised by another family, then maybe you would follow in your grandparents' footsteps and not Peter's. However, it was made clear the day you ran off with me to kill the Kyro Demon that you were as stubborn and hard headed, and no matter what she did, you would never be the Guardian she wanted to run the council," Shasta explained.

"She knew about that night," I interrupted, shocked that she never brought it up.

Shaking his head, he finished. "There's more. She knew all of it, and the only reason she allowed it to go on for so long was because she was hoping you would get yourself killed fixing the problem for her. When she realized you were too good to die, she went on to plan B. Allowing you to live with humans, and you fell right into her trap."

I ran my hands through my hair, something I did when I was stressed. I couldn't wrap my mind around all the information. I felt betrayed by the people I trusted—my family. This whole time she wanted me gone. Was she the only one, or were there more people involved? I paced back and forth, counting to myself, something I did when I was getting myself worked up. I was pissed, beyond angry, but there was nothing I could do about it. Even if by some miracle, Shasta got me off with his big plan he had yet to tell me about, I still wouldn't be able to prove her vindictive scandal. We would go on hating each other, hoping the worst for one another, and living together with this big secret.

It wasn't really the life I wanted to live; I just wanted to be free to make my own choices without the world falling apart around me. I looked over at Shasta. Sometime during my mental hissy fit, he had left for a moment to refill my coffee, yet again, and I had already downed half of it. My hands were shaking and I didn't know if it was from the caffeine overdose I was having, or the fact that I really wanted to hit something.

"I have a punching bag in the other room, if that would help," Shasta grinned.

It definitely wasn't a bad idea, and it would keep me from either hitting Shasta or breaking one of his priceless artifacts. He snapped his head towards me, piercing me with a look that said, "this is my badass glare, and don't you dare break my things." We both walked back inside, heading straight for his workout room to release some pent up rage. The rest of the information would have to wait.

Chapter 8

Derek stood in his suite with his family. He paced around from one side to the other, trying desperately to calm his nerves before he did something stupid to jeopardize the life of himself and his family. The room was large, with two bedrooms on either side, both looking out at the city of London. A small sitting area and a kitchenette lay flush with the front door. Across, there was a balcony. Beyond the balcony was the courtyard, an area so exquisite it was hard to believe you weren't standing in your own fairytale.

Jack sat at the desk, writing something in his notebook, while Sarah and Lucas sat on the plush white couch. Over the year since Alikye left, Derek watched as his family drifted apart. She wasn't the only one to blame for it, not really. They had all made their choices. Jack took to his work, sitting side by side with the council, in Alikye's place. Lucas became a completely different person. He fought harder and studied longer. He was an empty shell, numb to the world; shutting everyone out, including his brother. Derek saw it every time he looked into his brother's emerald eyes.

Six months after the choice, as the council liked to call it, Anastasis called for Derek, offering him and Lucas a chance at a job. The job was to become a council hunter, a job that was rarely given to anyone besides Legacies. Derek knew it was so that Ana could obtain as much information about Alikye as possible. To Derek's relief, Lucas declined the offer. Derek knew Lucas blamed Alikye for many things. He heard him say it over and over. Alikye was supposed to love him, to be with him, but she chose a human boy to love. Derek watched as Lucas slipped up, out of anger, and told the council everything he knew about the human boy.

****

"What the hell did you do, Lucas?" Derek yelled.

"It's not going to matter whether they know or not. Alikye doesn't care, so why should I?" Lucas spat back in Derek's face, storming out of the room.

"You have no clue what you've done!" Derek roared at Lucas's back.

****

Lucas's statement about the human was the turning point in the trial. If Ana had believed Alikye left just to go to college, she would have made her come back, and all would have been forgiven. But loving a human, telling a human all your secrets, choosing a human over your own kind, was unforgivable. Regardless, Derek didn't blame Lucas for the verdict. Deep down, he knew Ana would have found any way to charge Alikye; Shasta told him as much.

His parents' statements were the same as Derek's. They told the council Alikye was an asset, she was the most powerful Guardian to ever exist, and they would be stupid to dismiss her as anything else. Derek spoke of her strong points. He told them she just needed time to sort out her past.

During that statement, Derek found Shasta's eyes. If looks could kill, he thought, he would be dead where he sat.

Shasta was pissed. He basically told Ana and the rest of the council that they could all shove it. He would stand by her side no matter what. If they wanted a war, bring it. It was something Derek should have said.

It was hard on Derek to watch Alikye walk away from him. It was months later that Derek finally realized how happy she really was. The council had told his family to stay away from her. Derek never did. Jack didn't either. They were both there the day Alikye won state. They watched as the whole school cheered for her, as her human took her in his arms and kissed the living shit out of her. Her smile was the brightest they had ever seen.

They were there the day she graduated, when she accepted her scholarship to UNC in front of all her peers; they heard the pride in her voice, saw the spark in her eyes. They were there a week ago when she moved into her new house, when she wrapped her arms around her human, staring into his eyes, and when she kissed him. It was at that moment that Derek knew she had done the right thing. The love and passion in her eyes was something they had never seen before, and had finally found. She needed that life. It was the only way he knew she would survive.

****

"Maybe this was the right thing to do," Derek had once said to his mother. "You all act as if she committed a crime."

No one answered. Sarah wouldn't have any talk of the situation.

"And you call yourselves her family," Derek shook his head, walking away.

"That little girl ruined everything!" Sarah yelled.

Derek froze, slowly turning around. He had never heard his mother say such hateful things about a person she claimed to love.

"You raised that little girl since she was three," he reminded her.

"And all she has ever done is bring this family heartache," she barked back.

****

Sarah was hurt by what Alikye did to her family, specifically to her son. She had told Derek many months ago, and he knew she still felt that way now. Jack would never argue with his wife, so it was Derek who brought on all the arguments. It wasn't until the verdict that Sarah finally shed a tear of sympathy.

Afterwards, the council hunters took Derek and his family into custody, locking them up in a room until Alikye was found. Ana proclaimed that if anyone said or did anything to help Alikye escape, they would suffer the same fate. Derek was outraged. He would have left right after the verdict was read, if they weren't so quick to detain him. Before it was given, though, he noticed Shasta jump out. It was then he knew the results couldn't be good. Ana did nothing to stop Shasta; everyone knew it was because it finally gave the council a reason to kill him. Knowing Alikye would be warned and protected, Derek breathed a little easier.

****

Derek finally quit pacing the room, rage bubbling up inside him. In the blink of an eye, he ran to the other side of the room, grabbing a vase from the end table and throwing it against the wall. Hundreds of tiny pieces exploded in the air, scattering across the wooden floor, water spraying everywhere.

Jack jumped to his feet. "Son, that's not going to help anything," he said softly.

"No, but it feels good!" Derek yelled. He ran his hands through his hair, pulling at the ends. "We can't just sit here. She can't do this."

"We don't have much of a choice, now do we?" Lucas grunted, standing up from the couch. "She brought this upon herself."

"Are you serious? So, you think she should die?" Derek asked.

"I didn't say that. All I'm saying is—"

Before Lucas was able to finish his sentence, Derek grabbed another vase from the end table and threw it at him. Lucas saw it coming, ducking out of the way and letting it hit the wall behind him. It shattered. This wasn't the first time they had gotten physical with one another. Lucas had a broken heart, and didn't know when to shut up, and Derek was sick and tired of his mouth.

Derek shot forward, going after his brother. Pulling his arm back, he was just about to make contact with Lucas's face when Jack got in between them. He pulled Derek aside, pushing him into the other room. Jack shut the door, locking it before he turned to face his angered son. Derek glared at his father, taking deep breaths.

"You need to calm down, Derek. This isn't easy on any of us, and you're not helping by getting in your brother's face. He's having a hard time with everything," Jack scolded him.

"You heard what he said, Dad. Broken heart or not, he shouldn't blame her for living her own life," Derek said, referring to Alikye. "You saw her. She's happy. Why is it such a big deal that she chose a different path?"

"The council doesn't know how to deal with change, son. You have to trust that Shasta will get to her in time. Kye will figure out a way to fix this," Jack said, reassuringly.

"What if she can't? What happens if they catch her?" Derek sat down on the bed, putting his head in his hands. He rubbed his eye, wiping away a stray tear. "She called me the other day, but I sent it to voicemail. She probably thinks I hate her."

"She knows you love her, son. I think when this is all over, and she is safe, it's about time we all have a long talk and forgive her."

Derek knew Jack missed Alikye like crazy. She was his daughter, even if they didn't share the same blood. It didn't matter to Jack. He loved her.

A small smile pulled at Derek's lips. The thought of finally talking to Alikye was all he needed to calm down. He nodded. "Yeah dad, I'd like that, but I don't think Mom's gonna go for it."

"Let me handle your mother. I hurt for your brother. He loves Kye, but sometimes it's just not meant to be, and maybe this Andy guy is who is meant for her."

If anyone would understand lost love, it would be his father. If Jack had been strong like Alikye, he would have fought for Alexandra a long time ago. Jack confided in Derek a few months ago about once loving someone else, before he was chosen to be with Sarah.

"Andy, huh? Not human boy anymore?" Derek laughed. They never called him by his name.

"It's about time we use his real name, don't you think?" Jack winked.

Chapter 9

Death. It's such a small word, but with so much meaning to it. The absence of one, the end of a life, a soul which has become vacant from this world to move on to another. It all ends with death, and for the first time in my life, I didn't want to die.

When I was a child, I didn't care if I was taken from this world, knowing that I would go to a place where I never had to feel again. It wasn't until Andy, Kady, Greg, and even Amanda, that I realized that living was the greatest gift of all. That love, friendship, compassion, and laughter were the best parts of life, and I would be a fool to give it all up without a fight.

Sweat dripped from my body as I took a few more hits. I had been in this room for over six hours. After the first two hours of throwing my fists into the punching bags, Shasta decided on hand to hand combat and sword training. After a very bloody session, he called it quits, going on about how he needed to get things ready for our guests that were to arrive any minute. In reality, I kicked his ass, and he couldn't take another stab in the gut.

I grabbed my towel, wiping away the blood from my face and stomach, and allowing my markings to heal me and take the pain away. Only the physical pain, though, because even the magic in my Enochian tattoos couldn't take away the emotional pain I was experiencing.

"Hey, baby. Shasta said you would be in here. You look a mess," Andy said, coming into the room. I closed my eyes for a moment, feeling the warmth from his body; the pull I felt whenever he entered a room; a sudden calmness, like a drug running through my veins. I turned toward him, throwing myself into his outstretched arms. "I know. Shasta told me everything."

I buried my face into his chest, holding back tears I refused to let go of, not wanting to give the council the satisfaction of knowing they were finally breaking me.

"How could they? They were my family," I said in a muffled voice.

"I don't know, but we are going to fix this so we can go home," he responded.

"I can't do this without you," I admitted, thankful he had come, even though I had told him to stay. Deep down, I needed him, his strength, his courage, and his love for me.

"Baby," he said, grabbing my face so I could look into his sapphire eyes, "I wouldn't be anywhere else. I will never be anywhere away from you."

He ran his finger down my cheek, tucking a loose curl behind my ear. His hand was soft, yet rough at the same time. It was a familiar touch I couldn't live without.

"Why do you put yourself through this? You could be dating a normal girl, with a normal life and normal drama, but instead you get caught up in all this supernatural stuff. You never complain or make me feel guilty about getting you into this mess," I asked, already knowing the answer, but wanting to hear it again. Honestly, what normal person would actually want to live my chaotic life?

"Because I couldn't live without you, and if that means being part of the real you, then I have no choice but to get tangled up in the supernatural. I'm not saying that I wouldn't prefer a normal life. Sure, it would be a lot easier, but I couldn't imagine a day without you. I love you, Kye, and that means I will love you forever. I will be at your side through thick and thin, through heartaches and heartbreaks, through the good and the evil, through clear skies and rainy nights, through—" Andy trailed off, fighting through his laughter. I playfully punched him in the arm, mouthing the words, "thank you." Even on a bad day, he could always make me smile.

For the rest of the day, I slept wrapped up in Andy's arms. By the time the sun started to disappear behind the city, I was finally ready to hear the rest of the plans to keep me alive. After finding out what Anastasis did to me, I had been avoiding Shasta all day, not wanting to hear anything else. However, after a heavy workout, long shower, and hours of well needed sleep, I was ready for some food and to find out everything. How much worst could it get?

I walked out to the balcony with Andy in tow. Shasta and Amanda were in a deep hushed conversation that stopped when they noticed me entering. Amanda was curled up in Shasta's lap, profusely running her hands through her hair. Shasta had laid out food on the patio table, along with a few cans of Mountain Dew that, of course, made Andy shake his head in annoyance before grabbing a bottle of water for himself.

I gulped down an entire can, grabbed the second one, popped the top, and put the opening to my lips, only taking a few sips. After piling our plates high with snacks, we all settled down. I waited anxiously for Shasta to begin to explain my fate that, right now, lay in his hands alone.

"Let's just say your father wasn't too keen on Ana being third chair on the council, and with the Van Der Will Legacy gone, he knew nothing would stop her from taking first chair. After your grandparents died and Peter took to his position, Ana did the same to him as she has been doing to you; she tried to remove him by using absurd accusations. He knew that if anything ever happened to him and your mother, Ana would stop at nothing to destroy you. So together, with the help of Natalia, we devised a plan, knowing one day this would happen. Only, we had something else in mind, but that's a different story—" Shasta began.

What the hell!

How could she get away with something like that for so long? Furthermore, why hadn't my father stepped in when he had the chance? All of this information was too much to bare; Anastasis's plot to destroy me, sentencing me to death, finding out that Natalia had something to do with this, and that she was still alive. I was being toyed around with just for my position on council, which I didn't even want. There had to be more to it, more to this story. I glanced back up at Shasta, asking him silently to finish. I had no words right now.

"Darling, there is more to it, more than you can handle right now. All I know is, in order to save you, we need to find Natalia. She must take her seat as head chair, granting you immunity against your actions. Once she is sworn in, Ana can't touch you," Shasta continued.

"That makes no sense. What's to stop Anastasis from granting the same death sentence on Natalia that she has on me? Technically, she would be charged the same, only she was known to turning evil, the evidence alone would have her killed the minute she stepped in front of everyone."

This had to be the worst plan in the history of planning. Natalia was no way my saving grace, and her fate would be far worse than mine. There was no way out of it. I didn't even know what my true crimes were. Was it the fact that I left to live a normal life or that I fell in love with a human? It's not like I killed anyone. Maybe if I explained that to Anastasis, and relinquished all my power to the council, she would let me go without a fight. I could go on living my life how I pleased.

"Alikye, please trust me on this one. Natalia has something that can save you. She has kept it safe for over seventeen years for your father. Strolling in to explain your case isn't going to do anything. Ana wants you dead, and nothing will change her mind. Please don't do anything stupid until you meet Natalia. Please," Shasta begged.

I guess it wouldn't hurt to hear Natalia out before I took matters into my own hands. I nodded once.

"So, where do we find Natalia?" Andy asked.

He sat beside me, squeezing my hand. I wanted to know what he thought about the whole situation. It couldn't be easy for him to drop his life and head out on this wild goose chase, surrounded by the supernatural. I looked to Shasta, pleading for him to tell me something. I felt bad asking him to dip into Andy's thoughts for me, but I was desperate.

He loves you. He's scared for you, but he has no regrets, and I don't think he ever will when it comes to you. He knows what he's getting into, and he wishes he could do more. He also feels this unnatural intense pull to you, and, well... Shasta thought, as a grin spread across his face.

Got it. Now get the hell out of his head, please, I sent back.

Shasta burst out laughing. I threw my empty can at his head, but he foresaw it coming, literally, and ducked out of the way. Sometimes he knew how to ruin the perfect moment.

Andy's eyes shifted from mine to Shasta, before breathing in a heavy breath, rubbing the bridge of his nose. He hated when I had private conversations, feeling like I was keeping something from him. Even though Shasta could read anyone's thoughts, it was impossible for him to communicate with humans the way he and I could send messages back and forth.

The human mind wasn't strong enough to receive messages, so it frustrated Andy that only Shasta and I had such an intimate ability. I shot Shasta another evil glare, telling him to shut the hell up. Amanda didn't seem bothered by our craziness. She knew how Shasta felt about her and how I felt about Andy. I wished Andy would get the memo.

"Sorry, mate, it's not that easy. Peter never told me where to find her. He only gave me the first piece of the puzzle, and that person should have the second," he said, getting back on topic.

You've got to be kidding. Of course, nothing could be that simple in my life. Shasta could read my anxiety, so he went on.

"However, the woman we need to see is here, and she should be able to explain a lot more."

"Okay, so where is she?" I asked.

"Umm," he mumbled.

I took a deep breath, feeling Andy's warmth engulf me as if he knew he needed to calm me down. Shasta had no clue where to find her; I could read it all over his face.

"Shasta, are you serious? I swear I'm two seconds from killing you!" I screamed. His so-called plan was not a plan at all; it was more like pulling bull from his ass, hoping it worked.

Shasta put his hand to his chest, faking hurt, but grinning like a hyena. "Alikye, love, that hurt."

"Okay, enough with all the dramatics. What exactly do you know?" Amanda asked sweetly, smiling up at Shasta.

"Well, since you asked me so nicely, without threats to my life, her name is Isabella Valentino. She lives not too far from here, and once we are close, I'll be able to sense her," Shasta explained.

****

By morning, we had made our way to the heart of the city. People were everywhere, enjoying the beautiful sunny day. Set up around town were numerous tents and booths, selling things like artwork and hand-crafted masks. The smell of food filled the air; from gourmet Italian to everyday foods you would find in America. Shasta and Amanda walked off to do some shopping. Of course they would, while my life was on the line. Amanda couldn't pass up a chance to use her credit card. Shasta reassured me by explaining that he was also going to find a guy who knew a guy that could tell him where to find Isabella. So, Andy and I took the opportunity to do some sightseeing and spend a little time together on our own.

"You know, last year I was thinking about bringing you here with me. I knew then that all I wanted was to be with you," I said, lacing my fingers with his as we walked down the street towards a park.

Andy stopped walking, pulling me to him. He wrapped his arms around my waist, placing his forehead against mine. He didn't say anything as he took a few deep breaths, breathing me in. I could feel his body pulling me deep into him, an electric pulse racing from him to me and back again. His heartbeat quickened, causing my body to shiver with excitement. It was always the same feeling when we were touching, like our bodies were each other's batteries, fueling our energy.

"I love that feeling," was all he said, before crushing his mouth to mine.

I melted into his kiss, forgetting all about the craziness in my life. It was only the two of us, alone together. I couldn't help but giggle into his mouth. He pulled away, smiling at me.

I was lucky to have him in my life. So, I decided that I needed to cherish every minute, every memory, because I knew deep down that one day I would get my happy ending with him. I will sit on the beach, watching our grandchildren play in the ocean. I will get to see my beautiful daughter, that has her father's eyes. I'll smile at my loving husband, and my life will be complete. Andy gave me the strength I needed to push on and never give up. I swore to myself that, no matter what happened, it's exactly what I had to do.

We grabbed some food, and settled down beneath a large tree. After an hour passed, we decided we might as well do some shopping, since this might be the only time we could, and Shasta was still busy with his own errands.

We stopped by a shop selling one-of-a-kind Venetian masks, the type you see at a masquerade ball. Andy took pictures of me goofing off, trying them all on. The last one I tried on, I had to buy; it was stunning. The mask was the color of sapphires, with silver running around the edges, and a silver bow was placed on the right side that looked more like half of a butterfly wing. It was small and delicate, only covering the top half of my face, stopping at my nose.

I bought a few additional things that I knew Kady would love. I hadn't really had the chance to talk to her. It was safer for her not to know where exactly we were staying, but she needed to know we were okay for now.

I felt eyes on me as we walked from shop to shop. I was always taught to trust my instincts. I turned to see who was watching me, but I saw no one. I opened my senses, but in that instant the feeling was gone. Andy noticed my hesitation, and asked if everything was okay. I shrugged my shoulders, walking into the next store.

As I began to relax, an intense feeling grabbed my attention. A shockwave ran from Andy to me as the bell rang above the door, signaling a customer was walking in. I turned quickly to see a girl around my age, with dark thick hair and dark eyes, looking right at Andy. A sense of familiarity rushed through me. She wasn't a Guardian, that much I knew, but there was something different about her. Her eyes moved from Andy's to mine, and then she smiled like we were old friends.

I shifted my body in front of Andy's, looking for a way out of there. She didn't look as if she wanted to harm me; it was more like she knew me or Andy. The girl started towards us, not taking her eyes off Andy the whole time. I didn't like the way she was looking at him. I turned to see that he had the same confused look on his face. He never once took his eyes off of her.

"*Ciao, come stai?*" the girl asked in Italian.

I didn't want to seem rude, but she was pissing me off. I cleared my throa,t grabbing her attention, and in perfect Italian I answered, "*bene, non ci conosciamo?*"

She didn't seem fazed by my attitude.

"*Mi dispiace, basta guardare familiar,*" she responded.

By this time, Andy was shifting back and forth, completely lost. "Can we please speak English?"

"She thought she knew us, and said we look familiar," I translated for him.

Andy moved his body out from behind me, stepping closer to the girl. I tried to shift to block him, but he held my waist, positioning himself in from of me. His eyes never once left the girl's stare. The room started to feel warm, an intense heat surrounded us. I didn't like it, and I didn't like the feelings I was getting from the two of them. They both turned to look at me as though they felt the same thing.

"I'm sorry, and who are you?" I snapped.

"Maria," she said in perfect English, with an Italian accent. "Are you American?"

"Yeah, we're here on holiday," Andy spoke up, before I had a chance to answer.

"Ah, *si*—" Maria trailed off, still not removing her eyes from him.

I grabbed his hand, pulling him with me towards the door.

"Well, Maria, it was a pleasure, but we should be going," I said.

Before she had time to answer, we were out the door and turning down an alleyway. One street after another, we made our way as far from Maria as I could get us.

Andy didn't say a word the whole walk home, probably thinking the same thing I was. This feeling was something different, like I could trust her, even though I didn't want to. Two parts of me were pulling in opposite directions. One part told me to go back and talk to her, ask her questions, find out everything there was to know about her. The other part was telling me to run, get on the next plane, and go someplace no one could find me; maybe the Amazon rainforest or Antarctica, somewhere less populated with humans.

I stopped abruptly, turning my head back and forth. Should I go back? Maybe she could help me. No, you idiot, trust no one. Oh my god, my head was about to explode. I ran my hands over my face vigorously, contemplating my next move.

"Baby, what's going on with you, and who was that girl? She looked like she wanted to eat me," Andy said, pulling me into his arms. I let his warmth engulf me.

Taking a deep breath, I responded. "I don't know. She could be a number of things. I'm kind of a supernatural magnet. Things out there can sense I'm different, but depending on how strong they are, they can rarely pinpoint what I am, until it's too late."

"She didn't come off as something out to hurt us. I mean, she was just a kid," he pulled away from me, looking around as if he was checking to make sure the coast was clear. "She wasn't a Demon, right?"

I shook my head. "No, Demons I can sense right away, just like they can immediately sense I'm a Guardian, hell, a Legacy," I silently laughed to myself. Demons I could handle. It was the unknown that bothered me.

"Honestly, I don't think she was evil, but, like I said, she could be a number of things."

I racked my brain for a creature that wasn't evil, but also not human, that he may have heard of in a fairytale.

"Um—like a water nymph, or land nymph. They won't necessarily bring harm upon humans. They keep to themselves, hiding out in nature, but if you ever come across one, don't mess with their homes. They might come across as beautiful godlike creatures, but they can be vindictive."

Andy's eyebrows lifted and then fell. He rolled his eyes, taking my hand as we walked down the cobblestone streets.

"I don't know why I act surprised every time you mention something new to me," a deep rumble vibrated threw his chest. "So, are these supernatural nymphs like hot chicks that run around naked, forcing guys to like, you know—" he wiggled his eyebrows up and down, a devilish grin stretching across his beautiful face.

Now, it was my turn to roll my eyes. It still amazed me how natural it felt to talk to my human boyfriend about my supernatural life. The fact that he was still by my side, knowing how screwed up my life could get, and not wanting to run for the hills, made me love that boy a hundred times more each day. Every day, no matter how deep the crap I was in with Demons or my own race, I still wouldn't choose to have it any other way.

I needed to fight for what I loved and what I wanted with my own life. If Andy and my friends, even Shasta, could accept me after everything, then screw my family and my race. I was better off with humans and semi-good Demons. Well, okay, maybe only Shasta; he was the only Demon I liked.

"Yeah, babe. Why don't you go find one, and she can make you her sex slave?" I chortled.

"Aw, baby, are you jealous?" Andy laughed.

I punched him in the arm, causing him to grunt. I wasn't gentle about it either. He pulled his hand from mine, rubbing his bicep. I laughed at his shocked face.

"Damn, girl. Remind me not to piss you off anymore," he said playfully.

Chapter 10

Andy and I were alone when we got back to Shasta's. Shasta told me earlier that today was a bust, but I knew he spent most of the day shopping with Amanda. Wow, leave it to him to go off playing while I fought for my life.

Stupid Demon.

Whether the reasons were because Amanda needed to or wanted to, Shasta just wanted to make her happy. Amanda, like Andy, didn't really say much of anything regarding my situation, but I knew they both were scared. Not for themselves, they were safe, but because they both loved me and Shasta, and they wanted us safe.

I grabbed a drink from the kitchen, making my way outside to the porch. Andy was off doing something around the flat, probably snooping around Shasta's private collection of crap. I let him. I settled down in one of the plush chairs, pulling my legs up under me. Grabbing my phone, I decided it was about time to call Kady.

My stomach rumbled, stopping me mid-dial. Sometimes, eating all the time really got in the way of my life. I was comfortable and didn't want to get up to make a sandwich. Andy must have read my mind, because, right as that thought crossed my mind, he came walking out with a plate of food. He set it down next to me, kissed me gently on the head, and headed back inside.

Okay, that wasn't weird or anything, I thought.

"Um, hey," I said, stopping him before he shut the doors.

He raised his eyebrows, waiting for me to finish. I pointed to the plate. He didn't say anything, just smiled.

"Did you develop mind reading abilities and conveniently forget to tell me?"

"I just had a feeling, baby, that's all. Call Kady, she's probably worried," he said with a wink.

"Okay, seriously, what the hell is going on with you?" I joked. "Oh my God, you were taken over by aliens, weren't you?"

Andy walked out, taking the seat next to me. He picked up my Mountain Dew, taking a small sip.

"You know, water won't kill you," he said, putting my drink back down. "Babe, I figured you were hungry, so I made you something to eat. It's not that hard to guess, since you eat like," he trailed off, counting on his fingers, "a thousand times a day."

"First of all, I do not. I eat as much as you do. Second, you just so happened to know the two things I was thinking at the exact same time," I responded.

"Two?" he raised his eyebrows, thinking. "Oh, what, calling Kady? Again, not hard to guess," he said, standing up. "and no, I'm not Shasta. Even if I could read minds, I wouldn't invade your privacy like that."

****

In the morning, while we were all sitting around having breakfast, Andy mentioned the night at the bar to Shasta. He wasn't too happy to learn that Shasta had been reading his mind, and that he was running off to tell me about it. Shasta shrugged it off, not finding it to be a big deal. That set Andy off.

"Are you shitting me?" he yelled, standing up from his seat. "Stay the hell out of my head. I don't appreciate you running off to my girlfriend, spilling my personal shit."

"Babe, chill. I already told him to stop," I grabbed his hand, calming him down with my touch.

"At least until she tells me otherwise, mate," Shasta smirked.

Andy was seeing red. I felt the heat rolling off his body as he yanked his hand from my grip. He walked into the house, slamming the door.

I took a deep breath, but before I could talk, Amanda butt in.

"Fix this now," she snapped, getting up from his lap and heading toward the door. "If I ever find out your digging in my head, it will be the last thing you do."

Now, it was my turn to smirk.

"You know this is your fault right?" Shasta smiled. Everything was always a joke to him.

"My fault? How? I asked you to do it a few times to make sure he was alright, not to spy for me," I replied in defense.

"Because, love, it's my job to keep you safe; that includes your heart. Therefore, I have to make sure he thinks I'll always be there," Shasta said, pointing to his head, "so he won't mess up."

I knew he was talking about Andy cheating on me. Shasta nodded, reading my mind.

"He would never do that," I whispered.

Shasta's eyes softened, making them look transparent. Black curls fell in front of his face as our gazes locked on each other.

"I know that. Your love is—not humanly. Your hearts are connected as if one can't beat without the other. Your love is pure, unbreakable. In the end, you won't be able to live without each other. Sweetheart, your mate is the only other person in this world I would trust with your life."

"Then why do you do it? You know how humans feel about being violated like that," I reminded him.

Shasta's face lit up. "I don't do it for him; I do it because I'm scared for you. You shut yourself down, and hold all your emotions in. Hell, most of the time you block your mind from me without even knowing it. He knows every emotion, everything you feel, without you having to tell him. So I do it to make sure you're okay," he replied.

I was struck hard by his comment. I don't know if it was from closing myself off to him or him confirming that Andy felt what I felt. I was told as a child that once you are bonded to your mate, you could literally feel what the other felt. But, Andy and I weren't bonded, and I didn't think we ever could be since he was a human.

Before I could ask Shasta how that was possible, Andy walked out with Amanda by his side. They both sat down at the table, eyeing Shasta. Andy was the first to speak, and what he said surprised me more than it did Shasta.

"You're forgiven, but next time you want to know how Kye is really feeling, just ask. I'll tell you anything," he said.

I guess he heard us talking. I would deal with the bonding matters later.

****

"Andy, can you really feel what I'm feeling?" I asked, needing to know if it was possible, because I felt like it was one-sided.

I never knew how Andy really felt. I knew, without a doubt, he loved me more than anything. Other than that, I knew nothing more, which was why I was always asking Shasta to check. Maybe, because he was human, I would never get to feel him in that way, but he would be able to feel me. Jack used to tell me it was the greatest feeling in the world. At the time, he was talking to Lucas and I about being bonded together. What if it was never the same with me and Andy?

"Nah," he said, pulling me out of my thoughts. "Babe, I don't actually feel you, per se. I just know you well enough to know what's going on in that pretty little head of yours."

"It just feels one-sided. I wish I could know what you're thinking sometimes, what you're feeling," I lowered my head, studying my naked nails.

"Alikye," he placed a finger under my chin, raising my head, "you know, baby. Trust me."

Before I could say anything, he crushed his mouth to mine, setting off a swarm of butterflies in my belly. I tangled my fingers in his messy dark hair, pulling him closer to me. Without breaking our kiss, Andy fell into my chair, pulling me on top of his lap. Warmth engulfed me as our bodies smashed against each other. I wiggled around for a moment, trying to get comfortable. A deep growl vibrated up his chest.

Andy pulled away, breathless.

"Baby, you can't move around on top of me like that unless you want me to... you know," he wiggled his brows up and down.

The idea alone had me coming undone, and it didn't help much when his hands moved under my shirt, rubbing circles on my skin. I was torn. I wanted so bad to make him mine. I wanted to feel him inside me, mind, body, and soul; loving me, worshiping me, but I was scared shitless. I didn't know what it would mean to give him everything.

I stared into his eyes as they darkened with hunger. Without giving it another thought, I lowered my mouth to his. Andy licked my bottom lip, wanting access into my mouth, which I gave to him. His tongue found mine, sending bolts of electricity down my body.

Our heat collided together, consuming us in invisible flames. Andy lifted my shirt over my head, breaking our kiss for only a second, before finding my lips again. His lips then moved down my chin, my neck, along my collarbone, before stopping at the swell of my breast. He pulled back, watching me. I was lit up like a Christmas tree by now, outside in the open for the entire world to see. My Enochian markings became more visible; blue symbols crawled up my arms, down my back, around my ribs and stomach, before stopping at my thighs. Andy watched in awe as the symbols and lines connected.

"We should go inside," Andy growled. It was the sexiest sound in the world.

I nodded, not trusting my voice. Instead, I moved my lips to his neck, licking and nipping at his skin. A shiver ran down his back, and I loved that I could do that to him. He stood up with me still on his lap. I wrapped my legs around his waist as he walked inside. The whole time I tortured his neck and face, before finding his mouth and crushing my lips to his. I moaned as he dug his fingers into my thighs, which only set him off again. Andy pulled back once more, leaning his forehead against mine.

"I love you," I said.

"I love you, too, pretty girl," Andy whispered.

Heat spread, pooling in my belly. My eyes fluttered shut as my breathing became heavy. I didn't want to stop. I wanted to feel his lips, his hands, all over my body. I wanted to be his forever, but not today. I still wasn't ready, and he knew it. That didn't mean we couldn't make out a little bit.

We finally made it to our room, both of us breathing heavy. I pulled at his shirt, realizing he was still fully clothed. I yanked it over his head, tossing it on the floor. Still in his arms, we made our way over to the bed. I relaxed in Andy's embrace. He nipped and licked down my stomach, sending shivers racing up my spine. Unbuttoning my jeans, he pulled them down my legs, leaving hot kisses in his wake. He was driving me crazy, slowly exploring every inch of me.

He finally stood, crawling on top of me, supporting his weight with his arms.

"God, I love you. You feel so good," Andy grunted, looking down at me. His eyes were dark, and I could only imagine that mine were just as dark. While he was looking into storm clouds, I was seeing the ocean's water during that storm. He lowered his head, meeting my lips. I bent one leg, resting it against his thigh, while the other lay flat on the bed.

I lifted my hips, meeting his. A deep, torturous growl erupted, and I took advantage of that. It was my turn to drive him crazy. Before Andy even knew what happened, in less than a blink of an eye, he was on his back. I straddled his legs, never once breaking our kiss. He was so freaking cute. I wanted to spend the rest of my life in this bed with him, but knew the reality of the situation wouldn't allow it. I rolled away from him, snuggling my face into the hardness of his chest.

"I think I'll just lay in this bed with you forever, if you don't mind." My eyes closed on their own accord, as Andy's hands moved up and down my spine.

"You definitely won't get any complaints from me," he said as he nuzzled his face into my neck.

His breath was coming out hard and fast. He sniffed around my head, making me laugh. I screamed when he pinned me down with one hand, using his other to tickle me. I was just about to push him off me when a loud bang came from outside our door. Both of our heads snapped in the direction of where the sound came from. Andy's cute butt was saved from getting tossed across the room. Lucky bastard.

"Kye, get your butt out here. We've got shit to do," Shasta demanded.

One more bang, and Shasta's footsteps disappeared down the hall. I dropped my head, laying my cheek against Andy's warm hard chest.

"I really hate that guy," I muttered.

No, you don't. Let's go, we have a life to save, Shasta sent, interrupting my thoughts.

"You're lucky. That guy just saved your butt," I smirked at Andy, rolling my head.

Shaking his head, Andy stood up from me, pulling me with him. We both started to grab our clothes off the floor, until I realized my shirt was outside. I went in my bag, grabbing a grey tank top and a pair of Andy's basketball shorts. I looked over at Andy. He had a devilish smile on his face, similar to one a panther would wear before pouncing on its prey.

"Oh, really? Do tell, sweetheart," he winked.

"I was about to go all Kung Fu ninja on your ass, sweetheart," I mimicked his wink.

He walked over to me, cupping my face in his hands. He placed a gentle kiss on my lips.

"Keep talking like that, and I may need to pin you down again, using my manly willpower and awesomeness," he whispered against my lips

A chill ran up my spine. "Go take a cold shower, Romeo. I'll meet you out there."

Amanda met me in the hall as I stepped out of my room, dangling my shirt from her finger. Heat ran up my face as I snatched my clothing from her, tossing it in my room and shutting the door.

"We will talk about this later," Amanda laughed.

"Um, no offense, but isn't it a little weird to talk about that? Given he's your ex and, well, you know—" I trailed off.

It wasn't as weird to me. I wasn't human, so that kind of emotion was never the case. The two of them dated, I knew that. They had been intimate, I knew that, too. I didn't know if talking about me being intimate with Andy would be uncomfortable to Amanda, and I really didn't want to share details about it.

Amanda barked out a laugh.

"Sweets, please, that shit's old news. What Andy and I had is nothing compared to what you two share. I know how big of a step it is for you to take. I mean, believe me, I'm so glad I'm not stuck only being able to sleep with one guy for the rest of my life," she paused, scrunching her perfect nose. "But, hey, it's not like you have a choice. All I'm saying is that we're friends, and if you need to talk about anything, girlie, I'm here."

I didn't know what came over me, but I hugged her. She tensed up for a second, before returning my hug. She really was a great friend, even though we fought all the time. It was times like this when it mattered. We pulled apart, both shaking our heads. We were thinking the same thing. Who would have thought?

"Hey, before we go out there, how are you really doing with all this?" I asked, looking into her bright, hazel eyes. The sadness was present, but she was good at covering it up. She smiled, shrugging her shoulders.

"I'm not really sure. I love you both. I don't want to see either of you hurt, but I feel helpless. What can I really do, besides be here for support?" she asked, referring to Shasta and me.

"Babe, honestly, that's something both Shasta and I need right now. I just feel guilty—" I said before Amanda interrupted me.

"No. Both Andy and I are fine, trust me. We are all going to be fine. I can feel it," she said reassuringly.

Chapter 11

"How was shopping?" I scoffed.

I sat at the table directly in front of Shasta, my arms holding up my head, with my elbows on the table. I glared into Shasta's eyes. Like the man he always was, everything being laughable and a joke, Shasta threw his head back and laughed. Sometimes, the urge to hit him was too enticing. Best friend or not, he was pushing my buttons.

"Shasta, you have been out all day. Have you found any new information yet?" I shrieked.

"Love, calm down," Shasta smirked.

Calm down? How was I supposed to calm down? My time here was limited. If we didn't find some way of reversing my death sentence, Andy and I didn't have many more days together. Rage bubbled in my veins. I didn't know what I was angrier about; Shasta joking at a time like this, or him interrupting Andy and I.

The thought of bonding with Andy regularly popped into my head, wanting to feel what it was like to bond with my mate. As unfair as it would be for Andy to have me ripped away, I didn't see the harm on his end, considering he was only human.

When two are mated and one dies, a part of his or her mate dies along with them. Like losing a child or parent, the pain never goes away. You learn to function and get on with your life, but loving another so passionately would cease to exist. Two Guardians who have lost their mates have been known to find comfort in each other, helping one another through the tougher parts of grieving. They both know they will never love each other more than just companions, but it's better than being alone for the rest of your life. If anything was to ever happen to me, Andy would get another chance to love again. At first, it would be hard. After time, the pain would dull, even after we were mated.

Just then, Andy came up from behind me, placing his hands on my shoulders. His heat shot through my veins, calming me instantly. My heartbeat slowed at his touch. One minute, his touch drove me crazy, causing my body to spasm uncontrollably. The next, he had me feeling absolutely tranquil, like hitting a switch on the both of us, depending on the mood. Andy's hair was still wet from his shower. Long strands fell in front of his face, covering his dark eyes. I stood up from my chair, hugging my body against his as I turned to face Shasta.

"Figure this out before I do it myself," I said, turning to Andy. "I'm gonna call Kady. She's probably worried sick."

Andy grabbed my hand, squeezing it.

"Yeah, pretty girl. Sounds good. I'll stay out here and help Shasta come up with a way to find Isabella," he replied.

"I'm quite capable of handling it on my own, you know," Shasta leered.

"Yeah, because it worked out so great the first time," Andy retorted.

Shasta's smile pulled wider; his eyes sparkled off the overhead lighting. Andy was becoming very brazen when it came to Shasta, like Shasta was nothing more than a normal human. Comparing the two, there was only a little more than a few inches between them, but they were both lean and toned. If Shasta were human, he may have found his match.

"Aw, Kye, your little human lover is finally growing a pair of balls, how sweet," Shasta teased.

I was not getting involved with these two anymore. Was this how Kady felt when Amanda and I bickered constantly? Maybe I should work on being a little nicer to her. This was just annoying. I headed inside alone.

"Okay, Demon boy, I'll show you a pair—" Andy's voice trailed off as I shut the door behind me.

A second later, Shasta's loud, obnoxious laugh echoed through the walls. The phone interrupted the sound, ringing in my ear. Finally, on the forth ring, Kady picked up.

"Umm, it's way too early," she mumbled, her voice thick with sleep. I counted silently in my head, wondering the time difference.

"Sweetheart, it's like eleven in the morning there; it is not too early," I laughed.

Here, the sun was soon to set. Families were making their way home to settle down for the day's end. At home, the day was just getting started.

"Oh my god. Holy hell, Kye. I have been going out of my mind here. What the hell is going on? I tried calling, but no one answered their phone. Then I thought, of course they aren't, everything there is crazy. Well, guess what? Everything here is crazy. I had Guardians standing outside our house for two days. Don't worry, I was careful," she stopped to take a quick breath. I heard her feet shuffling around her room. From what I could tell by the sounds coming through the receiver, she was heading downstairs.

Greg's voice sounded through the speaker, asking how we all were doing. Before I could speak, she was back to her rambling a million miles a minute.

"Alikye, are you still there? What happened? Did the line drop?" she buzzed.

The sound of laughter slipped through my lips. Only Kady could go from dazed and groggy to overzealous in 2.5 seconds.

"Alikye!" she screeched.

"What? I'm sorry, but it's not like you were going to let me get a word in."

I wiped a stray tear from my eyes, trying to control my laughter.

"Oh, right. So, anyway," she began again.

I imagined her sitting on the porch with a cup of coffee in her hand. Greg may be sitting next to her, on his laptop or reading the paper. I wanted to be with them, sitting on that same porch, my feet resting on the table with a book in my hand. Instead, I was in one of the most beautiful places on Earth, and I couldn't even take the time to enjoy myself. The past year had been so easy. Why couldn't they just let me be, let me live my life? I wasn't hurting anyone.

"So far, we're safe, but if we don't figure out something quickly, it's only a matter of time before they pick this place," I explained. Italy was pretty much off the grid, which was one of the reasons Shasta set up home here.

"Kye, can I ask you something?" Kady muttered, sadness filling her voice.

I could hear caution in her question. She took a deep breath. I knew what her next question was; she didn't have to ask.

"Amanda thinks everything will be fine. Andy believes the same, but honestly, something bad is gonna happen. I can feel it. Dealing with Demons and monsters is easy, because they are predictable and irrational. Dealing with my own race, I don't know what their next move is, or how many steps they are ahead of me. I can tell you one thing, though. I'm the most powerful of my kind, and I have Shasta, so the odds are in my favor," I answered.

I paced the room, twisting a curl around my finger. Outside, I could hear arguing. Amanda must have joined them, because I heard her screech, going on about how annoying the guys were acting.

"I'm scared," Kady muttered. Greg's voice was soothing in the background as he told her everything would be ok. "I wish I could have come with you. I should be there," she finished.

"I know, but its better that you're not. I don't even want Amanda and Andy here. As much as I need Andy, I don't want him here," I admitted quietly my voice breaking slightly.

Putting Andy's life in danger was more painful than anything I had ever gone through. It was too bad that a part of me was too selfish to let him go— to tell him I didn't need him.

"We will get through this, all of us. Then, in August, we will all be in school together. I love you, Kye."

I smiled at her enthusiasm. That's my girl.

"I'll have Andy call Greg later. I love you, too," I said.

We hung up.

****

"Okay, I may have an idea, but it has to happen tonight," Shasta said when I walked through the door.

I took a seat, laying my legs on Andy's lap, as I watched the sky darken. "Good to know you two figured something out before killing each other," I responded keeping my eyes focused on nothing in particular.

"Well," Andy said, shrugging his shoulders.

"These two are idiots. It was my idea," Amanda gloated.

I raised my brows in question.

"Think of it this way; go to the places she would normally go, and ask around. She grew up in this town, right?" Her hazel eyes locked on Shasta's.

"Yes, love. We met in a small café on the other end of town the last time I saw her. She seemed to fancy the place, and the guy serving us seemed to fancy her," Shasta wrapped his arms around Amanda's waist, pulling her closer to his body. She rested her head on his chest.

"So, you think she was a regular there?" I asked.

Shasta nodded.

"Okay, that's good. Let's go."

I moved my legs from Andy's, standing up at the same time he did. Shasta and Amanda remained seated. Before I could say something, Shasta beat me to it.

"You go. I have another place to check out first. It is a few blocks away, but it should only take a minute."

I watched him questionably, but he was already in my mind answering my unspoken question. ***Trust me, love. It has to do with you, but if we want to find this woman tonight, we need to split up.***

****

The café was quaint; a one story brick building on the corner, adjacent to the water. Under a canopy that blocked away the sun, tables and chairs spilled out over the sidewalk. A small ding sounded as we walked in the door; the smell of coffee engulfed me.

With Andy at my side, we walked up to the counter, grabbing the attention of the barista. She smiled sweetly, asking for our order in Italian. I ordered us both a coffee, handing over the money. The girl called the order over to a second barista. The café was nearly empty, with the exception of one couple in the corner and a single man reading a book. The first barista kept herself busy, wiping down the counters and cleaning the dirty dishes. I took the opportunity to get some answers.

"*Mi scusi*," I waved over the counter.

She hung up a few more cups, before taking a towel from the back rack and wiping off her wet hands.

"*Sto cercando un amico*," I continued.

"You American?" she asked in broken English.

"*Si*," I answered, "I was wondering if you knew a woman, maybe in her late fifties. She used to come here all the time. Her name is Isabella Valentino."

The girl shook her head. She furrowed her brow, holding up a finger. I nodded.

We grabbed our coffees, taking a seat at one of the high tops. A few minutes passed before the girl returned. She didn't know Isabella, and neither did the second barista. They were both fairly new, and hadn't yet gotten the chance to know the regulars by name. When she asked what the woman looked like, I shrugged. I had never seen a picture. She apologized, asking us to come back tomorrow; one of the senior baristas would be in during the morning hours.

"So, what now?" Andy asked, taking a sip of his espresso.

I closed my eyes, taking a few deep breaths before beginning. "We hope that Shasta got more information than we did. If not, we wait until tomorrow."

I drank the rest of my coffee, bringing my cup over to the bussing station. Just then, heat engulfed my body, setting my skin on fire. I looked around.

Andy sat at the table, scanning through his phone, oblivious to his surroundings. Something was coming, and I didn't know what; I could sense it. I spun around, looking for a rear exit. It wasn't a Guardian I felt, and even if it was, they wouldn't risk being seen by me until we were alone. The hair on the back of my neck stood up, and goose-bumps covered my skin.

Andy's eyes finally locked on mine. They darkened when he saw my expression. He knew how to read me now, and right now I was on high alert, scanning information in my mind. I let the world around me blur. Lights flickered overhead, and the scent of lilies fluttered across my nose. A warm hand interlaced in mine, bringing my world back. The heat I was feeling before was washed away in a cooling sensation that replicated having a bucket of cold water dumped over me.

"What happened?" Andy's voice sounded worried.

"I don't like the uncertainty that they can be just around the corner, and we wouldn't know any different. Demons I can handle, babe, mostly because you can handle them. What happens when they send Derek or Lucas after you?"

"They wouldn't dare," Andy answered. "One, because I know them better than anyone. I would feel them coming from a mile away. Two, they would never agree to it, even if Ana didn't give them the choice."

"Yeah, but Shasta said they outed you at the trial. They didn't even stick up for you. Lucas told Ana about us."

Andy ran his hands through his hair roughly, pulling at the ends.

Shasta told us yesterday that Ana never knew about us until Lucas's confession. I couldn't blame him; he was broken. I had left. Out of rage, he told anyone that would listen about what I had done. It just sucked that it was Ana who was listening this time.

"They wouldn't, trust me. He had every right to be pissed at me; I broke his heart," I said.

Andy hated that I defended the boys after they couldn't do the same for me. What he didn't understand is that it wouldn't have mattered. In the end, it would have made matters worse for them. Ana had a vendetta against me. Nothing was going to stop her.

Before I could say anything more, the door dinged once again, grabbing ahold of my attention. I turned my head, finding myself face to face with a pair of dark exotic eyes. A smile tugged at her lips. I opened my senses, but felt nothing. Everything I felt a few minutes ago was gone. She was human. I had to believe she was, because my gut was telling me I could trust her. Then again, I could be wrong.

"Hello again," Maria said.

Chapter 12

A soft knock sounded on the door. Derek got up from bed, expecting it to be Lucas. It had been a few hours since they had spoken. After Derek went after Lucas, Jack stepped in, telling both boys to go their separate ways for a while. So, Derek locked himself in his room; it wasn't like he could go anywhere else, because Ana had hunters stationed at the front door. If he or Lucas wanted to go anywhere on campus, they would need an escort. It was absolutely ridiculous, but there was nothing Derek could do about it.

Not too long after Jack left Derek's room, Anastasis showed up at their door. She told the family that Alikye had evaded the hunters with Shasta's help. When the hunters showed up to take Alikye in, they found only a house full of humans. Derek laughed silently, thanking God for Alikye's normal human friends doing normal Saturday night things. Needless to say, the hunters had no other choice but to stand back and allow Kye and Shasta to get away. Ana had a fit about the situation, asking everyone to leave while she came up with another plan. Ana's plan must have been to use Derek, because while Derek stood at the front door watching Ana take a seat next to Jack, he knew what was to come.

"Mr. Davenport, I must say, your girl has a way of outsmarting some of my best men. Can I be sure you were not the one to warn her days ago, and what happened at the house was not a ploy to keep my men at bay?" Ana hissed, clearly aggravated that Alikye wasn't yet in custody.

"With all due respect, ma'am, you should very well know I had nothing to do with that, seeing as I have been locked away in here since the trial," Derek responded as politely as possible.

He knew the game Ana was playing. She would start by accusing him, threatening him and his family, until she would finally bargain with him to join her side to bring Alikye in. Derek was too smart to fall for that. He knew how to play the game, thanks to Alikye.

"Very well, but if I find out you were in any way part of her escape, I will not think twice when I take you in with her. Then, after your trial, that I will win, I will not be saddened by your death. Do you understand me, sir?" she sneered.

"Anastasis, I think that's enough. I will not allow you to belittle my son, accusing him of things that were clearly impossible for him to foresee," Jack interrupted.

Ana turned to Jack, none too pleased by his contempt. Derek saw it in her eyes as they flashed crimson. She brushed her black, silky hair over her shoulders as she scoffed.

"My sincerest apologies, Jack. It was never my intention to accuse Derek. The reason for my visit is to ask Derek for his help."

The lie fell off Ana's lips as she watched Derek intently. Derek played along, knowing not to call her out in front of everyone. Derek excused himself from the room, asking Ana to follow him. He walked out onto the balcony with Ana in tow. Once outside, Derek shut the door, gesturing for Ana to have a seat. Once seated, he looked out to the courtyard, watching as the other Guardians went on as if another Legacy wasn't about to be eliminated.

"Why are you doing this? If you just left her alone, she would have been willing to give away her title," Derek said.

Two hunters stood at the bottom of their building, watching carefully while Derek and Ana spoke, as if she needed added protection while behind the walls of the council. Ana took her title too seriously sometimes, thinking there were others out to destroy her.

Two years ago, he would have laid down his life to protect Anastasis. His opinion of her was most respected. Then, at the start of the trial when Derek and his family were forced to stay, and after listening to how she described Alikye as being a disease that would one day end the human race, Derek was revolted. For the first time, he saw the truth behind her evil eyes. Ana thrived on power, and would stop at nothing to carry around the highest title, ruling all Guardians. In doing so, Alikye's legacy would have to be ended.

"It was not a decision to come lightly to me, young sir. On the contrary, it was the hardest decision I have ever made, and I wish I had not been the one to make it. You have to understand, given the power I have, sometimes the choices made are not the easiest. If I allowed Alikye to go unpunished for her crimes, it wouldn't be long before more would follow her lead," she stated as if she had said it many times before. Indeed, she had. After the trial, she had to keep the Guardians from turning on her for ending a young girl's life.

"With all due respect, Anastasis, what is the reason for your visit?" Derek had enough of this conversation, and already knew where it was going.

He was right. Ana asked for him and Lucas to go to Alikye's home in North Carolina, and interrogate the humans on her whereabouts. When Derek objected, and informed her on his right not to be involved in a family matter of such importance, Ana could do nothing but walk away.

****

Derek put a target on his head that day. Turning Ana down for the third time would not sit well with her. He would need to watch his back to evade Ana's wrath.

Derek opened his bedroom door to find Seth and Avalon, two of Anastasis's hunters, standing in front of him. They were both Legacies, but would never hold a title to the council because they weren't the first born in their families. They were in their late twenties and lethal. Years ago, they turned off their emotions to become better hunters. It was like going head to head with an advanced, trained robot. No one walked away from them. Without a word, they led Derek and his family down to the courtroom, where the council did most of their work.

The council was set up by four different buildings on over 10,000 acres, framed by a fifteen foot brick wall. There was only one way in and one way out, protected twenty-four-seven by Guardians. The main building was the size of the White House, and was used for business. The apartments were in the top left corner of the property; two buildings, both four stories high with over thirty rooms in each, and in the center was the courtyard.

On the far right side, away from the housing, was the training facility; three stories high, with over ten different rooms, used for everything from working out, swimming, running, or fighting with every weapon known to man. Underneath the building was where the council built the prison.

Not only did the council and their families live on campus, but it was open to any Guardian for as long as they needed to stay. The only building that was off limits was the one that held the courtrooms and Legacies' headquarters, which is where the council lived. Other than that, any Guardian was welcome.

Once outside the courtroom, Seth and Avalon told the family to be seated, before disappearing into the room. Minutes passed in silence before Derek finally spoke.

"What do you think she wants now?" Derek asked, none too pleased by the intrusion.

If Ana asked him to find Alikye one more time, he was going to flip out, and that wouldn't be good for anyone. Her game was starting to get old, and his stress level was at its highest. If Derek was human, he would be dead by now. Alikye was still missing, he and Lucas were at each other's throats every second of every day, and his parents weren't doing anything to help the situation.

"It has something to do with Alikye. That would be my guess," Lucas said, looking anywhere but at Derek.

"Yeah, probably, but I already told her we wouldn't help. Why would she keep asking? Something's up. I have a bad feeling about this."

Ana had sent hunters to gather Derek and his family, so it couldn't be good. Maybe she caught Alikye, and they were on their way back. No, that couldn't be the case. Who would have enough power to catch her? Shasta would just get her out of there in a matter of seconds. Alikye was one of the strongest Guardians, stronger than any hunters. She had a darkness inside her that prevailed against both Heaven and Hell. Partnered with Shasta, Ana would fail.

There was only one way to catch Alikye. Her only weakness was Andy, her human love. Ana was twisted enough to use him to catch her, too. That's what worried Derek the most; that Ana would go as far as hurting a human to get what she wanted.

"Son, let's not think like that. This could be just another one of her games. Don't buy into it," Jack whispered.

"Jack, that's enough. Anastasis could be listening," Sarah retorted.

"Who the hell cares? I'm sick of being her prisoner. This isn't right," Lucas said.

"I'm with Lucas on this one. She has no legal right to keep us. We haven't done anything wrong," Derek agreed.

"Boys, I'm happy you both are finally agreeing on something, but this isn't the time or place," Jack hushed them. Just then, Seth walked out, waving them all in.

All nine council members were seated at the table. Ana sat in the middle. Seth took his position at one end of the table, while Avalon and two more hunters stood on the opposite side. Derek looked towards Carter, who bowed his head, looking utterly defeated. Carter was one of the members who fought to save Alikye, but was outvoted seven to two. He also argued that the two names standing in for the Legacies not yet old enough to take their title shouldn't count as a vote. Either way, it was still five to two.

"So glad you could all make it. I have some somber news, and I wanted you to hear about it first," Anastasis praised.

A sinister smile pulled at her lips. The bad feeling Derek was having earlier got worse. As Jack was about to speak, Ana put her hand up to silence him and anyone else who was about to talk.

"Avalon, here," she pointed a finger at the girl with long blond hair and violet eyes, "she stayed behind after Alikye and Shasta took off. It wasn't long before Alikye's human friends followed, but they were smart about it, and it seems we lost track of them somewhere in Chicago. Anyhow, her other two human friends remained at the house, and although they tried to keep the situation low key, left alone they seemed to have a lot to say."

Seth and Avalon took one last look at Derek before exiting the court room. Derek's heart pounded in his chest as he waited for Ana to finish. He looked over to his family, and saw the same look of horror that mirrored his own. Even Lucas look tortured.

"Anastasis, cut the games and tell them. We don't have the time for this," Carter snapped. Carter held the second seat on the council. If Alikye took her place, he would move back to third. Now, he would always hold second.

Ana snapped her head towards Carter. There was nothing she could do to him other than sneer. Derek took pleasure in her shocked expression.

"Very well. As I was saying, we have found a location on Alikye and Shasta. It seems they are hiding out in Italy, and I have sent my best to capture her, dead or alive. The reason for you being here is that I have a proposition," Ana said, looking only at Derek. "Call Alikye, and warn her once more that we have found her. Tell her to give herself up, her and Shasta, and no blood will be shed. When she is brought here, I will allow your family your right to say goodbye."

Chapter 13

"My madre will be cooking dinner around eight, if you and your boyfriend would like to join," Maria asked politely. It wasn't uncommon to invite strangers over for a meal in Italy. Meeting tourists on the street and welcoming there home was part of their culture. Most families even placed a light or candle in their front window. It was their way of saying you were welcome to stay the night in their spare room for a small fee. It was something I would never feel comfortable doing, even if I were just a human living in America.

I also knew how disrespectful it was to decline her offer for dinner. I felt deep down that she had no intentions of harming Andy or me. I also felt some kind of weird connection towards her, so I smiled, telling her we would love to join her. I let her know we were here with two more friends, which she ensured me were also welcome. After, I sent Shasta a message via mind read.

"Alright, love. I'm on my way now," Shasta sent back, taking the directions from my mind.

We headed off to Maria's house. It was a good twenty minute ride down the country roads right outside the city. A small cottage sat on top of a hill, and a little white fence traced the outline of the yard. A cobblestone walkway dotted the ground from the street to the front porch. On either side were gardens with every type of vegetation. We walked into the house; the smell of fresh basil and herbs filled my nose. Before we made our way to the kitchen, a woman in her late thirties came out, wiping her hands on a dish rag. Maria was the spitting image of her, so I knew right away this woman must be her mother. They spoke to each other in Italian. Maria told her mother we were tourists from America, and we would be staying for dinner. Maria's mother was more than delighted to entertain guests.

"What are they saying?" Andy whispered in my ear.

"Maria was explaining to her mother that we are staying for dinner. Italians love having guests, and always make enough for an army."

"Shouldn't we be out looking?" he moved his head back and forth.

I shrugged. "There is nothing we can do tonight, and it's rude to just turn them down for dinner. Plus, I'm starving, and this is real authentic Italian," I wiggled my brows up and down.

"Of course," Andy grunted. He knew me so well.

The woman made her way towards me, stopping suddenly to take a good look at me before turning her gaze on Andy, and then back to me. She cocked her head to the side, eyes scrunched together. I watched as she smelled the air around her, so subtle that only I noticed.

What the hell.

A blast of heat shot towards me, engulfing me in a tunnel of soothing warmth. I closed my eyes, taking in a deep breath.

The sweet laughter of the woman in front of me broke my spell, bringing me back to the present. I stood by the door, trying to place her. I knew from the moment I met Maria that she was supernatural; but I still wasn't sure exactly what she was. Her presence wasn't threatening. If anything, she made me feel safe. That didn't mean I had to drop my guard and trust her. Not until I knew what she was.

"Oh my," the woman said in perfect English, "I have heard so much about your kind, but have never had the pleasure of meeting you." Her accent was thick like her daughter's.

Electricity shot through me, causing my heart rate to spike. Damn it, she knew what I was. Not many creatures could sense me; only very powerful ones. I wanted to bolt, but there was also a calming sense from being around her. I was so confused, and she noticed it, too.

"Oh dear, my apologies. I forgot that you have no knowledge of me. Why would you? They don't speak too much about us. By the way you're looking at me, I assure you that you are safe with me. We are not here to harm you," she continued.

She ran her hand down my cheek, and I let out a breath I didn't realize I had been holding in. My world froze as colors wrapped around the woman and me, and a warming effect surrounded us. For a minute, I felt sleepy. In a blink of an eye, I was back in the living room, back to my normal self. Did she really just spell me?

As fast as I could, I grabbed Andy, placing my body in front of his.

"What are you?" I snapped.

She didn't even flinch. "What's your name, dear, your last name?"

She answered my question with a question. Her smile never left her gorgeous face. Maria sat in the corner, looking rather confused by her mother's strange actions.

Shasta, I need you. I think I'm in trouble, I sent.

Talk to me love. I'm coming around the bend, Shasta sent back.

Just get here. She knows I'm a Guardian. I don't know how, but she knows, I pleaded with urgency.

It wasn't that I was scared of this family. It would be easy enough to grab Andy and get out safely, but I felt that I couldn't leave. I didn't want to; curiosity was getting the best of me. I needed to know what she was, and how she knew what I was just by looking at me, because she was very much human. Before I had the chance to speak, Shasta burst through the door, stopping suddenly in front of the woman.

The woman stepped back, scowling. Her once happy face was now hard as stone. She lifted her hands in the air, whispering something. Suddenly, Shasta was thrown hard into the back wall. Amanda's screams echoed through the living room. I spun around fast, moving in hyper speed. I pushed Andy and Amanda out the door, and shut it hard before turning around to confront the woman. With one look, she brought me to my knees, a splitting headache pounding in my ears. The air around us vibrated with a light humming of electricity. I grabbed at my head, willing my markings to come to life. In a loud outbreak of color and sounds, indigo blue surrounded me, blocking out her magic. She pushed harder into my head, but years of learning to block Shasta out worked wonders on keeping her at bay.

I knew something was off about her. She had picked up Shasta with her mind, throwing him a good twenty feet. In the time it took me to get Andy and Amanda to safety, she had used her mind powers again, putting Maria under the protection of an invisible shield. She stayed close to her daughter, keeping me away as well. If she was a human witch, she had no chance against me, but she seemed too strong to be just a witch. Her power came from ancient times, and her draw to me was supernatural.

"You're one of the dark ones," she spat.

"Clearly you're one to talk. Now, I'm gonna ask you this one more time. What are you?" I screamed.

"You cannot defeat me. Your kind is no match for mine," she responded.

"What the hell are you taking about?" I was confused.

"You turn your back on your own. You are a disgrace, and I would like nothing more than to free your soul," she hissed.

Stop it, both of you!

We turned quickly to Shasta's voice in our heads. He was standing in the corner with a shit-eating grin on his face, and his large arms crossed over his broad chest. The woman said something under her breath, and a whoosh of air ran through me. Colors spread around the perimeter of the room, slamming straight into Shasta.

Nothing happened.

Shasta's grin widened like he was expecting another attack on him and knew he would be safe.

You can't hurt me, he sent.

I could see in his eyes that another blast would send him across the room. Whoever this woman was, she was much stronger than both of us.

Shasta didn't move from his position; he stood like a statue, staring us both down. With the three of us staring at each other like a Mexican standoff, it felt like an eternity before another word was spoken.

"Isabella Valentino, we have been looking for you," Shasta said with a laugh.

"WHAT!" My head snapped to face him. This was the woman who was supposed to help us. This was the woman with the answers to where Natalia was hiding. Well, hell, this would be interesting.

I ignored Isabella, and walked over to Shasta. Grabbing him around the arm, I pulled him to face me. My face was burning from anger.

"Demon, you came to destroy me!" Isabella yelled, drawing our attention back to her.

"I thought you said you knew her," I roared at Shasta, "and that she had the information we needed."

"You will never get it. You can try to kill me for it, but I won't work against them to help you," she spat again.

"SHASTA!" I shouted. Of course nothing was going to go as planned. Of course my life couldn't just be easy.

"Alikye, calm down. She doesn't know me because she isn't the one Peter entrusted with the information; it was her mother. Isabella here," he gestured over to the woman who was now white as a ghost, "was off at university when the arrangements were made. I'm sure with the passing of her mother that she was left with all the clues."

"Macayan, you're her. I was told you would come," Isabella held her hand to her chest like that little revelation surprised her. "I was told he would come, too, but never did I imagine I would be working with a Demon. I guess my mother left that part out."

Chapter 14

It has been said over the centuries that a creature so powerful could one day wipe out the race of all evil in a single battle. With the combined forces of the angels, the world would become a paradise where humans could live in peace. These creatures were made purely of magic, and existed through different dimensions. I've heard talk about their kind over the years, but they were spoken about as if they were a myth.

We all settled down in the living room. Andy sat next to me with his hand tightly wrapped around mine. Maria sat at the opposite end of the same couch, while Amanda sat on Shasta's lap on the small recliner next to us. Isabella made a pot of coffee. She placed cups around the table, a jar of sugar cubes, and cream, before joining Maria on the couch. Isabella had explained to us earlier that, although Maria knew nothing about my kind or Shasta's race, she was drawn to me. That was how she found me. She said she could feel a strong connection, and at first she thought she knew me. Her mother told us that our energies had a sort of supernatural detection compound, which also explained how she knew Shasta was a Demon, and how I could sense one without even knowing it was there.

Isabella and her daughter call themselves Veneficus, a very powerful bloodline of Warlocks. Over the centuries, Shasta had become acquainted with a few Veneficus families, but most were either in hiding and rarely practiced or stopped using magic generations ago. I personally have never met one. I was told the true Veneficus bloodlines were destroyed centuries ago, and that they were extinct. Yes, witches existed still, but they were one hundred percent human and practiced through Earth's elements. Veneficus were not human, but they took on human form. Their power came from their world. Lucifer tried to recruit them into his army long before he was cast down, but they refused, wanting to live in peace with humans. They wanted nothing to do with war. They were eventually drawn to our world after their world was destroyed by the same element now destroying ours—power.

"This is unbelievable," I said. To think I would be working with this kind of power, side by side with an actual Veneficus to save my life, was unreal. I had to give it to Shasta; maybe he did know what he was doing after all.

"I heard that," Shasta blurted out, slicing the silence in the room.

He ran a hand up and down Amanda's arm, whispering in her ear. She smiled her beautiful smile, and I had to wonder how she was taking everything so well. How could she believe that in the end everything would be okay, when even I didn't believe it myself?

Andy scrambled around on the couch, bouncing his knee up and down in a nervous motion. He was freaking out; I could see it in his eyes. One thing after another was happening, and I couldn't imagine how overwhelming all this was to him. No matter how many times he said he was fine, I knew he wasn't from the moment he walked into this house. Something had him spooked. He wouldn't talk at all, and the heat rolling off his body in waves was suffocating. I rested my hand on his leg, sending a bolt of electricity down his body, letting my energy consume him until he relaxed. I remained stuck in his gaze, watching as his dark eyes soften and his rapid heart rate slow to a much steadier pace.

Someone cleared their throat. I turned my head in Shasta's direction, only to be caught by his hard stare. I guess I missed something important, because all eyes were on me at that moment. I didn't even hear anyone speak; I was too preoccupied by Andy.

"What did I miss?" I asked sweetly, trying to lighten the mood. I watched as Isabella turned her eyes on Andy, ignoring my question.

"Andrew, it seems odd for a human to be part of this," she stated accusingly.

I furrowed my brow, wondering where she was going with this, and why she was showing even an ounce on interest in a human. Before Andy could answer, I interrupted.

"So, what's the next step in finding Natalia?"

Andy turned to me with a disapproving stare. I just shrugged my shoulders. I felt I could trust her; I knew that much. Her kind was never known to be evil. Like us, the Veneficus were forbidden to harm humans. When they came here not long after humans did, they swore to live in peace, never to use their magic in any means that would cause harm to another person. It was then that Michael granted them access. Regardless, I still didn't want her to know anything about our relationship. Andy and Amanda were bystanders who needed to be ignored.

Isabella understood. Before answering my question, she stood and walked down the tiny hallway into a room I could only assume was an office. A few moments later, she returned carrying a stack of manila folders, similar to the ones Shasta had shown me earlier. The thickness of the pile made me realize the work I had cut out for me, and how much more complicated my life had just become. Was it too much to ask for just a single slip of paper with a big red arrow pointing to an address, with the words, "Go here?" No, instead I get the words, "Go here, don't die. Go there, don't get killed, and maybe one day you will find what you're seeking."

I took the envelopes from Isabella, handing half of the papers to Shasta. Although my mind worked three times faster than the average human mind, along with my eidetic memory, I figured having Shasta's help would speed up the process. I scanned through my half, reading the information my father had written down many years ago. I couldn't help but wonder what he was thinking about, or what he was doing at the exact time these were written. Was he holding me in his arms, cooing me as I cried? Was I running around his feet, begging for his attention, while he smiled down at me? I could picture the young version of him, so handsome and strong. His bright silver eyes matched mine, and dark brown hair falling in waves around his neck.

Reading the words he wrote pulled at my heart. It was his handwriting, his thoughts, on this single sheet of paper. As much as it pained me, I wished for just a moment I could smell his cologne on the paper. I remember his smell being woodsy with a hint of pine. It was like smelling Christmas every day; a comfort I came to love even more with the ability to celebrate the holiday as a human with the people I loved most in this world. I was so young when my parents died. The memories I had of them seemed too little.

****

The cold chill ran over my body as I ran outside. The afternoon sun shined bright in the sky, reflecting off the snow. Shasta sat on the tailgate of my father's truck, doubling over in laughter as I stuck my tongue out of my mouth to catch a snowflake. All winter, I waited for the sky to open up. Until last night, the ground only stayed frozen. Right before bed, I looked out my window to catch the first fall of snow.

"Go to bed, baby girl, and tomorrow the world will be covered in white." my mother's voice cooed as she pulled

the covers up to my chin. She kissed my forehead before getting up to turn out the lights.

"Mommy, can we make a snow man please?" I begged, my small three year old voice coming out in little squeaks from all the excitement.

"Yes, honey, anything you want. I love you, baby."

"Love you, too, Mommy. Love you, Daddy. Love you, Shasta." My father and Shasta stood at the bedroom door smiling down at me.

By morning, the ground was blanketed by a fluffy white sheet. I turned to see my parents on the porch with steaming cups of coffee in their hands. Shasta had always been my favorite person; he cared for me as if I were his own kin. Every week, he would jump in to see me. I thought it was the coolest thing in the world to see him teleport, especially when he would take me with him to different places. I was the luckiest girl in the world. Sometimes, he would stay with me for days. It didn't matter whether he was working on a case or not; I was his number one priority.

"Shasta, come play with me puh-lease," I squealed, jumping up and down.

"Anything for you, darling."

I giggled at the word of endearment he used for me. He made me feel special. No one had a friend like I did, and I was his favorite. I was told that if anything ever happened to my parents, Shasta would take care of me. I was sad because I didn't want them to get hurt and leave me, but I loved Shasta. He made me feel safe, too.

We spent the next hour throwing snow balls at one another before finally partnering up, rebelling against my parents. By the time we went inside, our bodies were frozen with ice stuck in our hair. Mommy lit a fire in our fireplace, while Daddy went into the kitchen, coming back with a large pot of homemade chicken soup and four small bowls. Shasta laid a blanket on the floor in front of the crackling fire so we could all sit and enjoy a nice hot meal together. Daddy also made homemade bread; it was my favorite. After dinner, we made hot chocolate and used the fire to make s'mores. It was the best night of my life.

****

My world around me blurred as I was brought back to the present. With tears in my eyes and a smile on my face, I turned to Shasta. I never remembered that memory until now. Bits and pieces of my young life would come back to me, but nothing was ever that vivid.

"Did you?" I asked, choking on the lump in my throat. A heavy silence fell over the room. Andy held tight to my hand, rubbing his thumb back and forth against my knuckles.

"You were always such a cute little thing," Shasta's smile reached his eyes. "Always so demanding, and wanting me at your side all the time. You worshiped me."

"Oh, puh-lease," I said, using my most child-like voice and rolling my eyes for extra dramatic effect. "I guarantee you made that part up."

"Sorry, love. Besides Peter, I was always your hero," he said as he flipped through the papers causally.

"Well, all I can say is children are naïve; they're impressionable. Don't think too much into it," I joked.

Shasta's ice eyes met mine. He smacked his hand to his chest, faking hurt. We both knew, once upon a time, I idolized Shasta. Even now that he gets on my nerves and has the attention span of a five year old, I not only respect the man, but I love him, too. He was my family. When he does stuff like letting me see memories that are locked away, I can't help but think that life without him would be a little less full.

"Thank you," I said sincerely.

"Anytime you need to be reminded of the time spent with your parents, I would be more than happy to share that with you." Shasta's hands tightened around his file. He was fighting to hold back his emotions. Like me, since his father was a fallen angel and his mother was human, his emotions were heightened. "Okay, enough of reminiscing about the past. It's time to get to work."

Chapter 15

Growing up in my world, you learn what's real and what's not. Somewhere along the line, someone has uncovered the truth behind a myth or a movie. If you asked me if vampires are real— which, for the record, broke Kady's heart when I had to explain to her that Edward was only fiction— I would tell you no. Greg won that bet on Team Vampire versus Team Werewolf. Yes, werewolves are real, and they aren't something you want to cuddle up with, because they will rip out your throat without thinking. That was a fun night.

Anyway, looking through files on dimensional portals had my head spinning. Hypothetically, I knew they existed, but it wasn't our magic to use. Therefore, we were forbidden to conjure up a doorway. As I read further on, it became apparent that my father not only knew how to use that kind of magic, but he also created a doorway to another world—a world where Natalia had been living for the past seventeen years.

I flipped through the file once more, committing it to memory. I placed the finished one down on the table, picking up the next. Isabella caught my eye as she lifted the file I had already read, and tossed the papers into the fire without hesitation. My jaw hit the floor as I watched years of hard work erupt in flames.

"What the—" I trailed off, watching the papers turn into nothing more than a pile of ash. It wasn't that I needed those files for future research. It just saddened me to watch something of my father's burn into nothing more than another memory of him. When Jack took me away, I kept nothing that belonged to my parents. Everything from that life was left back in the mountains of Colorado, where my home once was. It felt like that stuff belonged to that house, like I had no right to move it from the last place my parents lived. Shasta took with him most of my father's books and my mother's weapons. I kept the bow and arrows and my father's last name; his legacy, my legacy.

"It was meant only for your eyes. Now that you have seen what needed to be seen, it all must be destroyed," Isabella explained.

I let out a deep breath. What she was saying was true, but why? I still didn't understand how my father knew Ana would one day come after me. He was a planner, so I had to believe what he did made sense.

"Shasta, you're gonna have to explain to me what all this stuff means," I said as I rubbed the heel of my palms into my eyes. I was out of my league. "This portal crap is confusing."

"A portal is a doorway that connects two distant locations, separated by space and time." Shasta clarified.

He kept his eyes glued to the sheets in front of him. Amanda sat between his legs, checking others' statuses on her phone. She argued earlier that she wouldn't say anything on her social networking sites, but she couldn't live without them. I told her we couldn't take that chance. The Guardians would be keeping tabs on all my friends. Amanda was reduced to only looking, not commenting on anything, in fear they would be able to triangulate her service.

"Wow, did you just give me the definition? I already knew that. It doesn't explain anything," I grunted, causing Shasta to chuckle quietly.

"Okay, think of it as a mathematical equation. Both math and science make up a big part in creating doorways; like a black hole, for instance," Shasta began.

"Wait, you're telling me all this chicken scratch adds up to a final equation that can determine where and when a person can go, and that humans can use it too?" I asked.

"Well, yes and no. Let me finish, will you? Scientists have studied this stuff for years, only to come up empty. Although the main usage is conducted through what humans learn every day, the final piece of the puzzle that no one has been able to crack yet is magic. As you know, magic isn't something normal people practice. With the right spells, yes, a human can open up a doorway, but will most likely be going in blindly. What I can do is distinguish where exactly I want to go. I can pinpoint the exact location of where and when, but that's where it gets tricky," he continued.

"My mother created a certain key," Isabella interjected, finishing Shasta's thought, "in order to keep Natalia safe from both Demons and Guardians. If anyone was able to find out what Peter did, a key was placed in the stars so that only a certain time would be able to free her. It was bound by three bloodlines; a Demon of noble blood," she turned to Shasta, "a Guardian born with darkness, and a Veneficus from a forgotten bloodline. Three bloodlines must bleed on a doorway during a full moon of a summer solstice to release Natalia from her world."

"Okay, so I'm guessing that means Shasta, you, and me. That means we have three days until the twenty-first," I stated.

Shasta and Isabella nodded. Three more days I would have to hide to keep myself alive until the night we could call upon the stars to free a woman who was just sitting around in some world.

"Where exactly did you put Natalia?"

The question had been bothering me since the moment I found out she was still alive. What the hell had she been doing all these years?

"Not sure. No one really told me; only Peter knew," Shasta said.

"I'm also in the dark," Isabella added. "My mother helped with the blood and the magic, but Peter never said what came of Natalia after she vanished through the doorway."

"So, how do we know after all these years that Natalia didn't have some kind of mental breakdown being trapped in a place no one knows about?" I asked

They all shrugged.

"You do realize that she can come out, I don't know, crazy and wanting to kill us for putting her there. For all we know, you could have sent her to a hell dimension," I suggested.

Great, even this plan wasn't full proof.

"Alikye, love, I can't imagine what you have been going through the last few days, but I know it's been rough," he said gently, sympathy flooding his eyes.

It wasn't long before a spark flickered, erasing all sadness. A hard look took over; one I have only ever seen during battle. I couldn't look away, and I couldn't speak. He wasn't finished.

"I say this because I love you and would do anything for you, but please shut the hell up and trust that I can save you. All this negativity coming off you is suffocating. I can't help you if you won't let me, and complaining all the time is not helping anyone, including you."

I was never one to be scolded, not without a snarky comeback on the tip of my tongue. This was one argument I wasn't going to win. I watched Shasta for a minute, and saw how much he truly did love me and only wanted what was best for me. A barely-there smile shadowed my face. I shook my head in understanding, and got up from the couch, making a quick exit. Before the door slammed shut, I heard Andy yell something to Shasta, followed by Amanda yelling in agreement with Andy. I walked out to the garden, collapsing onto a bed of soil, surrounded by plants and herbs.

Drawing circles into the dirt, I knew what Shasta was saying was true. Two years ago, I was so broken my life meant nothing to me. A year ago, I made the only choice that seemed right for me. A week ago, I was happy with who I became. Now, I was giving the control to the council; letting them tear me down to the broken little girl I fought so hard to fix. I was looking for an excuse to let the darkness take me over, to live with the anger that consumed me every day.

"He didn't have the right to say that to you," Andy said from behind me.

His body slumped to the floor next to me, wrapping his arms around my waist. His one leg was bent upwards, leaning against my side, while the other laid flat on the ground stretched out before me. I sat snug between his legs, my back pressed tight to his chest. His lips met the curve of my neck, resting his face against my skin. Andy took a deep breath in and out, and it rippled down my chest.

"Maybe not, but he's right," I said.

Andy's head snapped up. I looked everywhere but at him.

"I'm pissed off all the time. I'm pissed at Ana for doing this to me, and at the council for allowing her to do this to me. I'm mad at my family for betraying me. I'm mad at Shasta for acting like he's okay with everything going on, and Amanda for thinking everything's going to be fine. Most of all, I'm pissed at you," I snapped.

I finally met his eyes, only to see the hurt in them. He didn't speak, only nodded his head as if he understood what I was thinking.

"I love you more than anything, but it pisses me off that you're okay with all of this. When I first told you what I was, I wanted you to leave and start a new chapter in your life without me in it. I knew that if we were together,

133

nothing good would come out of it. I knew that in the end I would only hurt you, but I was selfish and couldn't let you go. I will never be able to let you go. You are the most amazing person I have ever met. You have done nothing but love me through it all. Everything we shared together, I wouldn't trade it, not even for my freedom. I will never walk away from you. I will never be able to live without you, and I know you will never leave me either, which is why you are the one I'm pissed at the most," I finished.

Andy's eyes closed. He pulled me tighter against his body. I lay my head on his shoulder, looking up at the darkening sky. The late evening was quiet. Light whispers drifted around inside the house. They were all giving me time to myself. The constant pull I felt when I knew Shasta was in my head was gone. It was either me blocking him out somehow or he was giving me some privacy. Everyone inside was trying to help me, and all I was doing was complaining, that things weren't easy. Deep down I had to believe my family was trying, in their own way, to save me, too. The council members that I knew had my back had their hands tied. It was time I sucked it up and fought harder than I ever had.

"You're right about one thing, Kye. I won't leave you, not for anything. So I guess you're gonna have to get over being pissed at me," Andy said into my ear, kissing the soft spot on my neck just below my jawline. I rolled my head an inch to give him better access.

"You're gonna hate me one day. Something big will happen, and you will resent me. Love won't be the problem, and leaving won't be the problem. The problem will be the 'what ifs' in life that you'll have to face. In the end, we will be together. Then you will be able to forgive me, but for a moment in time you'll hate me," I told him. My lips touched his, and for a second I was lost in his warmth. All too soon, I pulled away from him, standing up.

The anger was gone; the fear, the hope, everything that made me human, I pushed it all down, focusing on one thing, and that was life. I put out my hand to Andy. Pulling him into my body, I wrapped my arms around his neck, digging my fingers into his messy grown-out hair.

"If that time ever comes, we will figure it out together," Andy whispered against my lips.

"That doesn't make me feel better. You are supposed to say it will never happen," I replied as his lips touched mine softly.

"You'll just argue that it will, so agreeing with you will shut you up faster. Plus, every couple says things to each other they don't mean. One day, will I wish for an easier life? Sure, but to hate you would be like hating myself, and, as you know, I'm too amazing and sexy to hate myself," Andy winked.

He moved his hands up my body to cup my face. I smiled at his playfulness and how he always made me feel better.

Chapter 16

The tickets were purchased and paid for with four aliases to hide our identities. Shasta wanted to jump to Rome. I said it would be better to travel by train for three reasons. First, it would give me time to think. Second, being on the move meant we would be safer than sitting like ducks waiting to be slaughtered. Third, we could go over a few more details before the full moon. My points were valid, so Shasta finally agreed to them.

After we had a large and delicious meal at the Valentinos', we headed back to Shasta's flat. We would be leaving in the morning. Isabella would leave the day of the summer solstice, and meet us at the place written on the paper. Until then, time had to be drawn out. Staying invisible was the key.

We took a cab into the heart of the city. Amanda wanted to see the city at night, and Shasta wanted to make her happy. I would have argued, but she had a point; going home wouldn't make time speed up. Music erupted from different corners of the streets. Lights were strung from one building to another, illuminating the city in millions of tiny lights that matched the hidden sky. People of all ages roamed around, laughing and singing; some dancing, some eating, most drinking. The energy passed from one person to another was contagious.

Shasta glanced over at me and smiled. I shook my head, smiling back brightly. He never apologized for yelling at me earlier. Why would he? He was right, and knew I needed a heavy dose of reality. Andy was still giving him the silent treatment. He just didn't understand how Shasta and I worked.

We spent the next hour walking the streets. By the time we made it to the front of Shasta's building, I was both physically and mentally exhausted. I could tell the same went for everyone else. Punching in the security code to the elevator, access was granted, and the machine clicked to move upwards. I rested my body against Andy. A yawn escaped my lips, and Amanda followed suit a second later.

"So, when all this is over, what happens? Do you get to come home with us?" Amanda asked.

"That's the plan. Natalia will take first chair, grant me immunity, and I'll either relinquish my second chair or live both lives. I'll fight when I'm needed, but other than that I'll finish up school and play it by ear I guess."

The elevator alerted us to our floor, and the doors opened. We all got off, tossing our stuff in the foyer. The rooms were located on the opposite side of the building, past the main sitting area and dining room. On tired legs, I led the way, but stopped abruptly. An invisible source slammed into me, flashes of color coming off my body in waves. There wasn't a chance they hadn't seen me. I put out my arm to stop Andy from coming around the corner, using my body as his shield. My heart pounded against my chest. I fisted my trembling hands, positioning my body into a fighting stance. I was too far away from any of my weapons.

Ever so casually, two Guardian hunters stood up from the couch, never once breaking eye contact. They knew me well enough not to strike first. I knew how this game was played. In order to get out of here alive, I needed to keep my wits about these two. Granger and Kale were their names; personally, I had never met them. It wasn't unexpected. They were both Legacies, but second born, meaning they would never be an heir to the council unless their siblings passed.

Hunters were the worst kind of Guardians. They were trained differently; trained to track their pray and kill. Although we were all taught the same, they were trained without their emotions. It was too bad for them that I trained myself the exact same way, but I also had something to fight for, which only made me stronger.

Shasta's hand came around my arm. Andy was out of the room and out of harm's way. I could sense him and Amanda moving farther away. With that knowledge, I relaxed my body, taking comfort in Shasta's arrival. I cocked my head to the side, glaring at my attackers. Their plan of surprise was in vain, because I would jump out with Shasta. Next time, they won't be so quick to ambush me.

"Alikye Macayan, you are hereby in the custody of the council. You will surrender to us, or actions will be taken. Dead or alive, you will come with us. If you choose to come along willingly, you will be granted your time in front of the council. Do you understand the terms of your surrender?" Granger specified.

"Sorry, boys. You should know me better than that," I mocked.

I nodded once, giving Shasta the go ahead to get me the hell out of here. He must have had a different idea, because I was still standing in the room looking at two men with no emotion on their faces. If they were to tap into their emotions, I'm certain I would be looking at two smug smiles. I grabbed for Shasta, only to be met with stillness. I called to him, but got nothing. I glanced quickly behind me. A state of shock showed on his face. I turned back to the hunters.

"Shasta, what the hell is going on?" I grunted through my teeth.

"I can't jump. I'm being blocked by someone," Shasta sounded frantic. He stepped up beside me, placing half his body in front of mine. Granger and Kale took one step forward, but stopped suddenly.

"What do you mean you can't jump? What the hell do we do now?" I ran a hand through my hair.

"I don't know. It's like something is keeping me here. It's like someone is holding me down. I can't move, and I can't read their thoughts either. Whoever it is, they're stronger than me," he replied.

Oh, crap. That didn't sound good. Okay, stay calm. I opened my senses to Andy. He wasn't anywhere in the apartment. We made a plan earlier. If anything was to happen, Andy and Amanda would run, head to the train station, and get out. A meeting spot was picked in advance.

The hunters were waiting for an answer. They would have to wait forever, because I wouldn't give them anything.

Shasta wrapped a hand in mine. Together, we would win, but not at the cost of the hunters. As much as it pained me to say it, they were of my race, and I wouldn't see them die at my own hand. Never would I stoop to Anastasis's level. Never would I let her take that part of me away from myself. A quick escape had to be made. I would fight; that wouldn't be a problem, but I would only fight enough to get out alive.

"We are waiting, Alikye. It's time for us to go," Granger stated.

I took a vigilant step forward, holding tight to Shasta. I hated to admit it, but I really missed Shasta's mind reading abilities right now. Luckily, Shasta and I had this weird way of reading each other. I squeezed his hand twice, and then drew a circle in his palm with my finger. I was a step from him, so our hands were hidden behind me. Granger nor Kale could see the exchange.

"Yeah, that's not gonna happen," I winked.

Their expression stayed stone cold, which wasn't a surprise. Granger shook his head. The moonlight filtered in through the large windows that covered one wall. Outside, the river glittered, matching the sky above. Granger pulled a sword from his back, holding it up between him and me.

"One last chance to surrender. I will not grant you another," Kale said sternly. From his back, he pulled out two large knives. Both were twenty-four inch blades, with leather-bound hilts and Enochian symbols etched into them. They were from Legacy families that had been destroyed long ago. Granger's sword had the same markings, but the name engraved into it was not his.

Anastasis had once said that the weapons belonging to the fallen families were locked away in safe keeping. How she got them to work for others was beyond me, but given the situation we were in right now, I'm guessing Ana had a witch in her pocket. That couldn't be good. Admittedly though, Ana was smart to have one. Between Shasta and me, we were an unbeatable team.

"How thick are your windows?" I whispered.

"Pretty thick," a devilish grin spread across Shasta's face, "but nothing we can't handle."

Granger cocked his head to the side. Twisting his neck, he turned towards the windows.

Wrong move, dick.

His entire right side was left open. As a trained professional, he should have known this. The problem was that these guys were cocky and fearless, believing nothing could beat them. Yep, I should know. Two years ago, I was the same, believing I was the best. I was lucky to still be alive.

Shasta took off, crossing in front of me in Kale's direction. I went after Granger in hyper-speed. One kick to the ribs was all it took. I heard several bones crack in half. Granger yelled out in pain, stumbling to the side before tripping over his feet and face planting on the floor. Right away, he started to heal; blue markings lit his body. I estimated thirty-seconds before he was up again. I kicked the weapon from his hand, and bent down to grab it. Out of nowhere, Kale's foot connected with my face. Blood covered my lip, pooling into my mouth; a sweet metallic taste. Pain shot to my head as my neck snapped back. I spit, leaving a trail of blood spotting the floor.

His knife came down hard; a sure hit that would kill me instantly. Before the blade pierced my skin, Shasta's hard body came at me. Like a football player tackling his opponent, we both hit the floor a few feet away. Granger was already up, sword in hand, ready to fight. I caught Shasta's eyes. Nodding my head to the window, I winked.

"Now," he said.

"Now," I repeated.

Together, we took off running. I went ahead of him in hyper-speed. We needed the extra speed to break through the window. I hit the window fast and hard, feeling the bones in my shoulder shift and pieces of skin split open. The glass started to splinter around the edges. With Shasta's added weight, it was enough to shatter the glass. Large pieces pierced my arms, face, and body. More pieces rained down on us as we fell through the air, down three stories. Beneath us was the river. Hopefully, we jumped far enough to hit the water and not solid ground. My stomach jumped to my throat.

Seconds later, I crashed into the river; feet first, submerged into a deep dark abyss. Cold water rushed through me, filling my lungs with filth. I heard somewhere that the waters of Venice were polluted and dirty. I wasn't human, so sickness and disease wasn't a problem. That didn't mean the idea of drinking and swimming in filth was my kind of party. Under the cover of the river, my body started to heal. I could feel the glass being pushed out of each wound. My skin was being pulled together. The right side of my body was pretty broken from the impact of the glass, but after a few seconds, the bones started to realign and fix themselves.

Finally, my lights started to fade. I pushed myself up, gliding effortlessly through the water. Reaching the top, I broke through the surface, sucking in a gulp of air. Shasta was already pulling himself out of the water. Bystanders yelled from a distance. Voices screamed to call the police; some were saying two people fell out of a window, while others were asking if we were okay.

Lights and sounds came from afar. Glass littered the ground around us. I looked up at Shasta's flat, and saw Granger and Kale staring down at me. They were smart enough not to follow because of the attention we drew. My clothes were sopping wet, and my hair was sticking to my face. More people looked out from their balconies, and some more were coming our way. We needed to get the hell out of there before they started asking too many questions. Shasta knew it, too.

"We need to run. I told Andy to meet us at the train station. It's a few blocks away," he said, grabbing my hand. I ran with him, far away from the people yelling for us to stop.

"Shit, all of my stuff is in my room. My bow and arrows are there," I complained.

We ran past a cluster of buildings, ducking between narrow alleyways. Sirens sounded a few streets over. Once we were far enough away, we slowed to a walk.

"That was close," Shasta laughed.

I shook my head, laughing, too. The situation was anything but funny, but it was better than freaking out.

"What the hell happened, anyway? By the way, that was great timing to lose all your abilities," I joked.

Yeah, but it looks like I got them back. Come on, he sent.

"They had a freaking witch. She bonded my powers to her. I could feel her close by in the next room. It hurt like hell, that's for sure," he said, breaking the silence. "Now that they know where we are, it won't take them long before they find us again."

The train station was straight ahead. Andy and Amanda were waiting at the front. Amanda was worried. As she talked, her hand went flying. Andy grabbed her, pulling her into him. Her shoulders shook as he smoothed her hair off her forehead. It broke my heart to watch them. We did this to them.

Stop it.

"You know, I liked it better when you couldn't read my mind," I scolded. We turned the last corner, walking up the steps to the station.

"Love, I might have some bad news," Shasta ran a hand through his dark locks, twisting the ends. It was getting longer, reaching his shoulders. He needed a haircut. He raised his eyebrows at me, judging me for thinking about his hair while he's about to deliver bad news.

"Hey, at least I'm working on not being so dramatic," I answered his unspoken thought.

"Yes, good job," sarcasm dripped from his voice. He twisted his face to a more serious look. "When that witch bonded to me, the only way to do that is through blood. Ana must have gotten my blood somehow since I refused to give it up because of situations like this," he flung his hand around, inches away from smacking me. "Anyway, now that she has a taste of my powers, she'll be able to find me within hours, or at least come within a twenty mile radius of my location," Shasta said, his eyes focusing on the ground.

I pushed down the anger, channeling the new optimistic side I was working on. "We'll figure it out," I smiled.

Shasta suddenly stopped walking. He grabbed my arm, yanking me to him. Putting his hand on my forehead, he looked deep into my eyes, studying me. His face was only inches from mine, his breath tickling my skin. Without a word, we stood there. As much as I loved Shasta, this was getting way too uncomfortable; I wasn't an affectionate person. Andy was different. Shasta took up too much of my personal space. I started to shift my weight from one foot to the other.

"Am I making you uncomfortable, love?" he asked, his voice sounding very serious.

"Uh, yeah, you mind backing off a bit there?" I whispered.

"Something's wrong, love," he whispered, too close to my ear.

My body stiffened as I looked around.

"Did you hit your head when you fell out that window, because never in my life would I have guessed you to be so calm about this all," a laugh broke from his lips.

I relaxed, letting out an annoyed breath. "Are you serious?" I smacked his chest, hard. "You scared the crap outta me."

He laughed harder, drawing the attention of both Andy and Amanda, who looked up at us with wide eyes. He finally pulled away from me.

"There's my girl. I thought I lost you for a moment," he joked.

"Jerk," I grunted.

Amanda came running at us, throwing herself into Shasta's arms. He picked her up, cradling her head in one hand while supporting her small body in the other. Andy grabbed me, hugging me to his chest. He took my face into his hands, studying me intently. He kissed me lightly. All too soon, he pulled away, but kept a firm grip on me.

"Why are you wet?" Andy looked down my body, and then over at Shasta who was still holding Amanda. I loved that Andy didn't ask if I was okay. As long as I stood in front of him, he knew I was fine.

My body shook as I tried not to laugh. Maybe I did hit my head, hard.

One look at me, and Shasta's grin widened as he answered Andy. "It's her fault. She had the brilliant idea to jump through my window into the river."

"What window?" Andy asked.

"In the same room as the hunters," Shasta shrugged like it was no big deal.

"Okay, how in the world did you have time to open it and sneak out? Those hunter guys didn't look like the type to just let you escape like that," Andy asked Shasta. His grip tightened around me, holding me close to his body.

"Who said anything about opening it? Nearly killed myself jumping through it. Unlike Alikye here, I don't have super healing powers," Shasta had a deep gash above his eye, but the bleeding had stopped after entering the water. It would take less than a day to heal.

"Oh, please. That fall wouldn't have killed you, and you know it," I said against Andy's shoulder.

Andy looked down at me with raised eyebrows.

"What?" I asked innocently. "It was the only way."

"Going through a window?" Andy questioned.

"Yes, and look," I pulled away from him, spinning around once, "no harm, no foul."

"Yeah except all the attention you drew," Shasta said. "Speaking of which, we really need to get going before the hunters come looking for us."

We stopped off at the gift shop to pick up a few things for the trip. There was no way we could go back and grab our things. The risk was too high, even for Shasta to jump in and out quickly. I bought a pair of running shorts and a T-shirt, changing quickly in the bathroom. My boots were soaked, but with a clean pair of socks it wasn't so bad; nothing I haven't handled before.

By whining about having to get to Rome to see her family, Amanda was able to use her charm to change our tickets to an earlier time. The guy behind the counter looked like he just wanted her to go away, so we got on the next train out.

Within an hour, we were pulling away from the station, hidden away in a private room with the curtains drawn. My eyelids started to feel heavy, and in a minute I was fast asleep. The last thing I remember was feeling Andy twisting my hair between his fingers while I lay my head in his lap.

****

Bright light streamed in through the open door. Outside, it was still pitch black. The steady movement of the train and the wind whipping against the metal lured me back to sleep. I curled up tighter on the small couch, pulling the blanket up to my chin. I realized, only then, that Andy wasn't underneath me anymore. I sat up and looked around the darkened room. Amanda slept peacefully on the other couch with Shasta.

I got up, leaving the safety of the room in search of Andy. The train was quiet; there were only a few people up reading or playing games on their phones. On the other side near the bar, I spotted Andy talking to one of the servers. She handed him a coffee and went to the next customer. He turned to make his way back to the room, but stopped when he saw me. After looking around for a minute, he made his way towards me.

"Baby, what are you doing up? It's four in the morning," Andy asked, taking my hand and leading me to a private sitting area near our room. I sat first and Andy took the seat next to me, placing a hand on my thigh. He took a long sip of his coffee before handing it to me. The sweet but bitter taste was like heaven to my taste buds.

"You weren't there, so I got worried," I answered.

"I couldn't sleep. I kept hearing footsteps outside. I guess I'm just a little on edge. I don't like being trapped in

147

a moving box. You know, if they happen to be here," he admitted.

"They wouldn't risk confronting me with so many people around. For now, we are safe. It's when we get off the train that we need to be alert at all times. Lucky for us, we won't reach our destination until tomorrow morning."

I was worried they'd be in Rome by the time we got there, and by then they would have called for backup. It's not like we were too proud to ask for help. Even I asked for help every now and then. I let a step by step plan start building in my head, so we had something to discuss in the morning. The train station would be packed, so there would be no chance of ambushing us there, but Granger was one hell of a tracker. If he wanted to, he'd be able to follow us without us ever noticing. First step was to find a safe place to stay, and get there without being seen.

****

"Why don't you just have Shasta jump you to a safe spot?" Amanda asked the next morning. We were all sitting around in our cabin having breakfast. That thought had crossed my mind.

"If they know where we're going, they'll be tracking us. They know you're with us. If I take Kye away with me, you two are easy prey. At least Kye knows when she's being followed by her people, since she was pretty much trained the same," Shasta explained.

At school, I took extra courses in being a hunter. Knowing I was the only child of my Legacy, becoming a hunter was never going to be an option, but I wanted to learn to be the best. I wasn't trained the same as them, though; not as many hours put into my training, but enough to know when I was being followed. Maybe.

"Love, stop pouting. You are not to blame," Shasta said to Amanda. I was quickly pulled out of my own head, catching the end of what the others were saying. "You are going to get wrinkles," Shasta's tone was serious.

Amanda's head snapped towards Shasta. She was scowling. Andy fell to the floor, holding his stomach as laughter bellowed out. I looked around just in time to watch Amanda slap Shasta in the face. I smiled proudly at her technique. I taught her how to fight without breaking a nail or pulling hair.

"What the hell?" both Shasta and I said in unison. Although, we said it for totally different reasons. I was confused, and Shasta was sporting his signature devilish smile. That smile always got him into trouble.

"Read my mind one more time, and I will stab you in the gut," she pointed a butter knife at his face. His smirk faded. The knife wouldn't kill him, but it would hurt like hell for a few days.

"But," Shasta whined.

"No buts. Do I make myself clear?" she jabbed the knife closer to his eye this time.

"Yeah, idiot, does she make herself clear?" I smirked. I caught Amanda's eyes. She smiled quickly before scowling again at Shasta.

He was outnumbered, and the one thing you don't mess with is two pissed off chicks. He wasn't that much of an idiot. Shasta held up his hands in surrender. "Okay, fine. Sorry I read your mind, love. It won't happen again," he winked at me right as Amanda turned her head towards Andy, who was on the floor laughing like a lunatic.

Idiots, both of them. The day Shasta stopped invading the minds of people will be the day I become queen. Never gonna happen, I thought.

"You two are dip-shits. Can we please get back to figuring out a plan?" Amanda barked.

Andy settled down, rolling over to lay next to me. I sat on the floor, legs stretched out and crossed at the ankles.

He scooted around until his head was in my lap. I shot him a dirty look.

"What?" he asked innocently.

"Don't what me. I'm glad you think this is funny. Last I checked, you went all PMS bitch on him when he read your mind," I stared down at him, accusingly.

"Did you just accuse me of having a girlie meltdown?" he smiled.

"Yes," I said, just as Amanda said the same.

"Whatever. Anyway, I think what Amanda said earlier is a good idea," Andy continued, changing the subject. "Before we head out of here," he pointed to him and Amanda, "scout the area as best as you can. Then, get the hell out. We'll leave ten minutes later, grab some lunch, and do some shopping. That way we can keep an eye out for anyone who looks suspicious, and give you two enough time to find a safe location."

I was impressed. We all sat quietly for a couple minutes while I calculated the pros and cons in my head. They all knew me well enough to know what I was doing; flipping through the pages of my mind like a book. I saw the outline of Rome in my head as I scanned all the buildings. My eyelashes fluttered up and down like wings of a humming bird, while my eyes moved back and forth on their own accord. I was well aware of my surroundings inside the train, but when I put myself in this kind of trance without backup it could be dangerous.

I jumped back into the present. The world around me came back into focus. Shasta was in my head the whole time, seeing everything I just saw. His eyes were glazed over, taking a second longer to focus.

"It may just work," I said.

"Do you know how freaking scary you look when you do that?" Amanda said. "Back in school, I always thought you were off your rocker when you went into space mode."

"Thanks," I sneered. I looked down at Andy. He only shrugged.

"What? Sorry, but next time I'll record you. You're all," she imitated me the best she could, but she made it look like I was having a stroke, "something like that."

I could feel Andy shaking his head back and forth, trying very hard not to laugh. His shoulders shook, but he stayed quiet. I smacked his arm.

"I do not look like that!" I shrieked.

"Yes, you do," all three of them said in unison.

"You three suck," I hit Andy again, because he was the closest to me. He grunted, but continued to laugh. I ignored him. "Whatever. Anyway, as I was saying, we find a meeting place outside of the city. When the two of you feel like you're not being watched anymore, that's when you hightail it out of the city. We have a few more hours, which gives me enough time to teach you what to look for, and how to trust your feelings."

"What do you mean by feelings?" Amanda asked.

"Easy. You know that feeling you get when someone is watching you?" I asked. They both nodded. "Well, you need to trust it. Now that you know someone may be following you, paranoia will set in, so you two need to learn how to relax your mind to know the difference between the two."

"You do realize that's impossible, right?" Andy asked, trying to figure how he could clear his mind.

"Will you stop that?" I smacked his forehead lightly. "You look like you're trying to take a poop."

Oh, dear lord, somebody help me.

Andy unscrewed his face, pouting. I had to admit he looked so freaking cute when he did that. I wanted to squish him. I ran my hands in his hair, twisting my fingers around the longer strands. His hair was always so soft and thick. He never had to do much to it, besides brush his fingers across it. Andy closed his eyes, taking low, shallow breaths in and out.

When I felt his body relax, I started to explain in a low whisper.

"Now, find a place in your mind that's peaceful," I dug my fingers deeper into his hair, massaging his scalp.

"Mmmm, the beach," he slurred in a drunken stupor.

"Keep going sweetheart. Lose yourself in that thought. Feel everything around you as if you were there," I said, turning my gaze on Amanda, who was trying to hold back a giggle. Shasta was shaking his head.

Humans are so simple minded. Two-seconds worth of rubbing his hair, and he's a babbling idiot, Shasta thought.

Watch out, buddy. Your girlfriend's next. I smiled to Shasta.

"Sunny days," his eyes opened for a moment. A light blue ringed around his dark irises. "Hot sand, cool water breaking on shore, whoosh, whoosh," he made a motion with his hands back and forth between the empty space.

"Good boy. Now feel the water against your skin, the sun warming you. Hear the birds call for one another in the distances," I skimmed a finger down Andy's jaw, returning to his hair to play with the long strands. "What else do you see? Am I with you?" I asked.

"Mmmm, I like you in a bathing suit. Your smooth skin, flat belly, naked body lying on top," I threw my hand over his mouth before he could finish his sentence.

Crap.

My eyes widened in horror, heat scorching my neck. That was a first for me. My body had never reacted like this; heating up by private words being spoken out loud. I panicked. What else was I supposed to do? This moron, that I had put into a trance to clear his mind, was living a porno in his head, and it was starring me. I smacked his cheek hard, leaving a red mark on his beautiful face.

Andy snapped his eyes open, looking around the cabin confused. Sitting up from my lap, he rubbed his face, peeking through the cracks in his fingers. Light scruff dusted his face, making him look so much older and more handsome. Amanda had a stupid grin on her face, causing Andy to scrunch his face up in confusion.

It was Shasta, though, who threw us all over the edge. He was standing in the corner with his arms crossed over his muscular chest. Wavy black hair fell around his shoulders. He looked everywhere but at me. It took me a minute to realize that the look on his face was shame.

"Oh, gah! You son of a bitch. Do you see what happens when you get all up in everyone's head?" I screamed at Shasta.

He didn't say anything.

"Now you have a mental picture of me naked. Eww!"

More heat ran up my neck. I was getting the feeling this is how being embarrassed felt. I never really used that emotion, and I didn't like it. I felt sweat beads form around my lip and forehead. I wiped at my face with the back of my hand.

"What the hell are you talking about?" Andy snarled.

"You," I pointed to my not so subtle, sexually deprived, stupid boyfriend. "Shit, do you realize in my seventeen years of life, I have never once been embarrassed? Now I have a burning on my neck, and it's very uncomfortable!" I took a deep breath, rubbing away the heat the best I could.

Now I had three sets of eyes on me, all with different expressions. Shasta looked warily; he focused only on my eyes and nothing else. I could see he was struggling, but decided I would talk to him later. Amanda looked at me like I was completely off my rocker, and Andy still looked confused as hell.

Luckily, Amanda took the reins on this one, because I was still working on releasing the emotion that had my stomach in knots. The chemicals in my brain were on overdrive.

"Andy, first off, thanks for your very detailed porno of what you want to do with Alikye on the beach," she pointed to Shasta, "and for probably traumatizing my boyfriend for life, since I can only imagine what he saw."

Shasta looked down at the ground.

"What is she talking about?" Andy looked to Shasta. He still wouldn't speak. I tried to get inside his head to ask him what the hell was going on, but he kept me blocked out.

"I put you in a trance to give you an idea of how to clear your mind. When I asked you to think of a happy, calm place, you started mumbling about the beach. Then you went into detail about me with you on the beach, but I stopped you before you could go any further. Problem, though. Shasta was in your head and saw everything," I winced like I was in pain.

The whole situation just blew up in my face. It was uncomfortable inside this room with so many different emotions coming off of everyone. Just when I thought it couldn't get any weirder, Andy surprised me. He burst out laughing so hard. Within seconds, tears were streaming down his face. He grabbed onto his stomach, curling up in the fetal position on the floor. I didn't know whether to slap the shit out of him, or beg the floor to open up and swallow me whole. Damn this embarrassing emotion. It's useless.

"Andy!" I yelled. "Stop being an idiot and get up. This is not funny," I kicked him in the leg, but it only made him laugh harder.

Within minutes, Amanda joined him, and I saw Shasta trying really hard not to smile. He still wouldn't look at me.

I promised myself earlier that I'd lighten up. I was making good on that promise, until now. I couldn't change everything about myself, but I didn't want to anyway. The darkness and anger inside me was a part of me. I was a Legacy, and the best one out there. To catch me or kill me was nearly impossible. It was the negativity I had to lose. All my other traits were what made me uniquely me.

In this situation, though, it was different. I was pissed; not at Andy, he had every right to think the things he did. I just wish he wouldn't, and laughing at my expense wasn't helping. Shasta was an upside to the situation. Maybe now he would tread lightly when entering someone's mind. I was mad because I was feeling things I didn't want to feel. Day by day, human emotions that were useless to me were making an appearance, and that didn't sit well with me.

"I...oh, my god. I can't. I'm sorry..." Andy held on to his stomach, stuttering absurdly.

"For shit's sake, stupid, just spit it out," I grunted. I kicked his leg again.

After a good amount of time, everyone finally settled down.

"I'm sorry, baby, but that shit was funny," he said, breathless. "You should see your face right now." Andy looked towards Shasta, and started laughing more. I rolled my eyes. "And you. Stay the fuck outta my head or you're gonna see a lot more of my girlfriend."

"Andy!" Amanda and I yelled at the same time.

"It's not like it's the first time, but usually I get out quickly before anything happens. This time I was stuck. My head hurts," Shasta rubbed his temples.

"Shasta!" we all said in unison.

My face started to burn again. "Oh for shit's sake, make it stop," I mumbled, placing my face in my hands.

"What's wrong, baby?" Andy asked trying to take my hand.

"She's embarrassed," Shasta shrugged. "She's not used to that emotion. Give her a minute."

"Wait. What? You've never been embarrassed before?" Amanda asked.

"No. Why the hell would I want that? It's like jealousy; it's useless," my voice was muffled by my hands.

"Aw, baby," Andy chuckled, "you're cute when you blush."

I snapped my head up, glaring at Andy. His face was the picture of innocence and so full of love. I punched him hard in the shoulder, making him fall over. Yeah, that felt so much better.

"Ah, mate, I wouldn't do that if I were you," Shasta snorted.

"Ouch, damn, girl," Andy said, rubbing his shoulder. "That was not very nice," he pouted.

For the rest of the day, I worked with Amanda and Andy on trusting their instincts. The only problem was, until they face being out there, they won't really know how they will react. When faced with fear, humans aren't able to control the way their bodies work. That was another emotion I never had until Andy came into my life, but I was still able to turn it off if the situation called for it. We all went to sleep early that night, knowing when morning came we would need to well rested in order to escape to safety.

A loud shriek sounded outside, followed by the pull of the train. Slowly we came into view of a large building packed with people waiting. We made it to Rome. I was almost home free. Almost.

Chapter 17

I closed my eyes, taking deep slow breaths in and out. Shasta stood near me in a protective stance. If anyone were to pay close attention, it would look as if Shasta was my bodyguard. I smiled to myself because, in a way, Shasta was my bodyguard. Loud chatter filled the room with words I ignored. I blocked them out, letting the world around me disappear. Like humans, Guardians had their own scent, their own signature. One minute with them, and already they were imprinted in my mind.

A small flutter of recognition spread through my mind. They were here somewhere, but the trace was weak. Whatever the witch was doing was making it almost impossible for me to find them. Shasta was without his powers again, so it wasn't hard to figure out he or she was with them.

Ana was such a hypocrite; always spatting off about how witches were untrustworthy and their magic wasn't anything we should be messing with, and yet here she was using one to track me down. Desperate times called for desperate measures. For them, the situation with the council was desperate.

Now that I had a general idea of the whereabouts of the hunters, I could avoid them enough to get the hell out of here. I opened up my mind to Andy, feeling his warmth and love. His imprint was my favorite. It reminded me of the beach, the salty air, and the smell of sunshine. If I stayed too long, I could get lost in him. Andy and Amanda were still on the train. I felt the hunters closer to me than them. I was on the other side of the station, closer to the back exit.

"They're about to leave. If the hunters catch their scent, we're in trouble," I said to Shasta's back.

He was looking around the room, scanning each face.

"Have they found you yet?" he asked.

"Yes and no. They know I'm here; their witch is powerful. For all I know, they could be right behind me, without so much as a warning. They could also have the scent of Andy and Amanda already. I really don't know what to do right now. Either way, we're screwed if they track any of us," I answered.

"I have an idea, but we need to get far enough from the witch for me to do this," he grabbed my hand pulling me to the exit. "Let's get outta here before they follow."

"I don't like leaving Andy unprotected," I said, mostly to myself.

I knew nothing would happen to him. The council didn't want him, and once they realized I wasn't with him anymore, they would hopefully leave him alone. It sucked more than anything to have a weakness. Andy wasn't just my greatest weakness. In my world, he was also weak himself. Protecting him, while protecting myself, was becoming too much. What I needed most was for him to go home, and let me deal with this on my own. How could I say these things to him without hurting his feelings? The last thing I needed was to lose him, or make him truly see that our relationship was ruining me in more ways than one. I felt like shit merely thinking these things. I was a horrible person who was asking for the perfect life.

Karma's a bitch sometimes. I really need to have a heart to heart with her.

Shasta and I took off running down the street as fast as possible. We looked like a couple of lunatics, but I didn't have time to care. When we finally stopped behind a large building structure about a mile away from the station, my breath came out heavily

Okay, give me a minute, and keep an eye out. The witch seems to be too far away right now. I'm not really sure of the distance, but I'm pretty sure he or she is powerful enough to be more than a few feet away.

Shasta closed his eyes. From the light fluttering of his lids, I could tell he was talking to someone in his mind, a power I've always envied. I scanned the empty alleyways and streets, watching townies and tourists mingling and enjoying the bright, sunny morning. The weekend was long past, but, like America, the shops and restaurant were filled to capacity. In the far distance, a large fountain sat. Children ran around the area as their parents yelled for them to not jump in the water.

The world went on like every other day; humans clueless to the monsters lurking around each corner, and the struggles my world and their world brought to me. They were carefree, happy, and oblivious to any kind of danger; a sort of life I would never get the courtesy of having, but that didn't mean I couldn't fight for my sliver of happiness.

"It's done, let's go," Shasta's voice broke through my thoughts. I turned to face him, watching as his eyes scanned the area I had just checked. For now, we were in the clear.

"Where'd you go?" sometimes when he was that deep in mind communication, he would disappear from this time and place to enter the mind in which he possessed. It was all rather fascinating, but it could also be dangerous, unless someone had his back.

"I asked Isabella for help in hiding Amanda and Andy. She spelled them, so they will go undetected for now. She's leaving in a few hours. With the hunters on our trail, she thinks it would be a lot safer for us if she was here," he told me.

"You think this is really going to work?" I asked. Shasta shrugged, keeping his eyes focus on the streets. "Really, that's it? I just find it hard to believe Ana's just gonna give up, even with Natalia back. She'll find another reason to try me."

"Doesn't matter. The real question is what you're going to do with your freedom. The choice will be between Andy and the Guardians. Ana won't give you both. Natalia's hands will be tied since this kind of decision has to be unanimous," Shasta said, concern laced in his voice.

He knew how important both were to me. I loved my family, and I loved being a Guardian. If given a choice to live a life of darkness, the choice would always be light, and Andy was my light.

"I guess there's your answer," Shasta said after reading my mind.

"Is that wrong of me?" I already knew the answer.

"No," his face stayed stoic.

"Will you still love me?" I smiled at him innocently. He shrugged, looking away. In a flash, I was at his side, smacking at his strong chest. "Alright, Demon boy, you go ahead and tell yourself life would be so much better without me in it."

"It would definitely be easier, that's for sure," he tried to sound all high and mighty with his sexy European accent, but I wasn't buying it.

"Jerk face," I toyed.

"Yeah, but you still love me," he said, pulling me out into the streets of Rome.

＊＊＊＊

"Um, why are we at the beach, Shasta? I know you want me to lighten up a bit, but sunbathing and swimming isn't going to help right now," I was very confused why we weren't hiding out. I knew he would never do anything to hurt me, or put me in harm's way intentionally. It was usually me putting people in harm's way, unintentionally. At least, in my mind it was never my fault.

I looked around at the small amount of people laying in the sand. All tourists. I hate to talk shit, but Rome wasn't known for their beautiful breathtaking beaches, unlike some of the other cities and islands that sprinkled the large, gothic, historical city.

Shasta stared off into the distance. A little way ahead of us was a privately owned harbor, hidden behind a cluster of rocks.

"Come on. They won't wait forever for us," Shasta said into the wind, grabbing ahold of my hand.

We raced down the beach, sand flying up around us. He stopped when we reached the rocks, crouching down to be unseen. Together we scanned the faces around us; all of them were human. Shasta let out a heavy sigh like he had been holding his breath for a long time.

"I can see a plan going on in that big ol' head of yours," I whispered behind his back.

"I'll fill you in on the boat," he stood up straight, jumping up on the rocks.

I followed behind, skipping from one slippery rock to the next. Any human would break their neck trying to attempt what we were doing. Lucky for us, no one was paying attention. There was no way this looked normal. We jumped across the makeshift wall, landing on our feet on the other side. A small building, no bigger than a one story house, hid behind the trees inside the harbor. One wall was entirely missing with three docks. A small speed boat was tied up to one of the docks.

We waited a couple of minutes before a woman in her late thirties came out of a room that was located in the far right corner. She looked from me to Shasta before smiling widely. I stayed quiet, having no clue what the hell was going on.

"She's full and ready to go. When should I expect you back?" the woman asked sweetly, handing Shasta the keys. Her accent was French, but she spoke English very well, and she seemed to know Shasta. The woman was human, no doubt about it, and from the look on her face she knew what Shasta was, and wasn't afraid of him.

"Thank you, Tanya. I'll be back in a few days. Tell that husband of yours I owe him big time," Shasta said politely, kissing the top of her hand.

I rolled my eyes. Shasta was a charmer, plain and simple, and girls were always falling all over him, even before he opened his big fat mouth. Even Kady still got flustered around him. It was hilarious to watch her face turn bright red, and hear her words come out as gibberish. It was even funnier to watch Greg letting it happen, most of the time shaking his head and laughing silently. Amanda and I were the only ones who didn't fall for his crap. It was one of the reasons Shasta fell for her.

"No need. We owe you our lives, Shasta," Tanya kissed his cheek. After she turned and said goodbye to me, she went back to her office or whatever room was behind that door.

"Okay, I don't even know where to start, lover boy," I said, hopping not so gracefully into the boat. Shasta ignored me, revving up the engine and backing out of the small wharf.

After a while, we were cruising at high speed through the Mediterranean Sea. I sat back in my seat, the wind blowing across my heated face. The ocean was beautiful and crystal clear, glistening like a million diamonds. For the first time in days, a sense of calm washed over me. Out here in the middle of nowhere, I was safe. No way would I be able to leave a trace this far off the shore. Shasta's face was just as relaxed as mine, and if I were able to read minds, I'm sure he'd be thinking the same thing.

"The portal to find Natalia isn't actually in Rome," Shasta started. I looked up quickly, about to say something, but Shasta put up his hand to cut me off. "Before you go all crazy bitch on me, let me finish."

I nodded once, telling him to go on, before I did go all crazy bitch on him.

"We are headed to the island of Ponza; a small place not too far from here. Amanda and Andy should already be there," he continued.

"How in the hell did they even get there?" I asked. From what I could see, the only way was by boat, and I didn't see any ferries around.

"I sent them to Anzio by train. The hunters were too busy with us that they didn't see them get back on another train. If they made it there in time, a ferry took them the rest of the way. I had Isabella give them directions to a secluded area of the island where Tanya and her husband own a small bungalow they offered to let us use."

"Well, aren't you one for secret agendas. Why the hell am I the last to hear about this, and who the hell is Tanya?" I yelled, taking my aggression out on Shasta. These secrets kept popping up last minute. "Agh! I freaking hate this," I got up in Shasta's face, my breath coming out in heavy puffs. I could feel the anger coursing through my veins, heat seeping from my pores. "No one tells me anything. I'm just this poor, weak girl who needs to be shielded by a bunch of big tough men," I said, gripping the side of the boat until I felt the tears in my skin. By then I was speaking to myself, turning my back to Shasta. Big mistake. I should have been paying attention to the sudden changes.

"Tanya is a friend of mine from Paris. Her husband's Italian. I've known them for some time now, but that's not important," his tone got sharper. "You're the one they want Kye. So, yes, you have to be the last to know so I can stay two steps ahead of them. They're your people. I can't take the chance of them reading you, and finding out about Natalia," he was glaring at me, his eyes growing darker.

Times like this, I could see and sense the Demon in him. He was never one to lose his temper, but when he did, it was scary as shit. I held my ground, because weakness only made the beast want to play. His jaw tightened, moving back and forth as he ground his teeth. I could see him trying to reel it in, but he was too far gone. Muscles bulged in his upper arms and chest, and his breathing came out thick. Silver swirled in his icy eyes like wind mixing with water or clouded venom, before they turned black.

This wasn't the first, nor would it be the last, time he went Demon on me. It was in his nature to fall to darkness. Once he was able to snap out of it, he would feel like shit for days. I understood fully how amazing it felt to have that kind of darkness call to you. It was like a drug; a high so powerful you wanted to get lost in it and never come down. Only, when you did come down, you felt guilty for craving it so badly.

"Reel it in, Demon boy," I growled.

"I'm trying," he said through his teeth. I could already see the blue coming back into his eyes.

After a long couple of minutes, Shasta took a deep breath, looking back to his normal self. He sat back down in his seat, saying nothing, as waves crashed against our still boat. In the distance, a mile or so away, I saw an outline of the island that was our destination.

"What happened?" I asked softly, so not to set him off yet.

"It's not you, if that's what you think. The stress and worry of the last few days are just getting to me. It's a lot more than I could have thought. Actually, love, you are also a pain in my ass," a small smile played at his lips.

"You okay now?" I wondered.

"Yes, love, just a little bit of my father's side is all. Nothing I can't handle," he started the boat up, and within the next hour we were pulling up to the back side of the island. This was stressful for all of us and I realized it wasn't just my life that needed saving but Shasta's as well.

To many hours spent worrying wasn't good for either of us. I needed to make it up to him. Maybe a day to do nothing but allow ourselves to relax would do wonders for us all. If Shasta and I weren't 100% good, one small mistake could be fatal.

Chapter 18

The island of Ponza was something out of a fairytale. It is the main island of the Pontine archipelago, which is made up of eight tiny volcanic islands, surrounded by beautiful turquoise water. Beyond the rolling hills and jagged white cliffs, a small town of pastel homes and shops sat snugly around the harbor. Music came off the island from a nearby street, just off the docks where boats of every size were tied up. Restaurants and bars dotted the street. I knew, without a doubt, Amanda would be begging to explore.

 Shasta passed the harbor, heading towards the back. Rising up from the water, off the sandy beaches, were algae covered boulders, hiding away a cluster of caves. He slowed the boat, drifting across the water. Some of the caves had high arches, almost like a bridge. Private homes sat atop the jagged white cliffs. I had never seen anything so beautiful. Although being here was not a vacation, it didn't mean I couldn't enjoy the serenity.

Tucked away behind some trees, Shasta pointed to a small home that looked out over the ocean. The house sat atop a cliff, a grass trail leading to the beach. Shasta tied the boat to the dock as I walked the perimeter. We took the uphill trail; a canopy of trees blocked out the sun the entire way. It was all beautiful and inviting. The front of the house faced the cliff. A small porch wrapped around it, and a hammock swung between two trees. The house was completely hidden from a person's view on three sides by trees of all shapes and sizes. It was secluded from the rest of the world.

"You'll be able to get to town without taking the boat," Shasta said as he pointed to the back of the house. "A hidden path through the woods leads to the main road. Someone's gonna have to take a trip into town for food and supplies."

"I need my weapon," I grunted, climbing the grassy hill.

"Yeah, I feel naked without my swords. I asked Isabella to grab them for us," Shasta said, coming up behind me.

I nodded my thanks.

The house came into view, and I had to stop to admire its beauty. These days, the little things were becoming my beacons of hope. My moods tended to shift more and more lately. It wasn't my fault, but as much as I tried to control them, it only made it worse. Add stress to that equation, on top of feeling betrayed, and it was no wonder I wasn't hospitalized by now. Instead, I started finding my escape in the little things to help center my emotions.

"So, about this portal, are you going to tell me where it is?" I bent my head, searching Shasta's eyes. A smile crossed his face, and he looked to the ground. "Umm okay," I muttered.

"It's under your feet, love. This island is known for its magic, hidden deep under the earth. It just so happens the back of one of these caves holds enough magic to create and open a portal," he explained.

"Whatever, I'll never understand this crap. Just let me know when you need my blood. I don't know why I ask," I replied, throwing up my arms exaggeratedly.

"No worries, love." Shasta laughed. "Now, let's make sure the humans got here okay."

Breathing out a sigh of relief, I watched as Andy and Amanda made their way out the front door. Walking straight towards Andy, I wrapped my arms around him. For the first time in hours, I felt relaxed just knowing they was safe.

The first thing I noticed when I walked into the small beach house was the smell. Besides the usual salty aroma, the scent of spices billowed out from the kitchen. My stomach rumbled, and my mouth watered at the deliciousness waiting for me a few feet away.

"Amanda ran into town when we got here. Figured we'd need food and supplies," Andy said, walking over to the gas burner, stirring the creamy tomato sauce.

When the water next to him began to boil, Andy pulled out a box of dried pasta to pour into the pot. Wiping his hands off on the towel hanging from his jeans, he walked out of the room for a minute only to return with a stack of folded clothes. He handed them to me. I smiled at his domesticated nature.

After changing into a pair of skinny jeans and white tank top, I walked back into the kitchen. I was overly shocked by the sight in front of me, stuck between wanting to laugh or just stand there looking like an idiot with my jaw on the floor. Never in my life would I have imagined Shasta acting so tamed; he walked around the table, setting it with plates and utensils. Watching him straighten the silverware, moving them back and forth trying to figure out the best positions for them, had me almost on the floor.

"What on earth are you doing?" I asked through my laughter.

Shasta looked up, pouting.

"Which side do the forks go on?" he picked one up, placing it on the other side of the plate. Studying it intensely, he moved it back to the other side. "I give up."

I couldn't help it. I sat down in the chair, laughing harder. Shaking my head, I took in a couple deep breaths before finally relaxing.

"Will you just set the stupid forks down? Who cares where they go? One will end up in my mouth anyway," I teased.

Once we all sat down for dinner, Shasta opened his mouth. Right away, I cut him off. I knew he would want to talk more about what would be happening in the next two days, but I honestly just wanted to have a normal meal for once, and to talk about normal things. After dinner, we could get back to the depressing matters of my complicated life. Andy grabbed my hand from under the table, running his thumb up and down my soft flesh.

"So what happens when I get back home? Shasta, are you gonna finally lay down some roots and stay for awhile?" I said around a mouthful of food, covering my lips with my free hand.

"Um, well, I haven't really thought about it. Does it really matter? I like Paris. It's easier just to go back and forth when I'm needed," Shasta shrugged like it was no big deal that he could move around the world in the blink of an eye.

"I really do hate you, you know that?" Andy grunted, shoving a piece of bread in his mouth.

"I second that. Alikye's abilities aren't that cool," Amanda retorted.

I pulled my face into a scowl, shooting daggers at Amanda. She rolled her eyes, not caring one bit about the insult she threw my way.

"I'm sorry. I wasn't aware that it was a contest. Please tell me again, Amanda, what can you do? What human coolness do you possess?" sarcasm dripped from my voice.

Shasta threw his head back and let out a loud laugh, which got him a smack across the head by Amanda. This crazy bunch, with their constant banter and loving nature, had my heart filled with bliss. I watched as my friends went back and forth, stuffing their faces with delicious food. Conversation flowed easily around the table; not once did silence hit my ears. I was happy that no one brought up any kind of business, and it soon seemed they wanted to talk about it as much as I did, which was not at all. For now, it

170

really felt like I could relax and enjoy my mini vacation, even though it wasn't a vacation. Tomorrow, I had plans that included lots of water, lots of sun, and lots of Andy and me laying in the hammock. It sounded like heaven.

"Babe, why don't we go watch a movie?" Andy suggested, handing over his plate to Shasta, who looked down at it like it was an alien creature. Let him figure out that they needed to be washed; it may take all night for that to happen. Perfect.

Curling up on the couch, Andy put in a movie. Afterwards, he plopped himself down next to me, pulling me onto his lap. Pushing my hair to one side of my face, Andy placed soft kisses up and down my neck and shoulder as the movie started to play. I shivered at his touch, leaning more into his hard chest. A spark lit between us, causing us both to jump at the sudden shock. Every touch always felt different, but also the same. Whatever supernatural magic was surging between the two of us intensified with each passing day.

"I'm going to get something to drink. You want anything?" Andy asked, lifting me up and off his lap.

I nodded.

The movie playing held little interest to me. Andy had this thing for old movies, which bored me half to death. I didn't have the heart to tell him I hated this black and white crap. The day started to wear thin on me, and I felt my eyes getting heavy. Instead, I focused on the noises around me. The heavy footsteps of Andy sounded in the kitchen. I listened to him for a second before wondering where the other two were. I opened up my senses, feeling Shasta on the other side of the house, and then feeling Amanda in one of the rooms. Andy turned in the kitchen, heading back towards me.

My eyes were still closed when I felt it; a featherlike touch against my spine. The muscles in my body locked up, threatening to rip from my skin. Deep blue ink seeped

171

down my arms, like rain cascading down metal. Within seconds, the lines connected. The glow was faint, but it was enough to have me alert. It wasn't until I heard Shasta's gruff voice boom across the house that I was on my feet.

"Alikye!"

Shit… Andy.

The door to my right shattered. Two blurs of light came at me in different directions. I was prepared, feeling pure energy race through my veins. What I wasn't ready for, what stopped me dead in my tracks, what stopped Shasta dead in his tracks after he raced into the room, was when Kayla switched directions. The Asian goddess, wearing black armor from head to toe, grabbed Andy by the neck, pulling him close to her small body. Her Legacy blade, a weapon made from the purest of indestructible metal, was held tight with the tip digging into his back. One clean stab and he would bleed out in seconds.

My body went rigid as I sucked in a heavy breath. Andy watched me, his sapphire eyes wide with fear. He stood as still as a statue, the blade so close to his skin. I felt for him. Every ounce of me felt the pain of watching the love of my life being held hostage.

Darkness overtook me. I felt it poisoning my blood. From the deepest parts of my tainted soul, I could feel the monster begging to come out. If I let that part of me surface, it would be over. They would be over.

"Kayla," I growled.

"Come with us, Kye. I'll let him go if you just come with us," she demanded.

Kayla pulled out a pair of silver cuffs, tossing them over to me. The metal was cold in my hands. Enochian magic covered the outside layer with words of binding and entrapment. Once these things closed around my wrists, there would be no way to get free.

Shasta moved towards me, blocking Maya from me. He was either protecting me from her or her from me. The heat from his body mixed with the heat from mine. One look into his eyes, and I saw what the effects of this situation was having on him. Darkness pooled in the depths of his eyes, swirls of black mixing with blue.

"Hurt him, and I can promise you, Kayla, that I will make you pay."

"I have my orders," Kayla spat.

Orders? Was I hearing her right? What kind of orders would make her go after a human to get to me? Ana. I knew she was desperate to keep me from turning eighteen, but there's no way the rest of the council would allow this.

"Orders!" I screamed. "He's human. What the hell are you thinking? No way will you hurt him."

Kayla puffed out her chest, standing a little taller to tell me she would, in fact, hurt him. "I'm sorry, Kye. Just come with us. You love him, right? Then put on the cuffs, and I'll let him go."

"Kye, don't," Andy growled. He screamed out when the point of Kayla's blade cut through his skin.

I lost it.

In the blink of an eye, I twisted around Shasta, taking Maya by the throat. Her scream sounded only to be cut off when I stopped any air from entering her lungs. Kayla shifted, but stopped when I grabbed a handful of Maya's hair, yanking her face closer to mine.

"Call off your sister, bitch, or the last thing you'll see is my face when I rip your head from your shoulders."

Every inch of my body shook. My heart pounded against my chest. A growl, low in my throat, vibrated through me, sounding more animal than human. I was running on pure rage. The human inside me was gone. A true warrior was now taking over my body. Persian blue lit up my skin as I held tight to Maya.

"Kayla!" Maya screamed.

"Have you lost your mind, Kye? You would kill your own kind for this human?" Kayla asked, releasing a little bit of her hold on Andy.

I saw his body visibly relax.

"Babe, please, just go," he snarled.

No way would he allow them to take me. He would sooner sacrifice himself, and that was something I couldn't live with. I shook my head once before turning back to meet Kayla's dark eyes.

"And you would kill a human because it's what Anastasis told you to do," I spat. "All because she is so desperate to have me killed since I fell in love with a human. Do you see how messed up that is? Kayla, give me two days, and I can end this. Tell her you couldn't find me, tell her I got away. Two days and I will have everything figured out. I promise no harm will come to you or your family, but if anything happens to Andy, I can promise you what Ana will do to you for losing me will be nothing compared to what I will do to you and your family. You will beg me for death. I will make it my mission until my last breath to make your world a living hell. Even after I'm done, I'll do it all over again to the ones you love. When I get through with you, not even your switch will do you any good!"

Kayla matched my dark stare. As a Legacy, she too lit up in blue. Not the same shade as mine, though; hers were lighter than my indigo blue. Kayla's markings appeared, as did Maya's. I hit a nerve hard, but I didn't care. Right now, they held my life in their hands. They had Andy. If it came down to it, I would sacrifice my own life, but I was giving Shasta time to come up with a plan to get us all out alive. There was no way could I do it. I was completely irrational to any decision making. *One weakness.* I have one weakness, and they played it against me. One thing caused me to lose sight of what I needed to do. Shasta promised to get Andy home alive, and even though we couldn't talk to each other, I prayed he held tight to that promise.

He owed it to my name and my family to keep me safe, to always protect me. A promise he made so long ago that I still didn't agree with, but he did, and he would lay down his own life for mine. Right now, I needed him to forget about me and focus on Andy. Without him, I would be nothing.

Kayla still held tightly to Andy. I kept my hands firmly around Maya's neck. Shasta stood next to me. The air around us was thick; not even a knife could cut through it. The only sounds came from the five of us breathing heavily. There was nothing else.

I never saw it coming.

Pop. Pop. Pop.

Didn't hear the sound until it ended.

Blood spattered across Andy's face. The force of three bullets hitting flesh and bone threw him a few feet away. Maya's piercing scream sounded around the room as the scene in front of me played out in slow motion. Standing in the corner of the room, holding a Beretta 9mm handgun, was Amanda. The look of fear filled her wide hazel eyes. Kayla fell to the floor in a heap of tangled body parts.

She wasn't dead. The bullets pierced through her chest, but they were human bullets, so all it did was knock the crap out of her. I let go of Maya, and she ran to her sister, bypassing Andy who was now on his feet, running towards me. Shasta intervened, pulling him and Amanda from the room. I was still in shock, and proud as hell for what Amanda just did. I mean, come on, that had to be the most badass thing I have seen in such a long time. How the hell did she know how to shoot like that? It was perfect and precise. Even with Andy so close to Kayla's body, she was able to put three bullets in her without harming Andy.

Holy crap.

"Alikye!" Andy yelled.

I turned, heading to the other room. A heavy weight plowed into my side, throwing me against the wall. The white wall cracked and crumbled around us as Maya and I went through it.

Why is it that when something is about to happen, someone feels the need to yell the person's name? I mean, all that does is throw their attention in the wrong direction. Twice now, all I've gotten is my name yelled out, instead of, I don't know, "Watch your left! Incoming! Bitch about to run you down!" *Come on, give me something better than just my name.* Now, I was inside of a wall with a very pissed off Legacy.

My right side throbbed. Blood slid down my stomach, pooling at the waistband of my jeans. I blocked a right hook to my chin, throwing my left hand into Maya's chest. Looking down quickly, wanting to see where the blood was coming from, I saw swelling around my ribs. A small, bloody bone peeked out.

As nasty as it was, I shoved my hand into my open wound, getting my bone to go somewhat back inside of me. It was painful as all hell, and while shoving my foot into Maya's stomach to get us out of the wall, I screamed at the pressure I was putting on my own body. The both of us tumbled to the ground in a mess of blood and tangled arms and legs. We were both panting, but neither of us were letting go. She yanked my head back, palming me in my nose. More blood cascaded down my face, mixing in my mouth.

Now, I was pissed. Not to say I was happy a minute ago, but now I was nuclear. I twisted my leg around her body, putting me on top of her as I slammed my fist into her nose.

Yeah, how do you like it, skank?

Maya rolled me until I was on my back, but I bucked her off. In a split second, we were both back on our feet, circling one another. A kick to my sore ribs did nothing when I grabbed her ankle, yanking it towards me. What I wasn't expecting, which I should have been because this girl was a ninja when she wanted to be, was her taking my weight as leverage when she twisted her body. She threw her other leg around my shoulder, pulling us both back on the ground. Her right foot planted in my gut, knocking the air out of me, but as she connected, my fist connected with her cheek, snapping her head backwards.

This fight between us could go for hours; there was no point, because we were both trained the same way, both Legacies, and both with equal stamina. At this rate, we would just end up destroying the house around us.

"Stop!" I hissed, pulling away from her.

She took a safe step back, wiping at her bloodied and battered face. She looked a mess, but I probably looked just as bad, considering I got the same amount of abuse.

Chapter 19

Maya and I stood toe to toe. This wasn't over yet. With Andy gone, she had lost her leverage, and fighting would do nothing but waste time.

"You really think this is over?" Maya spat.

"It will be," I said back in the same tone.

There was no changing her mind. Like me, she wouldn't lose. I saw her movements, knew what she would do next, and we were back to throwing punches again. Now, my anger and patience were wearing thin. I'd had enough of this. For four days, all I had been doing was running, fighting, and planning a future I didn't think would ever be mine. I spent my entire life knowing one thing, only to learn the truth of what living really meant. Now, everything was being ripped away from me, and I was sick of it. If Maya wanted a fight, she would get one.

I blocked a punch, then a kick. She did the same. We were dancing around each other, using the same moves and techniques we were taught back in school. At any rate, one of us needed to mix things up, or we would be here forever.

A thin layer of sweat covered my body. A quick glance around the house showed me the damage that had been done. Whoever these people were to Shasta, I really hoped they liked him enough to forgive me for this.

I jumped back, twisting around Maya, and slamming my foot into her knee. The loud crack could be heard over her screams. My knee came up next, planting itself into her face, and snapping her head back. Like I said, I was annoyed and wanted to get the hell out of here. I would have to take her out first.

She tumbled to the floor, her movement jerky. Finally, I had the upper hand. What I failed to take into consideration, because I was too busy dealing with this girl, was that Kayla would be healed by now. With Shasta getting my friends to safety, I was left to deal with both. So, as I stood over Maya's limp body, about to give her a final blow to her temple that would be lights out, I made a fatal mistake— I left myself vulnerable.

I didn't realize any of this until I felt the weight of a heavy body crash into me. I heard the sounds of metal cut into skin, and smelled the scent of blood. I've prepared for situations like this my whole life. I've always kept one ear open to my enemy, and always felt my surroundings, even when I was occupied. I always remembered that until my enemy was laying without a head, they weren't out of the game.

I left Kayla because I thought I was safe to handle Maya, and I left Shasta to take care of Andy. I closed myself off to finish this. I closed myself off from my surroundings, not feeling Andy still here. I didn't know if he would leave me, even though I knew he would never leave me.

I knew Andy would never leave.

I knew he would be right here.

He loved me.

He'd fight for me.

He'd die for me.

I stood frozen, rooted to the floor, watching his face soften, watching the dark blues in his eyes grow lighter as his life faded. I held tight to his body, trying to hold him up. My strength faltered as he gasped for air. I felt my own body falling.

Kayla had thrown her dagger. From ten feet away, there was no way she would have missed. I turned just as the dagger left her hand; the sharp blade headed straight for my heart. Then, I felt his body cover mine, protecting me. The blade sunk deep into his back, piercing through his lung. I closed my eyes, suddenly feeling the pain from his body shoot through mine.

Andy coughed, trying to get air into his lungs, his pleural cavity filling with blood. Blood splattered from his lips as he tried to speak. I watched, my eyes locked on his, unable to look away. The pain was so fierce; it felt like my soul was being ripped from my body. In that second, watching the love of my life struggling to breathe, to live, my world collapsed around me.

Andy slumped to the ground, taking me with him. I held him as tightly as I could. The dagger stuck out from his right side, lit up in soft blue. The metal cracked, turning a deep charcoal color. The hiss from the weapon sounded like bacon sizzling in a fryer, before finally disintegrating into a pile of ash. The weapon was no more.

"No!" I cried, holding one hand to his bleeding back. "No!"

My finger grazed his face, tracing his bottom lip. With the little strength he had, Andy turned into my touch.

"Baby, please, you can't leave me," tears poured from my eyes.

A small smile tugged at his lips as he brought his hand up to meet mine.

"Please, just hang on. I won't lose you Andy. I can't be without you. I love you," my sobs grew louder.

Rubbing his thumb back and forth over my knuckles, Andy mouthed words I couldn't hear. Struggling to breathe, he shook in my arms. I dropped my head to his chest, rocking him, as more blood poured from his body. His injuries were beyond repair at this point. His gasps came out harder. My emotional pain was nothing compared to the physical pain Andy was going through, drowning in his own blood as his lungs filled with the thick fluid. I could hear his body shutting down. I could hear his heartbeats slow.

My own screams sounded foreign to me as I yelled for Shasta. He promised Andy would be okay. He said they wouldn't harm him. When I looked up, I found Andy's eyes closed, and his breathing labored. I grabbed at his face, bringing my lips down to his. I needed to feel him one last time. His light grip on my hand stayed. I cried harder into his neck, not wanting to let him go. I never wanted to let him go. I knew when he took two more ragged breaths, when his body went stiff, when his eyes opened to lock onto mine one last time. I knew when he whispered, "I... love... you... baby." His hand dropped from mine, and he was gone.

This wasn't how it was supposed to end. Either we all made it out alive, or I sacrificed myself. Andy dying in my arms while protecting me from my own people was not something I would live with.

Anger started to build up inside of me; so much anger that I felt my own body shake with adrenaline. I looked around the room for the first time, seeing only Shasta and Amanda standing in front of me. The twins were gone. Amanda looked as broken as I did, in which she had the right. Shasta looked ready to kill someone. If the blacks in his eyes didn't tell me, it was the way his body vibrated. He was in my head, channeling my own anger. I felt him pushing around, trying to calm me. The longer he stayed inside me, the harder it was for him to stay calm himself. My anger took over him until what stood in front of me was full blown Demon; Abaddon's son in the flesh.

"Alikye, please," he growled in his only attempt to get out. His eyes shut tightly as he tried to pull away from me. I was too strong, and unable to let him go. He promised. He was supposed to protect Andy. Shasta roared as my rage exploded in my head. They would all pay for this. I would take down the entire world for this, starting with my own race.

I stood from Andy's body. One look at Amanda, and she understood. She ran to her friend, taking up my position, saying her goodbye, but it was too late.

Andy was gone.

He died saving me.

Andy was dead.

Another scream sounded. "Shasta, do something!" The walls shook with my anger. "NOW!"

"You need to let me go!" Shasta roared, still stuck in my head.

And I did, I let him go. I fell to my knees in front of Shasta, begging for him to fix this. He couldn't be dead. I couldn't lose him. No way could I live in this world without Andy in it. He was more to me than just my boyfriend; he was my best friend, and my other half. I might never understand why it was him that turned my entire life around. I might never understand why it was him I fell so easily in love with. I gave up everything for him, but it didn't matter, because I would do it again a million more times. I saw my future in his eyes. Every time our gazes collided, I saw a life worth living, worth fighting for. Now, it was all gone. Andy was gone.

Shasta knelt in front of me, taking me in his arms as my sobs grew louder. I watched as my body lit up, blinding my own eyes. My pain reflected in my own magic, as the markings tried to heal my emotional turmoil. My markings were meant to protect me, and save me from death. They held the power to heal.

My markings.

"Save him now," I cried.

"How?" he questioned.

"Give him my markings, Shasta,"

Shasta met my eyes, the sadness reflected my own. He knew what I was asking. Without my markings, my soul couldn't live in my body. The human part of me wasn't strong enough to hold an angel soul in it. It would tear the body to shreds. My soul would be released, and I would then die. Shasta knew all this. Although the transfer of power wasn't something that had ever been done, it wasn't impossible. No magic was impossible, and Shasta knew how to do it.

I held his stare, begging for him to do it. If not him, then it had to be someone else. If this was to happen, it had to be fast. From death, the mind only has seven minutes before it dies completely.

"I can't," he whispered.

"You will. If you don't, more will die," I meant every word. I would kill them all.

Shasta closed his eyes tightly. I knew this would be hard for him. It would be like losing Elina all over again.

"You can't ask me to do this," he begged.

"If he dies, Shasta, I'm dead anyway," I pleaded.

"And what do you think it's going to do to him? To wake up and find out you killed yourself to save him. How do you expect him to live in this world where you don't exist? How will I live in this world without you?"

"It doesn't matter. It shouldn't have ended like this," I said.

"I can't," Shasta refused.

"You will."

"I love you, Alikye. You're my best friend."

"I love you too."

Shasta nodded.

"Make sure when I'm gone, Andy lives," I looked over to Amanda. "Make sure he lives the life he was supposed to live. I need him to, and I need you two to make sure that happens. Tell him I did this because I love him more than anything, and this needed to be done. Tell him not to hold on when I'm gone. He needs to live."

Shasta closed his eyes, speaking in the language of my Legacy.

"Teach him to love again. He needs to love again, Amanda," I gasped as I felt the first pull to my body. Still on my knees, I held to my chest.

"Kye," Amanda screamed, starting to get up.

I shook my head for her to stay, putting out my hand to steady my vibrating body. The first wave of pain hit hard, shooting daggers through my head. I grabbed my head as my eyes started to water.

"Alikye," Shasta whispered.

"Keep going," I choked out. "Amanda, watch over Shasta, too. He's gonna try and disappear, but don't let him. Love him. Push him to keep going."

The second wave of pain felt like having my chest plowed into by a truck. I felt bones shatter.

"Why is it hurting her?" Amanda screeched. She jumped back from Andy's body as he took his first gasping breath.

If my heart wasn't in so much pain, I would be relieved. I saw the first marking appear on his body.

"She can't survive without those tattoos. Her soul is too strong for her human body," Shasta choked. More lines of magic came out next, as he chanted one verse after another.

Another heavy blow to my body took my legs out from under me. I flipped on my back, screaming as I felt my body burning like it was on fire. Every part of me hurt, but I thought back to the days with Andy and the nights we spent under the stars. The feel of his body always made me feel safe. I brought myself back to the feelings I got every time he touched me. I lived in the happy moments.

I dug my fingers into the carpet, arching my back, shaking as another shock hit me hard. What came next was a blinding light that surrounded me.

"I'm sorry I couldn't save you, Kye," I heard Shasta say. "I'm sorry."

The last wave of pain took everything out of me. Pain so fierce that I knew the last of my magic was leaving my body. I cried out, but not from the pain. I cried because I would be dead before I could say goodbye to Andy. He would survive, and that gave me enough relief. When he woke, the first thing he would see was me lying dead. He would have to live with the fact that I gave my life for his. I needed Amanda to help him heal from that. In my last moments of life, I found Shasta's mind. I told him what he needed to do now. He promised Elina that he would always protect her kin. I needed him to promise me he would always protect my family.

With my last breath, I could hear his promise.

Andy took my hand, intertwining our fingers. The sun was hot on my face, as I looked out to calming waters. The breeze blew past me, bringing with it the smell of jasmine.

"Do you feel it?" Andy whispered.

I turned my head, meeting his dark eyes. I smiled. "I always feel it."

"Why me?" he asked. "From the moment we met, I could feel it."

I took a deep breath, loving the taste of the salty air. "Because, a long time ago, they wrote our story in the stars. We were always meant to find each other." I said.

"I love you, Alikye," Andy's words sent warmth all through my body.

"And I love you, Andy. Forever."

Chapter 20

A meeting was called in, over the loud speaker, as Derek stood by the lake. He'd been planning really hard on an escape, but everywhere he went, he always had a shadow. Derek felt like a prisoner in a place he always saw as a second home. Now, he hated this place.

Jack had come to his room earlier, voicing his concerns. Alikye had yet again evaded being captured, even with the help of Sophie, a witch who had been an ally of the Guardians for years. Ana wasn't too happy when she received the news, and sent out a number of Guardians to help aid the two hunters. Jack was tired of waiting on the sidelines, and wanted to get the hell out and finally help his daughter. Derek, of course, agreed to help, too.

The Guardian that had been shadowing Derek all day stepped out from behind a cluster of trees.

"Let's go," he said, taking Derek by the arm.

Derek shoved him off, but followed.

The courtroom was filled to the max, and all council members were seated in their appointed seats. Derek looked around, finding his family waiting up front. He bypassed his father, heading straight for the podium, where he caught Carter's silver eyes. They were so much like Alikye's, but not as bright.

"What's this all about? I'm getting tired of being asked to betray Alikye. I won't do it, so stop asking," Derek said to Carter. He trusted Carter, and always had. He knew Carter held Alikye's best interest at heart.

Carter shook his head, looking around the room, "Kayla called. She said she needed to speak with us."

Derek's brows scrunched in confusion, "Then why the hell do you have the whole community here?"

Carter's eyes moved back and forth. When he didn't see Ana, he spoke softly, pulling Derek closer to him, "Anastasis called for this meeting."

Derek's anger surfaced, bringing out his crimson markings. Carter placed a gentle hand on his shoulder, silently telling him to reel it in. This wasn't the place to lose his shit.

After sucking in a calming breath, Derek bowed his head to Carter. He then turned on his heels, taking a seat next to Jack.

Jack was about to speak when Ana walked into the room, flanked by two guards. She swept her hand around the room, asking for everyone to take their seats. Like little minions, they obeyed. The room went silent.

"Glad everyone could make it. I called this meeting because after speaking with Kayla, she said she had urgent news on behalf of Alikye Macayan. We have yet to find out the extent of her capture, but for everyone's safety, I have called for backup," she announced. The smile that graced her lips was menacing.

Shivers ran down Derek's spine. He looked over at his father, who looked just as scared. It was time for Derek to finally do something about this situation. If they brought Alikye in this room, he would do whatever it took to free her, and they could all run. It was something he should have done from the beginning, but honor and duty took that focus away.

Not anymore. This time I will fight with her, he thought.

He was already putting into play what needed to be done, when the doors to the room burst open. Kayla and Maya both walked in, looking as if they just came from the battlefield. Blood covered Kayla's shirt, but Maya looked the worst. Derek smiled to himself, knowing it was Alikye who did this to them. When he didn't see any signs of Kye, his heart leaped with joy. Maybe she got away again.

Ana must have been thinking the same thing, because the smile on her face faded.

"What is the reasoning behind this meeting?" Ana started, but was interrupted.

Kayla stopped dead in her tracks, feet away from the council. She looked visibly shaken, her hands trembling at her side. Kayla's breathing came out in heavy pants.

"I... I didn't," she stammered.

"It was an accident. This wasn't supposed to happen," Maya finished for her sister. As her eyes found Ana's, Maya's markings burst from her skin. Her eyes flared fire as she turned, meeting Derek's eyes, then went back to looking at Ana. "This is your fault!" she screamed. "You told us to take him! You told us she would listen!" Anger poured out of each word.

Derek was taken aback by her outburst.

"What is the meaning of this?" Ana yelled. "You are out of line speaking to me like this."

"We need to leave now," Kayla whimpered.

In all the years Derek had known Kayla, she had never once looked as terrified as she did then. It was confusing, considering the things they see every day.

"She's coming," Kayla moved back behind her sister, as if needing the extra protection.

"Nonsense, girl. Now tell me where Alikye is," Ana demanded.

At the sound of her name, both girls trembled.

What the hell.

"Ana, you don't understand!" Maya yelled again, now looking at each and every council member. "All of you need to leave NOW!"

"Silence!" Ana's voice boomed.

"Shut up and listen to her!" Kayla screamed.

A loud gasp came from the entire room. Ana's eyes flared. Carter stood from his seat, about to speak, but Kayla's loud voice echoed off the room.

"Andy's dead."

Derek stirred in his seat. Next to him, Jack did the same. What the hell has been going on, and why would a human be dead? The room exploded in chaos. So many voices and sounds evaded Derek as he tried to pinpoint what was happening.

"And it's your fault!" he heard Maya yell over the crowd. "You told us to use the human as leverage to capture Alikye."

"I never said to kill him!" Ana yelled back.

The room silenced. Ana's shock was evident. She hadn't meant to say that out loud. Derek had to laugh; not at the situation that a human had died, but at what this would do to Ana. Then, his thoughts drifted to Alikye, and why the twins had warned the council to leave.

"She's coming," he heard Kayla cry. Alikye was coming here, and she was coming for blood. The love of her life was dead because of what Ana did, what they all did. They were all to blame.

Carter stood from his seat, glaring at Ana.

"You did what?" his voice sounded around the room.

"I did what was necessary. She needed to be stopped!" Ana yelled back, matching his tone.

"She's not a criminal. She has done nothing wrong besides fall in love with a human. You gave orders to use that human as blackmail, and it resulted in said human's death. HAVE YOU LOST YOUR MIND?" Carter's head shook. Derek watched in amazement at what happened next.

"Guards," he signaled for them to step forward. "I hear-by strip you of your position as head council member. Upon investigation, we will see to a trial, Anastasis," Carter laughed. Not a laugh meant for something funny; one so vicious it caused Derek to squirm in his seat.

"You have no right. I'm in first chair," Ana stammered.

"No, not anymore you're not," Carter scolded.

As the guards went after Ana, Ana yelled to the rest of the council, Carter demanded one thing after another, and it was Derek who only paid attention to the twins' words. She's coming. When she did, there would be no stopping her.

"Carter!" Derek yelled, standing from his chair. Jack placed a hand on his arm, but Derek shrugged it off.

"Carter!" he yelled louder.

Carter finally turned, but said nothing. Derek took his silence as a good sign. It wasn't always the greatest idea to interrupt, especially if you weren't a Legacy.

"We need to find her. This has gone too far, and you know it."

"Find her? Are you out of your mind? We all need to get the hell out of here!" Maya shrieked. "We don't need to find her because she's coming here." Now, she had everyone's attention. "You don't understand. Alikye is gone; her humanity died the minute Andy did. I have never in my life seen that kind of darkness. She's coming, and when she does, we are all dead."

"She wouldn't come after her own people," Ana stated, matter of fact, "and if she chooses to come back, her punishment is still the same."

Derek was beyond shocked. He turned to see what Carter would say about this. Carter was just as stunned. The two men watched as a guard placed Enochian cuffs on Ana's wrists. Even with her title stripped, she still had the nerve to throw orders. Derek went to speak, but Kayla's loud footsteps pounded on the floor. She stomped over to Ana. Before anyone could stop her, she landed a clean punch to Ana's mouth. Ana's head snapped back, connecting with the guard's shoulder. Another guard wrapped his arms around Kayla's waist, pulling her from Ana.

"She wouldn't come after her own people? Her boyfriend is dead because of us. She watched her boyfriend die at the hands of her own people. She's coming, and when she does, she'll come for blood."

A loud explosion sounded, causing everyone to freeze. Before anyone knew what was happening, the doors to the room burst open, pieces of wood flying in every direction. A loud roar had everyone, including Derek, scrambling to where the council members sat. The chaos had one or more Guardians on the floor, trying to get away. The room erupted in bright light. Derek grabbed at his ears as a piercing sound seared into his brain.

Shasta walked in, hands held high, as electricity shot from his hands. His eyes were black as night, and Derek knew Shasta had turned his switch. Standing before the room of Guardians was a full blown Demon, pissed to all hell. Derek saw all hell break loose as he watched Shasta stop in front of his peers. Eyes blazing, body trembling, Shasta caught Derek's stare. A second later, Shasta let out another roar that caused Derek to jump back, bumping into Carter.

Derek stood in front of Carter, protecting him from Shasta. More guards raced in. Before they made it two feet into the room, Shasta turned, lifting his arms. The guards went flying across the room, hitting hard against the farthest wall. Shasta then turned his gaze to Kayla. She moved back, ducking behind the guard who had grabbed her only seconds ago. Fear showed in her beautiful features.

It was Jack who spoke first, stepping in front of his son.

"Shasta, turn it back on," he spoke softly. He looked around for Alikye, but when he saw Shasta was alone, he continued. "There is no need for more violence. I'm sorry about Andy. It was an accident. Ana is being taken into custody, and Alikye can come home. No harm will come to her," Jack turned towards Carter, who nodded.

At the sound of Alikye's name, Shasta let out another death roar, causing everyone to shriek.

Where the hell was Alikye? Derek thought. Shasta turned to Derek, no doubt reading his mind. The blacks in his eyes swirled.

"Alikye is dead!" Shasta hissed. "She sacrificed herself to save Andy."

Derek's heart plummeted. A gut-wrenching feeling twisted in his stomach. Derek stumbled back, almost falling to his knees. Without looking away from Shasta, he took in deep breaths.

Shasta's head cocked to the side. His darkness came off of him in waves, crashing into Derek. Derek felt his fire burning his skin; he actually felt his skin burn. He could see Shasta doing it to him.

"You have no right to care. None of you have any right to feel anything. You did this to her. You all turned your backs on her when she needed you the most. All because she fell in love with a human, you crucified her. You," he turned to Alikye's family, "you get to feel NOTHING!" Derek felt a pull in his head. He screamed out in pain as Shasta dug around in his mind.

Derek saw glimpses of Alikye's life. He saw the darkness that surrounded her everyday, the feeling of loneliness, hurt, and betrayal. Derek screamed out again as he felt her pain; he felt what each day was doing to her before she left for Florida. Never did he fully understand what went on and why she was the way she was. So much pain and darkness consumed her. It was so fierce, he felt his own body trembling, and wondered how she ever survived. Then, the sense of calm washed over him. Images of Andy invaded his mind. He sensed the way Andy made Alikye feel, the way he chased her own Demons away, and how in the end she felt free. He never fully understood why she left, but now he did, and his stomach dropped.

"I have watched that girl grow. I have seen the struggles she went through, the darkness that lived inside her. Do you know how much it killed her to leave? You were her family, and for the first time in her life, she chose to be happy. You all repay her by taking her life. Do you know what I felt inside her when Andy died? What it was like for her to ask me to kill her to save her boyfriend? I had to rip her markings from her body; I had to watch as her soul was being ripped from her body. To fix your mistake, I had to kill my best friend!" Shasta roared.

Wetness coated Derek's eyes. He turned his head, finding his family huddling together. Sarah cried into Jack's shirt. The look on Lucas's face tore Derek to pieces. Never did any of them expect to hear those words. They had come close to losing her many times. They had believed many times that it would finally be the time she would go too far, getting herself killed, but deep down they all knew Alikye would always find a way to live. Of course, the one thing to finally kill her would be because she fell in love with a human.

Anger triggered deep inside at that thought. Because of Andy, Alikye was dead. Yes, most of his blame was on Kayla. Derek even allowed some blame on himself for turning his back on her, but if Andy would have just walked away a long time ago, if he would have just let her go, Alikye would still be alive.

"Are you here to kill us, Shasta?" Ana barked. She struggled against the guards around her that were either holding her or protecting her. "Did you come for revenge?"

Shasta's head snapped towards Ana. The fire inside his body erupted. The electric hum surrounding him grew louder. He growled low in his chest, and it vibrated through his body. Tremors racked him as he looked into the ruby eyes of his enemy.

194

"As much as it would please me to rip your heart from your chest, I made a promise, and I intend to keep it. For now, I will allow you all to live, but don't take lightly to my warning. If any of you come near me or Kye's friends ever again, or intend to bring harm to Andy ever again, I will not think twice before killing you. Do you understand?" he warned.

Shasta turned on his heels, heading for the door. Before he made it to the wreckage, Ana's loud voice echoed across the room.

"This is not over yet, Shasta. Just because Alikye is dead, what makes you think your sentence has been overturned? You're still wanted for treason," she boomed.

"Anastasis, that is enough," Carter barked.

Without any warning, Shasta had jumped to Ana, taking her face in his one large hand. Sweat dotted his forehead as dark strands of hair fell in front of his eyes.

"Unless you are 100% sure you can take me, Anastasis, I suggest you watch that mouth of yours. I may have promised Kye not to kill any of you, but trust me, with her gone I really have nothing left to live for. If I kill you, I'll go dark, and do you really want something like me going dark?"

Derek had to give Shasta credit. Only he could threaten Ana and get away with it. Even now, if Shasta threatened the whole council, they would more than likely let him walk out unharmed, because of what he had to do to Alikye. A bitter taste was left in Derek's mouth. His stomach still twisted in knots just thinking about what Shasta had to do, and the thought of the death of Alikye. He couldn't imagine what Shasta was going through, having to be the one to kill her. Was he angry at Shasta for doing it? Yes. Would he have done it himself if the tables were turned? As much as the answer should be no, it was yes.

Understanding washed over Derek. From the beginning, he had been wrong about Alikye. Now, it was too late to apologize. It was too late to tell her how much he loved her. A quick glance at Lucas showed he was thinking the same things. Lucas would go about his life without Alikye in it, ever. Then, it hit Derek. The gesture would be small in comparison, but he had to do it, for her

Shasta let go of Ana's face, this time disappearing altogether before some other idiot made a comment that would set him off. Derek had to get out of there before he too decided blaming his own race would help heal his sadness, before he decided to use anger to overshadow the sadness.

"I have to go. There's something I need to do," Derek whispered. He held back tears that threatened to spill, not wanting to show that kind of weakness. You didn't cry when a loved one died. It happened too often, and it was simply part of life to his race.

Jack nodded as he held tight to his wife, who looked more in shock than anything else. Carter, who had walked off to assist the guards, glanced over at Derek as he turned to leave. Carter waved Derek over. Even though he needed to leave, it would be disrespectful to turn his back on a council member.

"I need you to verify Shasta is telling the truth. Ana will be dealt with accordingly, but unless there is proof the boy's alive, I'll have to take the twins into custody. If he is indeed alive, I'll free them," Carter requested. His eyes closed his eyes for a second. When he opened them, they darkened, showing a hint of sadness. "I need to know Alikye is really dead. With her Legacy now gone, I'll take head chair."

Chapter 21

Twenty four hours later, Derek stood in front of the house where Alikye had once lived. Pain pulled at his heart when he thought back to the first time he was there. It was only a few weeks ago that he stood watching her unload a truck to start her new life. Back then, she was happy, full of life and love, and living free for the first time. Now, he would never see that light again.

He ran his hands over his buzzed hair, wishing he could pull at it. Instead, he dug his nails into his palms, welcoming the biting pain. It shouldn't be this hard to go up to the door and talk to the human boy who Alikye sacrificed her own life for, he thought, but it was. What would he say to him, and what if after seeing his face Derek blamed him for her death? It wasn't his fault, but deep down he felt it was. Did the human feel the same way, too?

Finally willing his legs to move, he walked up the stone path that led to the porch. Bringing his fist up to make contact with the door, he was interrupted at the last minute by someone clearing their throat.

"I wouldn't do that," the girl said. She had been crying, her eyes puffy and red-rimmed. The blond sat on a swing, curled up, staring at him like he was a plague.

He had met the girl a few times. Remembering her name was Amanda, he turned, taking a seat next to her. The moment was awkward. He rubbed at his face, wanting to speak, but not knowing what to say. Amanda looked as destroyed as he felt. She glared at him for a long while.

Reading her facial expression, he could see the hatred she held for him.

Finally, he cleared his throat to speak.

"I need to know he's alive," he told her.

"Why?" she snapped. "Why all the sudden do you care about any of this? She's been trying to call you for a month, and you couldn't give her two seconds of your time," Amanda sputtered, letting her tears bathe her face.

He closed his eyes tightly, fighting back his own emotions. Without even asking, he got his answer. Alikye was really dead. He saw it written all over the girl's face. Derek turned into his own mind, dimming the switch in his head. He was ready to lose it, and he first needed to talk to Andy. His emotions simmered. For the first time in a day, he felt the band around his chest loosen. The sound of the girl laughing brought him back to reality. Liquid gold eyes met hazel ones as he pulled his brows up in confusion.

"It's so freaking easy for you guys, isn't it? Well lucky f-ing you," her sobs grew louder. "Not only do I feel like my heart is being ripped out, but I also have to watch my friend slowly fade away from me, all because the thought of Alikye not being here is too hard for any of us to bare. What I wouldn't give to turn it off, all of it!"

Now Derek was getting angry, an emotion he liked.

"Do you really think it's that easy for me? I have known Kye my whole life. I loved her my whole life, and now the thought of never seeing her again is like being torn to shreds. Regardless, I still have a job to do. I still have to protect this place from shit you can't even imagine. I wasn't there, I know, and I'll have to live with that for the rest of my life. The least I could do for her is make sure the people she loved the most survive," Derek stated. Taking a few deep gulps of air, he went on. "I'm sorry. I'm so freaking sorry for what happened, but there wasn't anything I could do."

"You turned your back on her!" Amanda yelled.

"I had no other choice!" he matched her tone. "I need to see Andy. I need to know he's alive."

"No," she said.

"You don't understand. They will kill Kayla if I don't report back."

"Let them," she chuckled viciously.

"They will kill Shasta," he threatened.

Amanda's eyes widened.

"I hate you guys," she got up from her chair, moving towards the front door.

"You were never supposed to know us," Derek told her.

She looked back at Derek, matching his stare.

"Yeah, I kinda wish that was the case," she whispered as she opened the front door.

The moment he walked in, he wished he hadn't. Sitting on the couch, staring blankly at the wall, was the human boy Derek had met once. His dark hair was spiked in a messy way. Dark eyes met his, and if looks could kill, he would be dead. He didn't move or say anything. Instead, he comforted the small girl in his arms, rubbing circles in her back. The girl he knew as Kady looked worse than the rest of them; her usually tanned face was now pale.

A small part of Derek was angry that Alikye did this to them. She knew making this kind of connection with them would one day lead to this exact picture. At least as a Guardian they were trained to deal with this kind of tragedy. He felt for them, he really did, but he had a job to do, and couldn't afford to be distracted.

"What's he doing here?" the boy hissed. He could see the anger coming off him and thought twice about being here. In the end, his presence might make matters worse.

Kady's eyes flew open at the sound of her boyfriend's rough tone. She wiggled from his grip, moving from the couch to stand in front of Derek. She didn't look mad, just really miserable. Kady was different from the rest when it came to Derek. He had the time to spend with her over a year ago. She was a sweet little thing, and right away Derek liked her. What took Derek by surprise was when she wrapped her arms around him in a tight embrace.

"I'm sorry," she whispered against his chest. "I know you just needed time. I want you to know that she never doubted your love."

Her words shot straight to his heart, making his walls start to crumble. Derek closed his eyes, holding back his emotions.

"I never left her. I was here the whole time. I wanted what was best for her and, in the end, this was it. I just wish I could have stopped them."

"I know."

"I need to see him," he said, not having to say his name. Even his name hurt to speak out loud. Andy was the light that Alikye always needed. Derek would spend his life in debt to him.

"Kady," Greg snapped from the couch, "don't."

Kady turned to her boyfriend, the first sign of anger in her dark eyes, and said, "He was her brother. It's not his fault, and we have no right to judge their kind, Greg."

"Can't you just take our word that he's alive? They'll never know the difference," Amanda mumbled. She was doing her best to hold back the bitterness in her voice.

"He's not in a good place right now, dude. Seeing you will wreck him," Greg continued.

"He's right, Derek. Andy isn't doing well right now. Between the effects of his death, then being brought back to life only to see… this probably isn't the best time," Kady said.

"What do you mean by effects," Derek asked, startled.

"Shasta had to put Alikye's markings on him. I don't know, but it's like they're affecting him. He still has one on his arm. It looks like a burn in the palm of his hand, but it's a symbol of some sort," Kady answered.

Wait, what?

Now, Derek was very muddled. He understood a little of what Shasta did, but the Demon didn't stick around long enough to explain further. Never had a transfer of power been done. The magic was coded to each individual DNA. A name could not be put on someone else, especially not a human, yet Shasta attempted to do it and succeeded.

"I need to see him now," Derek's voice was urgent.

Three pairs of worried eyes met his.

"What's wrong?" Kady was the first to ask. Greg had already left the room, heading upstairs.

A moment later, Shasta appeared in the room. At first he looked confused, and then his features turned to pure rage when he saw Derek standing there. Derek took a step back, his anger also evident. How could Shasta be so careless as to give a human the marking of a soul, and a Legacy's soul at that?

Shasta's head cocked to the side, a threat obvious on his face.

"I warned you," he spat.

"You gave a human her marking," Derek hissed.

"What the hell is going on?" Amanda countered.

"Do you have any idea what you just did?" Derek ignored the girl, directing his question to only Shasta. Then, it hit him. How could he not see it before? "She's still alive, isn't she?"

Shasta didn't answer. The stunned look on the two girls' faces told Derek the answer. Shasta hadn't told them as much. After a second, Shasta relaxed.

"It doesn't matter, she's never coming back. Yes, her body still lives, but she's gone. She'll never return."

"You marked him," Derek continued. "You had no right using our magic."

Derek ran his hands over his head, jerking to the side to face the wall. His marking erupted red as his emotions broke to the surface. Lines connected, and symbols appeared, reaching around his entire body. Without any rational thinking, he pulled his hand back, thrusting it into the wall. The loud noise caused Kady to scream.

"Derek," Shasta hissed.

"What the hell does all this mean?" Amanda turned on Shasta, grabbing his face with her hands. "What's happening to Andy?"

"It means every second of every goddamn day I can feel her inside me," a voice sounded.

They all turned to see Andy descending the staircase. Derek took in his tortured features. Dark circles shadowed even darker eyes. His dark copper hair hung limp around his pale face, his bangs plastered to his forehead. Derek could sense the darkness that surrounded him, Alikye's darkness.

For a long time, no one spoke. Instead, Derek studied Andy's jerking movements, the way his hands trembled at his side, simultaneously closing and reopening his fists over and over again. A tick worked in his jaw as Derek heard the grinding of teeth.

He'd seen this a million times, whenever a Guardian died. To understand the effects it would have on humans had never been heard of or seen. Derek watched Andy intensely, his own emotions raging. He stomped over to Andy, pulling him the rest of the way down. Taking Andy's hand in his own, he stared down at the Enochian symbol. Pulling him towards Shasta, Derek held out his palm so Shasta could see what he did, see what Alikye did. This was not what he intended to happen when he arrived here this morning.

Finally, he spoke to Shasta, letting Andy go.

"Do you have any idea what you just did, Shasta? Are you out of your freaking mind? How in the world did she agree to this? She knew what was going to happen," Derek paused, taking his head into his hands. He let out an anger-infused roar. "She knew and did it anyway. Oh my god, this can't be happening," his mind went through a hundred different scenarios, contemplating his next move. If the council found out about this… A sharp pain radiated through Derek's head, but only lasted a second. He yelled out in pain, and then turned to Shasta, ready to kill him for shocking him.

"They will not find out about this," Shasta grunted.

"No, they won't," Derek said aloud.

Because if they did, they would take Andy, he sent to Shasta.

She didn't know. We both knew it was a risk, but him being human it shouldn't have happened. She thought the mark would disappear, Shasta responded.

Andy watched as the two men silently stared at each other. Derek knew that Andy was aware of what they were doing, but he felt it best that Andy didn't know what they were discussing. Except, for some strange reason, Andy did know what they were talking about.

Andy's voice came out rough, scolding the two men.

"You need to tell me what the hell is going on. I… This feeling inside is slowly killing me. I can… It's peaceful, but at the same time it pains me. I don't know whether it's me feeling this. It doesn't feel like it's me. What did she do to me?" he questioned.

"Each mark represents a certain magic. Each bloodline carries the same one that's imbedded in their DNA. It's what makes us each different. When two Guardians mate for the first time, the marking that carries their family name is transferred to one another for a split second, binding them together. Not only does it promise forever love, it also binds your soul so that you are one forever," Shasta explained.

"So…" Andy paused, his hand trembling as he looked down at his palm, the palm that held Alikye's name, burned forever into his skin. Realization hit Andy hard like being trampled on by a dozen bulls. He sucked in a hard breath, and it got stuck in his throat. "No… Oh my God, she… I…

I can't... breathe," Andy hit the floor, gasping for his next breath, the pain in his lungs triggering an all-out panic attack.

Derek watched in shock as Andy grabbed at his chest, digging his nails into his skin. On his right side, Kady screamed, crashing into her friend. Greg came running down the steps, taking his girlfriend into his arms, yelling at Derek to do something. Andy's face paled more, his lips turning a shade of blue. Derek fell to the floor. He pulled Andy to him, lifting him up with his arms raised above his head.

Shasta ran to Andy, grabbing at his face. Closing his eyes, he pushed through Andy's mind, knowing how dangerous it was to become trapped inside an emotional mind. Like Alikye, sometimes it was hard to get out if the other wasn't stable enough to let go. Andy's mind was a blur. Dark smoke clouded his head with shifting images, pulling apart small pieces of two lives. Still, Shasta pushed through the murky maze, trying desperately to find the light. Blocked memories pushed back at Shasta, causing him to lose his grip. Using his own memories to foreshadow Andy's haunted life, he was able give him the sense of peace he needed to calm down. Yanking himself back to reality, Andy slumped in his arms. His eyelids fluttered as the color returned to his face. Within seconds, his breathing evened and his body relaxed.

It was the longest minute of Derek's life as he watched Shasta navigate through the human's head to finally get him to calm down. Afterwards, he laid Andy on the couch, waiting for the inevitable. This was the exact reason he didn't want to say anything. Andy wouldn't be able to handle what Alikye did to him. He didn't want the boy to hate the girl he loved, but how could he not? What Alikye risked might be the thing that would destroy Andy, making this whole situation, and her death, futile.

However, Andy had known. Alikye must have told him enough of what would happen, because his reaction was one of terror.

"She said it wouldn't happen to me because I'm human," he spoke.

"It shouldn't have," was all Derek could say.

"I'm bonded to her forever, and she's not even here," the realization tore at everyone's hearts.

"I'm sorry," Derek whispered. The look on Andy's face was one of pure dismay.

"What do I do now?" he asked.

Part two

Chapter 22

A sense of calm washed over me as I stared out into the abyss of my afterlife. Peace, like nothing I had ever felt before, curled into every ounce of my soul like the darkness that had lived inside of me not too long ago had wasted away. Thinking back to the ones I loved, the ones I left back home, I felt overjoyed. Not a feeling I was used to but for the first time in my life— well, death— I was perfectly content.

A warm breeze blew past me, the scent of the ocean reminding me of Andy. That thought alone had my stomach feeling lighter. I'm sure reliving the memories in my head of the moments we shared should have had me in tears. The thought of never seeing him again seemed to be heartbreaking, but no other feelings, besides happy ones, invaded my mind. I knew that one day I would see him again. Maybe not anytime soon. To be honest, I hoped it would be a long time until the day when we would meet again.

Anyway, I was happy. I was a little confused as to why I was so satisfied, considering, but I chose to just go with it. After all, I was dead, and this was my forever. I smiled to myself; a slight giggle escaped my lips. Yeah, I just giggled. Never had that happened to me. Back in my life, I hated the sound of girls giggling. Maybe a tiny part of me was jealous of their carefree lives, while I risked mine everyday so they could live in their blissful, delusional world. Now, it was my turn to live for eternity in my own blissful haven.

So here I sat, for I don't know how long, on a bench that felt like a bed of clouds. I chose this place because something about the water always brought peace to me, like tasting the salty air on my tongue was a reminder of what I had, what I died for. The world around me was a blur of colors. The crystal blue water in front of me was the only thing I could see clearly. In the distance, I could make out the silhouettes of trees dancing in the wind. Like waking up after hours of sleep, it all had a dreamlike quality to it.

I realized it had been hours since I had last eaten, maybe days, but I didn't feel hungry. Come to think of it, I wasn't tired or bored either. I was just... I don't know. How long had it been since I said goodbye to Andy, to Shasta? It couldn't have been that long. I think I got here yesterday. Out of nowhere, I appeared here from the unknown. So, I took a seat, and haven't moved since.

"So what now? Where do I go from here?" I said to the wind. "Is this my first stop before I pass through the pearly gates, or did I already do that?" I didn't remember doing that or passing over some bright light. At the end of my life, as I felt the last of my magic leaving me, I remember a light surrounding me, giving my life to Andy.

"My child, you are not meant to be here," a voice said from the distance.

I craned my neck to the side, looking behind me, but seeing nothing but the usual blur of colors.

"Who's there?" I called out.

A chuckle carried on the wind.

"Alikye, you have yet again changed Destiny's plans. She is not happy with you," the man 's voice said. "She has sent me here to make things right," his voice was soothing, almost like velvet.

I watched in amazement as the blur of colors, like being in a kaleidoscope, started to take shape. A light so blinding hit me dead on, causing my eyes to water and my ears to ring. I shielded my face, feeling the first beads of sweat form on my forehead. I wiped at my face, rubbing at my eyes, but I still couldn't hide away from the beauty of the form walking towards me.

Still completely awestruck and muddled, I didn't move from my bench, as the hazy form started to take shape. A man, nearly seven feet tall, built entirely of chiseled muscles, glided through the blinding light. I watched, stuck in a trance, as I tried my hardest to focus on the man in front of me. Every time I was finally able to make out a leg or an arm, my focus broke again, and all I saw were the twisted lines of what a man should look like to me. From what I could make out, he was a beautiful man, the most beautiful creature I had ever had the privilege of meeting.

As I concentrated more on the man, I asked, "Who are you?"

"Look harder my child, and really see me. Look past the beauty, and see the truth in which stands before you. My light is prevailing, if not intimidating, but once you can separate what needs to be seen and what needs to be known, you will then see what is your right to see," he said.

Um, okay, because that makes perfect sense. Okay, so this guy liked to talk in riddles. Deep down I had a strong feeling I knew who he was, but it was hard to believe in such a thing, that something so powerful would come in search of me, not the other way around. Either I was in a lot of trouble for the messes I have caused in my old life, or I was just that awesome.

"I know who you are," I wanted to roll my eyes, but that would be rude.

"Then why do you ask?" the man, still surrounded in light, stood in front of me.

I wiped at my eyes again, the burning light causing tears to roll down my cheeks.

"No offense, Michael, but do you have to be so bright?" I refused to look up at him until he dimmed.

A laugh burst from his mouth, sounding like a beautiful song. The heat from his body lightened enough that I was able to open my eyes. Choking back a gasp, I was taken aback by the beauty of Michael. Long, blond curls fell in waves an inch past his shoulder, tucked neatly behind his ears. Eyes like liquid gold, surrounded by long thick lashes, bore into me. Michael's features were perfect, not one flaw I could make out. He had hard defined cheekbones, a straight nose, and lips full and pink. His pale skin was covered from feet to chest in blue Enochian scripture, far more breathtaking than mine.

What had me gaping at him wasn't the fact that he was shirtless and wearing only a kilt looking thing to cover his… well, you know. It was what was attached to his back; a span of ten feet, from tip to tip, midnight black wings adorned his body. I reached out, gliding a feather through my fingers. Soft to the touch, like cashmere, each feather radiated magnificence.

Michael, in all his beautiful glory, broke my spell with a touch of his skin, or with his soul. I'm not too sure without our shells if we had skin anymore. Anyway, that kind of thinking would only bring up too many questions. Running a hand down my cheek, Michael used one finger under my chin to lift my head. Still holding on to the feather attached to his wing, I met his golden eyes.

"You do know me, my child," Michael said.

"I wasn't too sure. Why would a man of your caliber come to me?" I questioned.

"You ask all the wrong questions ,Alikye. Upon meeting me, I would think you would want to know where you are, or maybe what all this means," he swept an arm around my surroundings, "but you are not like the rest of them. I have watched you your whole life, Alikye. Never have I seen a girl cause so much trouble. Not only have you riled up Destiny, but death seems to be unpleased by your behavior, too."

I didn't know whether to be confused by his proclamation or ashamed. My mouth screwed up, mirroring my scrunched eyebrows. Contemplating if I should apologize or defend my actions, I let an abundance of thoughts race through my head. Considering what the world was like, I wouldn't think my actions as too bad, but I was a Guardian, therefore I was to be held to higher standards. Too bad I never saw it that way. I smiled at my own thoughts. Even if I had the chance, I wouldn't have changed who I was or how I came to have the life I deserved, even if it was short lived. My mistakes from the past brought me to Andy, and he made me a better person.

I shrugged, deciding against speaking altogether. I was almost positive Michael had the ability to know what I was thinking, anyway. He nodded at my unspoken assumption, almost causing me to laugh. This moment wasn't as awkward as I would've thought it would be, perhaps because in a way we had known each other all of our lives.

Taking a deep breath, Michael finally took a seat, his gigantic wings folding into his body.

"That's not fair, you know," I pointed to his wings. Was I jealous? Hell yeah, I was. "I want wings."

Michael's lips pulled into a wide smile. Eyes sparkling like diamonds, he erupted into laughter. I couldn't help but follow suit. After all, I was sitting next to an Archangel in my own afterlife. What more could a person want? I rolled my eyes at my own thoughts.

After an eternity of laughing, Michael's gorgeous smile faded from his face, turning serious. "Alikye, you were never meant to die. Although death was pleased to have you, I was able to get to you first. You, my dear, have put a rift in many plans."

Chapter 23

"That is twice now that you have interfered with Destiny's plans," the mischief in Michael's eyes was shocking. Shouldn't he be more upset that I couldn't even follow simple plans as to live?

One side of my mouth lifted in a snarl. I was tired of others telling me how to live my life. Even after death, I was still doing everything wrong.

"You're not mad. You're not gonna smite me," I joked.

Michael barked out a laugh, rich and soothing like melted chocolate. I closed my eyes and absorbed his silky voice.

"I am not one to agree with all of her plans. From the beginning, it has been said that many situations that we both do not agree on, will or will not be what's best for mankind. In the likelihood that one might cause catastrophic damage in result of the supernatural, Destiny will try as she may to rewrite what has already been written, in order to keep peace. You, my child, have been her main focus for quite some time. Although, what she has written about you seems to make no difference."

"I couldn't let that happen," I looked past Michael, past the blur of the forest, to the pinkish sky above. I was beginning to love it here. The weight of a thousand pounds no longer weighed me down. I only felt relief, knowing I did what had to be done. "I brought him into my world. I wasn't gonna let him die because of my mistakes," the sad truth was that if Death really wanted Andy, he would have him.

"No worries, child. With your death, things may seem weary now, but I can assure you that soon it will all make sense," a smile played at his lips. "Although, as it seems your death," a pause, like he was uncertain whether he should speak. Michael tapped his finger against his thigh and said, "Never mind."

Yeah, okay.

We both sat in silence for a long time. I had so many questions, but some I didn't know how to ask. I went with the easiest one.

"How are my parents?" I hadn't seen them yet. I thought when a person died it was their loved ones waiting for them. In my case, I had no one. Hell, I couldn't even remember what happened between the time I gave my life to Andy until I found myself sitting on this bench.

Michael raised one eyebrow, making his rugged, masculine features soften. Screwing up his mouth in thought, he cocked his head.

"They are fine. They miss you. They wanted to be here to see you, but that is not possible."

"I don't understand. Why I can't see them?" I asked.

"All in due time, your answers will be found," and just like that the conversation was done.

Gotta love riddles.

I rolled my eyes, "So tell me, Michael, what's next for me?"

"Do not worry. I have many plans for you. Come, follow me," Michael held out his hand, his long, pale fingers were inviting.

I placed a small hand in his large one. Soft, like silk, but still rough with a warrior's touch, Michael's hand dwarfed mine. Warmth crawled up my arm, melting away any worry I had a moment ago about not seeing my parents. Tremors racked my body being so close to an Archangel. This had to be the coolest thing I had ever done. Holding hands with an Archangel was like epic on a scale that reached far past the highest point. These warriors might as well be Gods. I wasn't ashamed to admit that I was a little giddy, smiling like a fangirl.

Once past the forbidden forest, a clearing came into view, surrounded by hills as far as the eye could see. A doorway made out of deep cherry wood sat in the middle of the field, alone and misplaced, but judging by the haziness around the frame, I had a feeling it was meant to be there. Looking behind me, I noticed my place of peace was gone. The forest was now hills, stretching up to the clouds. After a five minute walk, we were in another part of this eternal paradise.

"Where are we?" I asked, taking leisurely steps towards the doorway. It called to me, wanting me to walk through to the unknown, like a beacon of light granting me passage.

I could feel the pain behind the wood, the sorrow of many lost souls asking to be set free. The pain twisted in my gut, tightening my lungs. For the first time in days, that peace I came to love dissipated, leaving my wounds wide open. I opened my mouth to speak, but nothing came out. Not knowing the right words to say had me at a loss. I was grateful when Michael came up to me, taking my hand again. The sudden rush of calm slammed into to me. The sadness was now gone.

Blinking back tears, I was stunned at what I had just witnessed. One minute I was happy, the next everything hurt. I thought being in paradise was only supposed to bring peace. I looked up, meeting a pair of golden eyes.

"You were never supposed to be here, Alikye. For years, I had made sure you lived. This one time..." he trailed off, looking out into the distance, "At least it was a sacrifice of love."

"I still don't understand?"

"Yes, but you will. Now come," he demanded.

As we approached the door, a light came on through the crack in the bottom.

"You were always meant to find Andrew, you know. Long ago, a prophecy was written that the two of you would meet," he paused, taking in my bewildered face.

I mean, yes, I've always known there was something supernatural about the two of us. It was in the first time we met, the first time we touched, some kind of electricity that connected us. Hearing it confirmed by Michael was reason enough to believe my suspicions. Maybe, just maybe, something more was in works here.

Before I could ask, Michael continued, "It has been a battle between Fate and Destiny for many eons now. Fate of course…"

"Aren't they the same thing? I mean, the definition of fate is destiny," I interrupted.

Michael's chest rumbled in humor.

"Don't let those two hear you say that. The human definition is what you just said, but know they are two separate souls with many different meanings; Fate is by chance, while Destiny is your calling. Fate worked against Destiny so you would find Andrew. Destiny is not pleased, as I have already told you."

Michael's hand slipped from mine, hovering over the doorway. It was then I noticed a lock was the only thing on the door; there was no handle to open it. With a flick of his wrist, a click sounded, opening the doorway.

"So why is it that Fate is on my side, but Destiny is so hell bent on destroying me?" I asked.

Michael raised his eyebrows, cocking his head to the side to meet my eyes.

"Not you, just your relationship with Andrew. You see, it's not that loving him, because he's human, is wrong. It's that loving him because of who he is will not end well for most. What Destiny fails to see, though, is trying to foil Fate's plan for the two of you only brought you one step closer to each other."

I breathed in a heavy sigh, feeling a headache coming on. At least, if I were still alive I'd be feeling a headache coming on. I didn't even know how to respond to that or anything that Michael was saying.

Beyond the open doorway was a black hole, a room so dark I couldn't even see my hand in front of my face. I relied on Michael to know where he was taking me. Holding tight to him, I wondered what would happen if I let go. Each step I took felt heavy, a pressure of suction gripping at my legs. What felt weird, though, was not being able to feel the air. I felt nothing, but somehow knew it was cold in there.

We walked for some time, neither of us speaking. Instead, we listened to the sounds of complete and utter silence. Not even the sounds of our breathing could be detected in this place. It felt wrong to speak, but something inside me wanted to scream, just to hear what would happen. Were their other souls like ours walking around in this dark abyss, or were we the only ones allowed in this place of perfection?

"There was a time long ago that Guardians worked side by side with Veneficus. As you know, they were a very powerful species," he started.

In the dark I couldn't see Michael's face but I felt him staring at me. When I said nothing, he continued, "Although Veneficus are far more powerful than your kind, they are a lot like humans when it comes to death."

Again, he paused, waiting on me to speak.

"I know all this," I said against the darkness.

"Yes, well let me just refresh your memory."

Another pause.

"Together, both races were unstoppable. As your laws state, you cannot harm a human," Michael continued.

I couldn't help but let the image of Andy dying in my arms flash around in my mind. Killed by my race, I let Andy get involved, thinking he would be safe because of these laws. Anastasis knew my weakness, and she used it against me.

"The same laws apply to the other race as well. When I gave them permission to enter our world, I did so under the condition they would not use their power for evil. Soon after, my brother saw fit to recruit them in his army, but they declined, wanting to live in peace. When the war started and Guardians were created, we asked for assistance when your kind started to die off all too quickly. In the end, my brother's army used humans again. This time, we had to sit back and watch the slaughter happen. Many Guardians died going into battle with the Demons that turned the humans."

Sadness laced Michael's voice. I remembered hearing stories of that fateful night. In a town inhabited by both humans and Veneficus, they lived together in peace and harmony. Until onne night when everything changed, and over 100 Veneficus lost their lives because they were believed to be human witches.

"1692," I whispered.

"Salem, Massachusetts," he replied, using the same light tone.

The veil of darkness lifted, revealing a peaceful, quiet day blanketed in a sheet of snow. The sun shone bright on a small town, the breeze enough to bite at my skin. I pulled my jacket tighter to my body, loving the feeling of actually feeling something other than numbness. The only sounds came from the heavy soles of my boots pounding into the rubble of the dirt road. On either side of me were fields as far as the eye could see. In the distance, I could make out a two-story wooden home.

"Where are we?" I asked, kicking snow off my pant legs. I was never really one for snow. The whole cold and wet stuff looked better in the movies.

"Salem, Massachusetts."

I turned to catch Michael staring at me, brows raised.

"Salem?" I questioned. This place looked nothing like Salem. Yes, it had that New England feel about it, but Salem? "Salem?" I repeated.

"Salem."

I took another look around. The trees behind me were bare of leaves, covered in snow. Looking past the winter wonderland, the woods looked fresh, like years of pollution hadn't yet touched them. The dirt road was framed by a wooden fence, rounded logs nailed to each other, pieces of grass sticking out from under the white fluff.

"When?" I asked.

A smile tugged at Michael's lips.

"There are facts that you need to know, Alikye. A story that belongs to you. To know the truth, you'll have to see the story for yourself. There is a reason why Destiny was so hell bent, as you say, to destroy your life. You, my dear, are the chosen one," Michael explained.

Rolling my eyes at his ridicules love of riddles, I jumped in front of him, stopping him in his tracks. With both hands in front of me, palms out, I tilted my head up to meet his eyes. He towered over my small frame, easily able to trample me, but with a smile still on his handsome face, he slowed to a stop, folding his arms across his chest.

"When?" I asked again, referring to the time in which he brought me.

"1692, January," he said, matter of fact.

This was going to be fun.

Chapter 24

January, 1692. Salem, Massachusetts.

Now, standing in the middle of the snow covered road, I looked around, noticing for the first time that we were indeed not in the present time. The bitter cold brushed against me. Even with the sun out, I couldn't stop from shivering.

"How come I can feel?" I asked Michael. Rubbing my arms up and down, my body started to warm up, but not enough to keep me comfortable.

"I let you feel so you can know the pain that tonight will bring," Michael replied. Apparently it didn't apply to him, because he was still shirtless in all his golden, tanned glory.

Out of thin air, a jacket appeared; it was thick and looked warm. I grabbed it from his hands, wrapping it tightly around my body. The warmth immediately swallowed me up.

"Is this real?" I bent down and grabbed a handful of snow. The cold numbed my fingers, bringing back memories of my life in Colorado as a child.

"Yes."

"Can we stop tonight from happening?"

"No."

"Can they see us?"

"No."

"So we're like ghosts, haunting this place. Can I move things around and scare people?" I wiggled my eyebrows for effect.

"Umm, no," he ran a hand up and down his jaw, keeping himself from laughing. "I have created doorways, hidden holes that can bring a soul to wherever they want to go. As a spirit, they can travel through time and space, but only as an invisible being. They cannot change the past. Some souls will spend eons traveling the past. It is absolutely enjoyable to see with your own eyes as history unfolds itself."

Down the road, a small town came into view. Large two-story colonial buildings dotted the grounds.

People milled around town, stopping to speak to one another. Women wore long skirts, looped up to keep out of the snow. The skirts were worn over petticoats, slightly shorter than the skirts. Over the peasant shirts, women wore corset-like bodices with shoulder straps. White stockings and black buckled shoes were worn under their skirts. The men wore knee length breeches with vests over their loosely fitted peasant shirts. The same as women, men also wore white stockings and black shoes with buckles.

Their clothes looked more like piles of rags, colors thrown together in a mess of fabric. I laughed, picturing myself wearing these silly garments. I walked farther into the crowd, lifting my hand to touch another person like I touched the snow, but I wasn't able to make contact. For a split second, I felt the person's warmth, but nothing more. Then, it was gone. The lady in front of me looked past me as if I were a ghost, oblivious to me poking, literally, at her.

The man spoke quietly to the woman, looking a bit nervous, speaking to the group about the witchcraft going on and the list of witches they had seen practicing. Already, many young girls were accused of being bewitched. The history, of course, was tainted. It wasn't months at a time that the Veneficus were placed in jail. The trials didn't last years as they interrogated innocent people, and it wasn't the devil they saw bewitching the children. Demons needed the job done, and in one night they were able to burn the town and destroy the lives of hundreds.

"I fear they will come for our children if we do nothing, sir," the woman whispered to the man.

"That will not happen. Tonight we will end the terror that the devil has placed upon us," the man replied.

The devil, my ass. These idiots were too brainwashed by their church to realize it was them killing innocents in the name of the devil, not the other way around.

"Patience, my child. I know it hurts to see the truth, but it's not their fault either. They were being played by evil," Michael spoke.

"But why couldn't we do anything? Why wouldn't they fight to save themselves? I understand it's not our place to interact, and we can't exactly hurt humans, but this," I waved my hands around at the numerous people plotting to destroy and kill others, "we should have been able to fight back."

"And if we did, we would be no better than them. We have laws for a reason, Alikye. What you need to understand is behind every evil is a good soul willing to sacrifice themselves for another. The Veneficus understood this, and were willing to sacrifice their lives to stay pure."

I did understand why we did what we did, in order to follow our laws. It didn't mean I had to like it. My race and the Veneficus race could rule the world together. We could fix everything that was broken about it. We were a force to be reckoned with, but we were trapped, chained to our laws. It was frustrating knowing so much power was being bottled up, never to be released on our broken world.

"Why am I here? What does Salem have to do with Destiny's plans for me?" I wondered.

"There is someone I want you to meet," Michael took off in the direction of what I assumed was the courthouse. His tall frame was hard to keep up with. Add the carpet of snow, and my abilities being gone, and I was stumbling around like a nitwit. I would think being dead and haunting the past I would be able to fly, but no. Not only did I feel 100% human, I was also cold and wet.

"Meet who?" I yelled across the opened area. "I'm pretty dead right now, if you've forgotten. I can't meet anyone," I kept yelling as I raced around the people, wondering if their dead selves were walking around watching their idiocy unfold.

"All in due time, Alikye," Michael smirked.

"Yeah, because I haven't heard that one yet. I would tell you I'm not getting any younger, but considering I'm already dead, I guess time isn't really an issue, huh?" I joked.

Michael stopped at the door, turning to meet my eyes, a smile wide on his face. He replied, "You are funny, you know that?"

"You're not so bad yourself, old timer. Anyway, who's this mystery person I need to meet?" I reached for the door, swinging it open. Voices erupted in chaos. Men and women yelling, children crying, chairs being scraped against the wooden floor were the sounds exploding around me. I took off running, knowing I wouldn't be able to do anything, but I needed to see what was happening.

A dark-skinned woman sat on stage as a man yelled in her face, asking her if she knew the devil. The woman cried as she answered over and over again, her accent thick but still easy to understand. I watched in horror as small children sat in the corner, some of them screaming, others repeating every word the woman spoke.

I walked up front, standing near the man, wishing I could hit him. Clearly this woman was scared and, from what I could tell, completely human. She begged to be released, but all the man did was laugh in her face. She was innocent, but ended up confessing just to stop the abuse happening to her. Another man in black moved to the front, roughly handling the woman, taking her from the room.

Next up, another woman was brought on stage. After her, another followed, all being accused, all being forced to confess. Hours went by as I watched. Michael pointed out each Veneficus, most not willing to speak. Not once did they break eye contact as the man in black pulled them away from their families.

"Come," Michael beckoned.

I nodded, not wanting to speak. I just wanted to do something. I didn't like the feeling of weakness, the feeling of hopelessness. I lost my control because I was dead, and now I would never be able to save another person.

Being dead was beginning to suck.

Once outside, night took to the sky. I shivered at the dropped temperature now that the sun was gone. More people stood in the courtyard area, huddling around one another for warmth. Homes were lit up by firelight, shadows dancing in the windows.

Heading over to one of the houses, I took a peek inside. A man and woman sat at a table, sharing a plate of food. In the corner, a dark-skinned woman cradled a toddler. The connection I felt to this family was overwhelming, like I had known them all my life. A burning sensation crawled up my arm, pooling in my chest. My head spun, the aching in my neck pounded against my spine.

"You feel it," Michael whispered against my ear.

Of course I felt it, how could I not. Every nerve ending was on fire.

"Yes, what is that?" I reached out, wanting to touch them. I needed to touch them. I had a strange feeling in the pit of my stomach. A pull in my chest told me to go inside.

"They are the Wardwells, a very powerful family, one of the first pure bloodlines. It has been said that, long ago, it was them who ruled their world. You, Alikye, have a connection to them. How this connection happened is a mystery to me, but stranger things have happened," he shrugged.

I blinked away my confusion. Just another piece of my crazy puzzle that made no sense. Why was I the one to be so different from other Guardians? Why couldn't I be home now, waiting for the next call, watching crappy TV while Lucas and Derek worked all night on last minute details? Since the age of three, my life has never been normal, by Guardian standards.

"Watch the child. It is because of that child that Destiny was thrown into your path," Michael countered.

"Who is he?"

"Charlie Wardwell. He just had his second birthday last week. In the next hour to come, he will watch as the humans take his parents. The woman holding him is human, a Native American enslaved by the town. Martha Wardwell took her in as the child's caregiver, and treats her like she is part of the family," he answered.

Michael waved his hand in the air, and time started to move. Like hitting the fast forward button, I watched as the people blurred, hurrying around each other with no knowledge of the presence of an Archangel interfering with time. The doors to the courthouse burst open, and it was then I felt them. A sick feeling twisted in my gut. The smell of death swam around me. I choked on my next breath, tasting the inky vile on my taste buds.

Standing behind the group of human men, dressed in black, their faces covered in dark fabric, were a handful of Demons. Using glamour, something known by witches, they appeared to everyone as just men. I turned quickly to see the parents of Charlie Wardwell jump from their seats, most likely feeling the same thing I was feeling. Their voices erupted in chaos, grabbing their son and his caregiver, stuffing them in what appeared to be a closet.

Speaking words that were not known to me, a light shot against the floor, framing the perimeter of the house. Dark markings, Veneficus markings, painted the floor.

"These will protect them from Demons, but not humans. What they failed to see is that by defending themselves against evil, they gave themselves away as Warlocks. The Demons you see shadowing the humans are speaking to them, making them believe their thoughts are their own. They are giving them the power to kill, believing what they are doing is for good, when really they are being tainted by evil."

Within seconds, the screaming started. The darkness was lit up by fire. Human women hid away in their homes, keeping themselves safe from danger. I turned just in time to see a couple ripped from their house, struggling against their attacker. Seconds later, a child was pulled from his mother. I ran as fast as I could, but realized there was nothing I could do. I was helpless, and made to only watch the tragedy unfold.

I grabbed at my head, the pain tearing through my body; not physical pain, mental pain from seeing the chaos in front of me. All I could think of was the Guardians' whereabouts. If they were here to destroy the Demons, maybe that would break the spell on the humans. Why weren't the Demons being destroyed? Veneficus were more than powerful enough to stop them, but they weren't doing anything.

Like cattle, families were steered into the middle of the courtyard. Thirty men surrounded them, others stayed on the sidelines to watch and listen. In history, it was written that a few people were executed in different ways while the crowds watched. Like most human history, the story was twisted and manipulated to meet human standards. In one night, over a hundred Veneficus were burned, hung, or stoned to death. All in one night, the town massacred innocent people for practicing witchcraft.

"Your people were off dealing with a war happening thousands of miles away, most likely caused by the same

Demons, as a distraction," Michael's voice came from behind, startling me.

I placed a hand on my chest to calm my pounding heart, not sure if it was from Michael sneaking up on me or the scene playing out in front of me.

"Why not kill the Demons?" I asked

"And expose themselves?" he countered.

"They are just letting themselves be slaughtered like cattle," my voice was faint, giving away my sadness.

"Everything happens for a reason," he said solemnly.

The first death happened twenty minutes later. A man was tied to a pole and burned alive. Next to him, a woman went up in flames, her burnt flesh mixing with the New England air. I covered my face to get rid of the revolting smell. Voices drifted around us; too many to determine what was being said. Cries sounded, mixing in with the screaming.

"Upon their deaths, the evil they bear will be released, and our town will be cleansed. Our children will be protected, and our women will stay safe. Upon the deaths of the Devil's servants, we will all be free," a man spoke loudly to the crowd.

The crowd erupted in applause as they lit the next pole in flames.

From behind me, the sound of a woman's voice caught my attention. Instead of sounding scared, she sounded pissed. My body shook as I met the eyes of Martha. Blue eyes, so dark, stared back at me like she could see me standing there. Her string of words were cut off when she stopped in front of me. The man holding her also stopped, but only to talk with another man. Long, dark hair fell over her shoulders, messy and unkempt like she'd struggled with these men.

"I can feel you," she whispered to me, her voice like silk. A shiver ran down my spine at her words. I stood wide-eyed and in shock. Looking around for Michael, to make sure I wasn't going crazy, I noticed he was gone.

"Keep him safe," she said. Then, she was gone, being pulled over to the others.

"What the—" I said, looking around.

"Like I said, your connection is strong, even in death," Michael said from behind me, again startling me.

"Was that the real her or the spirit her?" I asked.

"She was real. She couldn't see you, but she could feel the disturbance in the air. It told her she knew of you, but when and where, she could not be sure."

"Do you like riddles or are you just naturally difficult when it comes to giving straight answers?" I said sarcastically.

He raised his eyebrows.

"Never mind," I shook my head, turning back to the cries that masked the quiet night.

"Come," he said, holding out his hand for me.

Rolling my eyes, I took his hand. A rush of wind slammed into me, knocking me toward the ground. Before I hit the floor, I found myself floating. The wind carried me as I was lifted higher into the air. Hugging my body closer to Michael, the world blurred.

We touched down minutes later, my feet hitting the hard, snowless ground covered in hay. Above me, a roof protected me from the cold. I looked around, not knowing what was in store for me now. This night was turning into a nightmare. Now that I was able to feel, I felt exhausted. If I could, I would sleep, but I was still dead. Although, it seemed like a good idea. Once back to my paradise, I would be numb again.

The door to the side squealed, causing me to move. A head peeked in. After not seeing anything, the doors opened wider to reveal the Native American woman and the small child she held under her care. Looking at her, I noticed her torn clothing and bleeding feet.

"She ran for five miles in the woods to save that little boy," Michael explained. "She will only live for a few more minutes but, because of her sacrifice, Charlie will live."

I spun fast to face Michael.

"You're telling me the Wardwell bloodline wasn't killed off?"

When I was twelve, in history class, we learned about the true events of this night. Drexel, a Demon much like Shasta, born from a human mother but conceived by a Demonic father, held the truth of the events that occurred that night. Fifty bloodlines were said to be lost, forever killed off, including the Wardwells.

"Many of the bloodlines weren't killed off, but I do not have the admission to find where those bloodlines are hiding," he explained.

"Umm—" I was confused, again.

"Many different occurrences happened after this night. While Drexel took one of each bloodline, we were able to hide the rest. Now, the bloodlines are scattered around the world, most with no knowledge of the power they carry. Some turned to evil, having no other choice. Others ran scared, giving up their powers to stay hidden," Michael began. "There is a prophecy written that, in the time of need, both races must band together to defeat evil, and to save the remaining human race. It is also said that it must be the High King that calls forth the forgotten bloodlines, and the first chair of the Guardians will bring them together."

The little boy lay sleeping in the hay, curled into a ball. I watched him, somehow feeling responsible for his wellbeing. Keep him safe, the woman, Martha, had said to me. Was it this child I was supposed to keep safe? If so, how was I supposed to keep him safe when there was nothing I could do?

A Wardwell, a freaking living Wardwell. That was amazing all on its own. The fact that there were more, in present time, living, going about their lives as if they weren't the most important and powerful creatures ever to live, was astounding. This child in front of me would bring new... Wait, just because I knew about the child being alive, how would the others know?

"Why show me him if there is nothing I can do to tell the others? You do realize what this means, right? With him alive, Guardians could finally end this battle," I said, taking another step closer to Charlie.

The little boy stirred in his sleep, calling out for his Mommy. The Native American woman covered up his body, keeping him warm. She placed a kiss on his forehead before taking a quick peek outside. When all was clear, she took off running. Michael grabbed me again, just as I was about to reach out towards Charlie.

"Your death should not have happened," Michael said.

"Yep, I agree, but no way would I have let Andy die," I told him.

"His death would not have happened," he responded.

I glared at Michael, then rubbed my hands over my face. Shaking my head, I turned back to the small child. These riddles, partial answers, were becoming annoying. Why not just say, "Here is the story," plain and simple? Nope, I get games, puzzles, and an earsplitting headache.

Yay me.

"Okay, seriously, you are making absolutely no sense. You are going in circles with me instead of giving me straight answers," I gulped in a huge breath, clearly sounding frustrated. "Clear answers, please. Who is Charlie, and what does he have to do with me?"

"Charlie Wardwell is the bloodline of the High King that will one day bring forth the battle to end all battles."

"Yeah, I got that, but—" I raised my eyebrows. When he didn't say anything, I continued. "Charlie Wardwell is dead. We would have to find the ancestor of Charlie. How do we find his ancestor? I mean, honestly, that bloodline was known to be dead. How do we find a needle in a million different haystacks?"

I watched the child again, seeing the steady rise and fall of his chest. Dark hair fell in front of his eyes, his small chubby face unrecognizable. Drexel should still have the records of what happened, and he more than likely knew the Wardwell bloodline had not died off that night.

"Alikye," Michael said, bringing my attention back to him. His face was stone-like, pale, and beautiful. His eyes gleamed yellow, the swirling motion making them look like melted gold. "How is it you do not know the connection you feel for this child? Why is it you deny what is yours? Destiny may have had a hand in your life, but Fate made sure everything was set right. Your death was done out of love and sacrifice. Your death was not a death at all," he grabbed my face, bringing us closer together. Michael ran his thumb over the scars that still marred my face, scars that didn't disappear, even with death. My body shook as his next words slammed into me like a Mack truck slamming into a brick wall.

"Look into your head and really feel. You want to know who the new High King is? Alikye, this whole war tonight is about you. It is written that a Macayan and a Wardwell, a Guardian and a Veneficus, will fall in love. From that love, they will bring the ending for new beginnings."

I stared at Michael, unable to speak, wide-eyed and scared to death. I knew without him telling me. I knew what he was trying to tell me. This whole time, everything was making more sense. Everything was clearer. I couldn't breathe. How could I have not known from the beginning? How could I have gone this whole time believing it was normal? Did Shasta know? I didn't think so, but he felt it too. This whole time...

"No," my voice shook. "No, Michael."

"Yes, Alikye. Andy is the High King of the forgotten bloodline. Andy is a Wardwell."

Chapter 25

January, 1692 Salem, Massachusetts

There have only been a few times in my life that I have been stunned into complete and utter silence. Right now was one of those times. The words swirling around in my head seemed to be frozen in place before leaving my lips. I blinked continuously, like somehow that would make my words come out. Michael stared at me, golden eyes meeting silver ones. Andy? My Andy was a Wardwell, a very powerful Warlock. My Andy wasn't even freaking human.

I laughed, thinking about the night he found out I was a Guardian. That night Azaria, a Pagan god, had almost succeeded in killing me, tearing me apart like I was hamburger. Shasta was trying his best to put me back together. The others came in and watched as my body started to heal itself. Andy was so angry. He didn't know how to talk to me, let alone look at me.

"Are you even human? Because that shit that I just saw is no way human," Andy had spat out viciously. I winced.

He was freaked out and, of course, had every right to be. His whole life he believed the supernatural was fiction. I showed him it wasn't. It took him some time to warm up to the fact I was only half human. Wait until he found out that he was not at all human. I shook that night out of my head. How would I tell him? I was dead.

"We should go," Michael said.

I followed behind him, not sure what I would do next, or how to handle this new information. Looking back at the child, I knew he would be found soon, but it didn't sit well with me to just leave him.

"They will find him in the morning and raise him as their son. He will grow to become a fine young man, and one day leave behind his legacy," Michael reassured me.

Once back in Salem, as the sun started to rise, the scene that played out in front of me was so gruesome not even the sickest of people could imagine it. The bodies of men, women, and children were carried away from town, their corpses being placed in a mass grave. Many of the victims were nothing more than piles of ash. Bones that didn't have enough time to burn poked out, charred and disfigured. The worst of the victims were stoned to death, their flesh torn apart from the blunt force of sharp objects. Crimson painted their skin, making them look almost inhuman. The smell...oh my god, the smell was horrific. The air was thick with the scent of death.

I turned my face into Michael's chest, holding back tears. In all of my life, I have seen some bad things, but this had to be the worst. I have been raised around death. I watched as my parents were murdered at a young age. I killed my first Demon at fourteen, but this...I never imagined the hate and violence caused by a race so easy to manipulate.

"Can we please go now?" I whispered.

I felt Michael nod.

Within seconds, we were back at my place by the lake. Now, the pain was gone. My body completely relaxed. I took a deep breath, remembering everything, but not dwelling on the destruction that occurred at the hands of my enemy. I had so many things to consider now that I knew the truth—the truth about the missing bloodlines, the truth about Andy being the High King. I really wanted to be the one to tell him, to see his face when he found out he wasn't human. It was wrong on so many levels, but I couldn't help but laugh. I blamed the peacefulness of paradise.

I took a walk towards the lake, dipping my feet into the warmth of the water. A pleasurable balminess snaked up my limbs, pooling deep in my belly. I ran my hands through my dark auburn hair, resting my hands on the back of my neck. Michael appeared at my side, taking my hand in his. His touch was comforting, enough to let a smile pull at my lips.

Sighing deeply, Michael watched me for a minute before beginning.

"Lucifer is getting stronger. I have watched for many centuries now," he had a faraway look in his golden eyes, as he watched the ripples of the water lap against each other. "After all this time, he had found a way to break through the chains that bound him. I thought I had enough power to keep him locked up forever. What I wasn't betting on was all the betrayal amongst the good ones. Every day, evil prevails; every day that it does is one step closer to bringing Hell on Earth. I am not able to do anything from where I am. It was why I created your race, so that you would be able to keep peace. The more of you I created, the more my brother did, too, and because of his hatred for the human race, he used them for his game of world domination."

Taking his hand from mine, he ran it through his hair. I saw the frustration in his features. He blamed himself for all the pain his brother caused. I knew the feeling, except I always blamed myself for the pain I caused Derek and Lucas. I missed them dearly, and wished like hell I could see them one last time. I'd tell them how much I loved them, and see for myself that they were okay. I still wasn't sure how I could help in the situation, how I could warn the others, how I could tell Andy that he would be the one to bring an extinct race back together. I wanted to be the one, but I knew that was impossible.

"My brother has a plan, but I am not privy to that information, nor do I know what it entails. The only thing I do know is that the separation of your race and Veneficus's race was key. Now, this is where you come in," he turned his glare on me, studying me. I just watched silently, waiting for him to continue. "It is said that it must be the first chair of the Guardians to bring the races together."

I thought of Natalia. I thought of Anastasis and my Legacy. Because Natalia wasn't actually dead, she was rightful heir to the throne. If I was initiated in, I would take second, bumping Ana to third, but we missed the time to awaken Natalia. With the Macayan Legacy now gone, it wasn't possible.

We were screwed.

Reading my mind as it spun through many different scenarios, Michael laughed.

"So much you do not know, child. So much hidden away from your race for fear of the end. Your grandparents knew the truth, and yet kept it with them until the end. Anastasis, too, knew the truth. As you can see, she chose power over honor. Many years ago, for reasons that I do not know, your ancestors gave up first chair. Until the day comes when a Macayan asks for it back, only then can she rule her race."

"You're saying—but that's not possible," I shook my head in disbelief.

"Yes, Alikye, you are the rightful heir to first chair. It was your Legacy whom I created first, and it was you who Destiny has been after for many eons. Many secrets have been hidden from me. It was a risk I had to take, using parts of human souls to allow you to feel. The flaws in humans are now your own flaws in which I cannot fix. I was unaware of the deception; it was the reason I needed to somehow interfere without actually interfering," a long pause had me snapping my head towards a wary Michael.

"Alikye, I am sorry, but this was the only way to fix my own mistakes. I have always known you were different. A fire so bright burns inside of you, and that fire keeps your heart pure. As a child, you have always asked yourself why you were nothing like the others. It was because, since the day you were born, you were something extraordinary. You have always been the key to stop world domination. You are the key to save this world from my brother. It is why I needed to bring you here."

Like a deer caught in headlights, I glared at Michael, wide-eyed and shocked.

"What do you mean you needed to bring me here?" I growled.

"We needed to talk," he shrugged. "You needed to see the truth. I can't walk the earth, but I can bring you here for a short amount of time. Andy was supposed to intervene. He was never going to die, Alikye, but the only way to get you here, and get you home, was for you to sacrifice yourself out of love. It was not ideal, and if this plan went awry—" Michael explained.

"It would have been me who paid the price," I finished for him.

"It would have happened anyway. Eventually, they would have caught and killed you. This way, I was able to control the outcome. I sent Fate to intervene by putting Andy in the middle. I knew with his death I would be able to save you from your death. I am sorry," he stated nonchalantly.

I wanted to be mad. I could feel the anger boiling to the surface. Even in this place of peace, I was allowing my feelings to slip in. They were not as thick as if I was on Earth, but enough that I had to fist my hands to keep them from shaking. I pulled in my emotions, shutting them down before the rage could consume me. To say I had anger issues would be putting it mildly. Once my breathing evened out, I slumped in defeat. What was the point anymore?

"From the beginning, you all never even gave me a chance. I never had any control over my own life," I turned, leaving Michael standing alone.

In my head, I pictured a night sky, millions of stars scattering across the darkened plane. I saw bright lights of pink and blue, darting up from the ground, swirling around, reminding me of the northern lights in Alaska. I heard waves crashing against the shore, saw foam gather against the sand as the receding wave disappeared. The smell of salt enveloped me like a warm blanket on a cold night. When I finally opened my eyes, everything I saw, heard, and smelled was all in front of me, my paradise morphing into the image in my mind.

"I want to go home," I whispered to the night.

Michael appeared at my side, nodding.

I looked up, meeting his stare. A flicker of remorse gleamed in his eyes. All too quickly, it was gone, replaced by his stone-cold features that showed no signs of emotion.

"Do I get to go home?" I asked quietly.

He nodded again.

"How?"

"You must make Andy believe. Once he has unlocked his true self, he will be able to bring his race back together. You must find the missing bloodlines, find Drexel; he is the key to this. Take ownership of the council, they are yours to lead," Michael ordered.

I listened, silently, blinking rapidly. I gathered all the information Michael was telling me, not wanting to forget anything. This was my destiny, this was my journey. I was a fighter, a Guardian. I was a Macayan, a Legacy, the last of my legacy. As much as I didn't want to do this, I had to. As much as I wanted a normal life, to go to college and play soccer, I couldn't. My cards were dealt, and it was my duty to be extraordinary. Michael went on to tell me what I needed to do, how it was going to be me to change the ways of the council. No more secrets, no more deception.

"I still don't understand how you are gonna bring me back when I clearly died, but I won't question you. You obviously have a plan," a smile tugged at my mouth.

"Just know it was your sacrifice that allowed this to happen. When you gave up your life, you did so out of pure love for Andy. You gave up your markings, your magic, so that he could live. Your body still lives, hooked up to machines. While your soul is detached from it, your body will never wake, but to give back your markings is to give back your soul to the shell of yourself," he explained.

Michael placed a gentle hand on my face, cupping my cheek. His other hand grazed my shoulder, moving down my arm. As his fingertips whispered against my skin, blue lines started to appear. I watched in awe as the symbols of my race adorned my skin. My chest tightened, causing my next breath to catch in my throat. It was still weird to me that I even needed to breathe. Was their even a point to it? My thought was interrupted quickly as a spark of electricity shot through my veins. I froze, lifting my head to watch Michael, who was mumbling quietly to himself with his eyes closed. Another shot of pain raced across me, squeezing my muscles. Why did this always have to be so painful? Why couldn't my markings be like water flowing across my skin, instead of tiny knives scraping my flesh away?

"Michael," I gasped.

"Darling, be sure to do what I have asked," he paused as a light started to enveloped us. "Be who you are meant to be. Lead your race to salvation."

The light around us got brighter, blinding me instantly. The burning of my skin expanded across my body.

"Be who I know you to be."

An explosion sounded, throwing my body into the air. When I expected to fall, I never did. I reached around for Michael, but I was alone. Alone in the dark, I tumbled. Like Alice falling down the rabbit hole, it felt like an eternity before I hit solid ground. As the pain started to fade, so did the light that surrounded me. My vision started to blur and my head spun, until finally I couldn't keep my eyes open anymore.

Before I fell into darkness, the last thing I thought was, *"Where the hell am I?"*

Chapter 26
Present time

I awoke with a start, blinking through the blur of tears that threatened to spill. My eyes burned as they adjusted to the blinding lights around me. Pulling at the tube that was shoved down my throat, I managed to yank it out, causing me to cough. I was sore from head to toe, my body weak and broken. I felt around my chest and arms, counting numerous wires and tubes which were keeping me alive. The beeping to my right quickened, my vitals showing stronger rhythms. The once gone markings I gave to Andy now painted my body, with an additional one that adorned my neck—the mark of the council, first chair. It was the mark of Michael. Twisting my head around, I rolled my shoulders, stretching my stiff muscles.

Once I was able to pull myself up from bed, I realized I was home in Colorado. I took to work on releasing myself from being a human pincushion. The last thing I remembered was Michael putting his hands on me as a scorching pain ripped through my body. I could still feel it lingering, a dull ache, enough to let me know I was alive.

Michael had said he would send me home, even though the probability was hopeless. What he said had made sense. Had Shasta let my body die due to the beating it took as my soul left it, if he would have left me there to wither away and then burn properly, there would have been no way to return home to finish my duties.

I pulled out all the tubes, throwing back the heavy comforter. I wore a pair of clean pajama pants and a sports bra. Running my hands over my flesh, I felt a thin layer of oil and grime. First thing I needed to do was take a shower. I didn't even chance feeling my hair, in fear of finding it in a heap of tangles and filth.

Touching my feet to the cold, hard floor, I winced, holding my breath as if it would hold back the pain. If I remembered correctly, I heard and felt every bone in my body break. Fortunately for me, however long it had taken me to get home and the combined efforts of my marking, the pain was manageable. Although I stood on shaky legs, steadying myself on the bed so not to fall on my ass, nothing was broken. I was just tired and weak.

How long had I been gone? To me, I thought it was only days, but by the temperatures outside and the heat blasting inside, winter was soon to come or was already here. I was scared to look outside and see snow on the ground, which would mean I had been gone for months and not days. Walking down the hallway, I kept my hands on the walls to keep me upright, pivoting around the spot I knew my parents died. The area had long been cleaned and replaced, and it wasn't my first time being back here since their deaths. Actually, I've been back quite a few times. Every time I purposely stayed away from that spot.

Heading toward the living room, the scent of burning wood carried around the room, bringing back memories of when I was a child. The crackling of the fire soothed my stress-induced brain. I sat for a minute, looking around the room. Someone had been there recently. They even stocked the kitchen with food when I wandered there to grab a drink. Shasta must have been staying here. Pain gutted me, but this time it was from hurting Shasta in the worst way possible. To think, for months he had been living here, hoping for me to wake up when we both knew it was impossible, was heartbreaking. It was another reminder of losing Elina long ago. I scrubbed at my face hard, pulling back, shaking my head.

"Shower first, and then I call Shasta," I spoke to no one, hearing as my voice struggled to make words. I coughed in my hands, clearing the gruffness from my sore and raw throat. "Great, I sound like a dude." Another cough and grunt to clear my throat did nothing but make it sore again.

Turning on the shower as hot as it would go, I waited while steam gathered. Stepping under the stream of water, I felt my body become stronger; something about being clean always made me feel better.

I spent the better part of an hour making sure I scrubbed every inch of filth off me. It wasn't until I stepped out that the thought of Andy crossed my mind. I couldn't believe I didn't think about him or anything else, like my new destiny, but I'd been so preoccupied with making myself feel somewhat back to normal that I just didn't think. A part of me hated being back; the peacefulness I felt in my paradise was all consuming. For the first time, I felt completely free with no worries. I felt guilty for wanting that when so much needed to be done here, and I was the only one who could do it. The dreadful part of it all was having to prepare for a war that would eventually kill me. My emotions were on high alert, the feeling of loneliness, darkness, anger, sadness; it all came flooding back in one giant wave. I should be relieved to be home, but I wasn't. Maybe once I was reunited with Andy, things would feel normal again, which brought up the fact that maybe Andy wouldn't even want to see me after I told him the truth about himself.

Drying off, I felt a hundred percent better. I dressed quickly in a pair of jeans and a long sleeve thermal Henley tee. I pulled my black boots over my pants, lacing them up tightly. Inside one boot was a silver dagger I always kept hidden there. The other boot still carried the iron dagger Kady gave to me two years ago for Christmas. Looking around my old room, that didn't resemble a child's room anymore but an adult room with few things in it, I spotted my Sagitta (Bow) and Arcus (Arrows) laying in the corner. Lights filtered in through the cracks in the curtains, illuminating my weapon. It called to me, wanting me to hold it. It had been so long since I last saw my bow, and now that I was close to it, it lit up in blue, matching my glowing arm. I ran my finger up the soft metal, feeling the power within both it and me.

Grabbing my bow, I headed back to the living room. It was time to finally get this show on the road. Once I got some food in my belly and had a long talk with Shasta, my next step was to go see Andy. I was both excited and nervous about seeing him. Wondering how long it really had been, I took a quick look outside. A thick blanket of snow covered the ground. I scrunched up my features, groaning inwardly. When I left, when I died, it was summertime. Now, from what I remembered about Colorado, it was full blown winter.

Shasta! I yelled inside my head.

The first pull started, telling me he heard me. He didn't answer back. Instead, he fought me. An ache coiled around my brain like a snake trying to squeeze the life out of me. I laughed, pushing harder at Shasta. Whatever he was thinking, he didn't believe it was me calling for him, but a trick by my people.

Shasta, get your ass here now. I don't have time for this, I called again

A whoosh of air sent my hair flying around my face. The wet strands stuck in my eyes, causing me to shake my head.

A figure appeared before me, casted in shadows. The most intense icy blue eyes stared back at me, white flakes stirring inside their depths. His face was set in stone, his jaw ticking wildly like he was trying to keep his Demon side at bay, afraid it would be release.

"Alikye," he whispered, his European accent thicker than normal.

"It's been a while," I replied, grabbing Shasta's face so he could feel me. He stood as still as a statue, his arms at his side. "Shasta," I moved the dark strands out of his eyes. Shasta was so much taller than me, towering over my small frame. I had to stand on my tiptoes, and still I only reached his shoulders.

Finally, a light flutter of fingertips against my flesh caused me to shiver. Eyes locked on one another, Shasta moved his hand down my face, tracing the outline of my jaw. His other hand came up, running through my hair. Close contact with another always made me uncomfortable; I liked my space. Andy was the only other person I let touch me the way one would in an intimate approach. I loved Shasta, he was my best friend, and up until a year ago we never even hugged. This felt different. Letting him touch me, feel that I was really alive, was something he needed. Goosebumps covered my flesh when his fingers found my new marking. Tilting my head to the side to give Shasta a better view, I felt his breath dance across my skin.

"You're alive," he finally said.

"Yeah, apparently I'm not done here yet."

"You've been gone a long while," he continued.

"So I've gathered, but we really need to talk, and I need my old funny guy Shasta back right now," I shoved at his hands when they still hadn't left my body.

Shasta blinked a few times before finally realizing how close we actually stood. He took a wary step back. I could sense he didn't want to let go, in fear that once he did I wouldn't be there anymore. I have known Shasta my whole life, and never had I seen him look so sad. Guilt churned in my belly, and it hurt worse than I thought that I had done this to him, to them. I couldn't imagine what Andy was going through.

Andy.

Shasta's head snapped towards me, eyes wide. I was first confused by his change of character, until I realized the last thought I had was of Andy. Why was the mention of Andy in my head causing such a weird reaction?

"We should talk," Shasta said. He began walking past me, but stopped, turning to face me. "Please don't ever do that to me again. I can't lose you. The thought of never seeing you again—" he shook his head. "I nearly lost myself."

I took a seat in the kitchen, watching as Shasta busied himself making lunch. Every few seconds, he would look back at me, and I knew it was his way of making sure I was really there. I still didn't know how much time had passed, and I never asked about Andy. I wanted to, but I wasn't ready to know the truth. I did wonder if Andy had found someone new. If he was happy with school, and finally coping with me being gone. I asked Amanda to make sure he went on living, and to convince him to find love again. That was before I knew the truth. How would he take seeing me again, knowing that I was back? I knew there was no way around it, but something inside of me told me to just let him go. I wish I could.

Pressure pushed at my mind. I shot a glare at Shasta, who was finally smiling.

"You're blocking me love, why?" he asked.

I didn't know I was. I dropped my walls, letting Shasta into my head. For a moment, he stood frozen, reading everything. His eyes widened when he got to the part about Andy's true bloodline. I studied his face, knowing he was too deep into my head, his reality nothing more than a blur of colors. Behind him, whatever food was in the pan sizzled, releasing a puff of smoke. Oblivious to our lunch burning, I pushed at Shasta to get him back. It always felt weird to have another person in my head; it was like having two minds. I could see what he saw, hear what he was thinking, all the while hearing my own thoughts. For a time, we were connected as one.

"I knew he was different, I could see it in his head every time I went inside him. So many hidden doorways, so many blocked thoughts I couldn't pass. His mind is a blur, cloudy and distorted. It all makes sense now," Shasta said, turning down the stove.

"Michael said once he knows the truth, he'll be able to access those thoughts," I told him.

"Yes, but I'm afraid he won't take lightly to this new discovery. He hasn't been in our world long enough to understand what it means to not be human."

Changing the subject, I asked, "What did you want to talk to me about?"

Shasta's eyes casted down, and I knew whatever he wanted to talk about wasn't going to be good. He gave me a heartfelt smile, but it looked forced. After a long minute, he placed my food down, taking a seat next to me. We ate in silence, neither of us realizing how hungry we actually were. How long had it been since I last ate?

"It's the middle of February," he whispered.

I dropped my fork mid bite, freezing at this new knowledge. I've been gone for eight months. I turned eighteen, and wasn't even here to know it. I would be nineteen in July, only five months from now.

"It felt like I was only gone for days," I said, my voice cracking. For eight months, everyone I loved grieved my loss. "What about my family?" I had to know if they cared.

Shasta sighed, running a hand through his long, dark locks. A smile tugged at his lips, and it gave me hope that they still loved me.

"After you died, I went to see the council. I wanted to make sure the twins wouldn't die for what they did to Andy. As much as it pained me, and I wanted to see them pay, I couldn't allow another Legacy destroyed. Carter took head chair, arresting Anastasis. They were gonna let you come home. Carter was going to allow you back. Derek wanted to help from the start, but Ana kept him locked up,"

249

he met my stare and something stirred in his eyes. "Derek and Jack have been with you the whole time, watching you since the day you stayed in Florida. They never left you, Kye."

The weight of a Mack truck lifted, and my heart swelled with joy. Those words were exactly what I wanted to hear. He didn't mention Lucas and Sarah, and I didn't ask. At least Derek and Jack never left me.

"As for Andy—" he paused. Another minute ticked by without a word.

"Shasta! Just tell me!" I needed to know.

"He's had it rough, Kye. After he woke, I had already moved you here. When I got back, I had to tell him what happened. He was devastated. Amanda said he wouldn't talk for days. He is doing much better now, but something in him broke. He is not the same boy you once loved. Whatever I did to bring him back from death, weighs heavily on his soul. Combine that with your mark, your darkness—" he trailed off.

"What the hell do you mean my mark?" I interrupted. "Oh my god," realization hit me hard, causing my chest to ache.

"I am sorry, but yes. Andy and you bonded, and knowing what I know now, it is a lot worse than we first thought. Never had a Guardian and Veneficus bonded. The power alone is too much."

"But, how come I don't feel him? Why didn't I feel the bond when I woke? To be honest, the urge to see him is minimal. Shouldn't I want to see him?" I asked.

"I don't know. Like I said, it has never happened before. Therefore, I cannot answer your questions."

"I need to see him now," I blurted, standing from my chair. I raced to my room, grabbing my bow and arrows. Attaching them to my body, I strapped on a few more weapons I would need later. Within minutes, I was back in the kitchen and ready to go.

"Are you sure you can handle this right now?" Shasta asked, concern written on his face.

"Yes," I lied, because this was all too much for me right now.

So much needed to be done, and I didn't even know where to start. This new knowledge that Andy had bonded to me, and I couldn't even feel him, devastated me. He had been going through pain for months, and I wasn't here to help him. Yeah, he was going to hate me. He had every right to hate me. I knew this day would come when I would see so much hurt in his eyes because of something I did. It didn't matter that I would do it all over again. I did what had to be done, and that was that. Without dying, I would have never learned the truth. If I lived, Andy would be gone, along with many others. Two more Legacies would eventually die off, along with many more, had I not died. I never wanted to hurt Andy, but I told him time and time again that one day I would hurt him—that one day he would hate me. I guess that time had come.

I stood on shaky legs as I took Shasta's hand. He nodded once to me and, with a whoosh of air, we were both gone.

The end.

Coming soon…

Mark of Darkness is the third installment in, "A Guardian Series." Find out what happens next as Alikye's story continues.

About the Author

There isn't a lot to say about me. I spent most of my life living in a small coastal town in South Florida. The most important person in my life is my rambunctious seven year old mini me. And of course my right hand man, who isn't a man at all but a crazy hyper blue heeler named Syrus.

I love to write. Like most Authors my passion grew as I grew and then one day I said why not? So I came up with a story and failed miserably. It sucked and I had no clue how to develop my characters. A year later I took that story, another story I was working on and combined them. I then let my characters take over and Alikye's story was born. Since then more characters started to come alive.

When I'm not writing, I'm reading—A LOT. It's my guilty pleasure, boarding on obsessions. Yes! I'm the girl who will break plans with my best friend just so I can finish reading my next fixation.

My passion isn't only for writing; I have a big mouth and will stand up for anything I believe in. I'm proud of who I am and not afraid to voice my opinions. I will speak loudly for those who can't speak or are too scared to. And trust me everyone who knows me knows I love to talk.

I love coffee, gummy bears, sour gummy worms. Code red mountain dew. Music—all kinds of music. Tattoos, yeah I have a few. I have a crazy bucket list I would like to one day accomplish and when I say crazy, it's really not your normal travel the world. Although yes, one day I would like to travel the world.

I dislike one thing. Hate. We are all here together so why live in a world of hate, when love is so much more fulfilling.

I'm your typical crazy twenty something year old who sometimes thinks I'm still a teenager. My friends like to call me a nerd because of my love for sci-fi, fantasy and all things super hero. Thor may be my favorite, although he really isn't a super hero. Did I mention I might one day marry him—I wish. They also think I may be a little crazy due to my constant taking with the many voices/characters in her head. I can't help it. I love my characters.

Other than that, I'm just living my life day to day, loving every minute of it.

Don't forget to check out my Unwanted series, an adult romance. Unwanted Truth is available now.

I love to hear from my readers, so please if you love my books leave a review or let me know what you think, or if you just wanna talk, hit me up. Also to find out more about my upcoming books visit my facebook page or email me.

https://www.facebook.com/danielle.pepe.9
https://www.facebook.com/DanielleMPepe
pepe.danielle4104@gmail.com

Acknowledgments

There are so many people I would like to thank. First I would like to start with my family. Since starting my journey as a writer/Author, I've realized what a huge support system I have. I wish I could name everyone but unfortunately that would take too long.

My parents who I love dearly, especially my mom who called me at least ten times while reading Last of Her Legacy just to yell at me or ask me what goes through my head or just to tell me how great of a writer I am, I also have to thank her for being my unofficial manger, even though I still wouldn't let her read this book until it came out. Sorry mom, I love you but you have to wait like everyone else.

To my dad, who listens to me and gives me advice when I need it. He's a big reader, so we are always going back and forth so when I stuck, he's my go to guy. You know I love you too.

Thank you to my brothers David and Dominick. To my Aunts and Uncles and Cousins who are huge fans even though they aren't obligated to read my novels but they do anyways.

A **HUGE** thanks goes to my Beta readers, Kenneth Hayes Geary Jr, Shayna Brooks, Kaitlin Schultz, and Ally Collette.

I would particularly like to Thank, Rachel Mulcahy, another Beta reader who happens to also be my Unofficial P.A. You are amazing and I am so glad I have you in my life. Not only are you a million different things to me including my friend and my daughter's role model and favorite person but you are also my muse. You are the type of girl every writer wants to write about because not only do you have a heart of gold but I've also seen that fire burn inside you when you get annoyed. Thank you Rachel for everything, And I can't wait for you to be my official P.A and business partner years from now, until then I'll have plenty of books for you to read.

Now let's get to my **awesome, stylish, amazing** editor, who I have known since we were kids, Cori Chasmar, I am so glad you agreed to work with me and I see a long road ahead of us and love that you want to take this journey into the world of my own. On top of being my editor, it makes me happy to also have you as a friend. Love you girl and can't wait to come visit you on the West coast.

A huge thanks goes to Michael Fenimore of Fenimore Graphics, again you out did yourself. My cover is beautiful and you were able to stay with a certain theme for this series. We ran into each other by chance, working together at the same job, and even though you aren't there anymore, I'm glad I was able to snag you as my designer. I can't wait to see what the future holds and the many more covers you will be doing for me.

My biggest thanks goes out to my beautiful and wonderful and smart little bug, Alix. You are my everything, my reason for existing, and my every breath. I love you baby girl, to the moon and back. Alix you inspire me every day and every day I am the luckiest mom in the world. I know you're still too young to read my books, not because you can't but because I won't let you but I have a feeling you'll one day be my biggest fan. Love you kid.

And of course, a gigantic thanks goes out to my READERS........ Ya'll rock and I love you more than I can ever show.